Join my newsletter and get *The Lodger*—a twisted tale of obsession and betrayal—absolutely free.

Plus, you'll be the first to know about new releases, exclusive content, and the dark secrets I uncover in my next psychological thriller.

Sign up at: subscribepage.com/thelodger[1]

Because the most dangerous enemies are the ones who smile while they destroy you.

CW01499369

1.

The drizzle comes in sideways from Morecambe Bay, the kind that soaks you without seeming to try. It streaks the sash windows of our Victorian terrace, blurring the view of Scotforth's quiet streets where students hurry past with their hoods up, rucksacks clutched against the November wind.

The castle bells toll faintly in the distance, their bronze voices carrying across Lancaster like a reminder that this place has been weighing people down for centuries.

Inside, the radiator clanks its familiar protest while Josh's Fisher-Price garage plays its electronic tune for the hundredth time this morning. The sound should be cheerful—bright plastic optimism against the grey day—but it feels like mockery.

"Mummy, look!" Josh's sticky fingers tug at my cardigan, leaving jammy prints on the navy wool. "Car is fast!"

I glance down at his chubby face, all earnest concentration as he pushes a red toy car up the plastic ramp. Four years old and already more focused than I manage most days.

"That's lovely, sweetheart," I murmur, turning back to my laptop screen where a half-finished logo design stares accusingly at me. The client—a boutique hotel in the Lake District—wants something "fresh but timeless, modern but authentic." The brief makes my teeth ache with its contradictions, but the invoice will help with this month's mortgage. If I can actually finish the bloody thing.

The Nanny's Secret

J. Cronshaw

Published by Wyvern Books, Ltd, 2025.

THE NANNY'S SECRET

First edition. October 25, 2025.

Written by J. Cronshaw.

For Sammii.

My mobile buzzes with another email notification. Probably another client chasing work I promised for yesterday, or the day before. The cursor blinks in the design software, waiting for inspiration that won't come. Instead, I have *Peppa Pig* nattering from the television, Josh demanding attention every thirty seconds, and the persistent ache behind my eyes that's become my constant companion since becoming a mother.

The kitchen still bears evidence of breakfast chaos—Weetabix cemented to Josh's high chair, coffee rings on the work surface, his beaker knocked over and spreading orange juice across yesterday's post. I catch it before it reaches the bills and mop quickly with a tea towel. Small victory.

I should have cleared it up hours ago. But the logo needs finishing, and Josh needs entertaining, and somewhere in between I'm supposed to be a functioning adult.

I stare out the window again, watching a young woman with perfectly styled hair stride past in a raincoat that probably costs more than I spend on clothes in six months. She moves with the confidence of someone who's never sat in pyjamas until noon, paralysed by the weight of her own inadequacy.

The other mothers at Dallas Road Primary have that same assurance. Gemma Harding, who teaches at the grammar school and always looks like she's stepped from a magazine spread. Sarah Whitworth, whose three children are permanently scrubbed and dressed in coordination. I bet she has a cleaner on speed dial.

They make motherhood look effortless, while I feel like I'm drowning in the shallow end.

I had plans once. A first-class degree in graphic design from Central Saint Martins, a portfolio that landed me work with decent London agencies. I was going to be someone who mattered, whose work meant something. Instead, I'm pushing thirty-five and designing logos for provincial hotels while my toddler wipes his nose on the sofa. The sofa he seems to believe is his personal handkerchief.

The guilt hits like a familiar punch to the stomach. Josh deserves better than a mother who resents her circumstances, who looks at him and sees everything she's given up rather than everything she's gained. He's beautiful, bright, affectionate—a miracle I waited years for, went through three miscarriages to have. The silence of those hospital corridors still echoes sometimes, the crumpled scan photos I keep in my bedside drawer a reminder of what I nearly lost forever.

So why do I feel like I'm suffocating?

"Mummy sad?" Josh has abandoned his cars and is studying my face with the unsettling perception children possess.

"No, love. Mummy's just thinking." I reach out and ruffle his curls, soft as silk under my fingers. He leans into my touch, trusting and warm, and something loosens in my chest despite everything.

But he's right, isn't he? I am sad, tired, lost in a life that feels too small for the person I thought I was. The rain intensifies against the glass, and I imagine it washing the whole street clean, carrying me somewhere I can start again.

Outside, Lancaster carries on without me. Gulls circle inland from the bay, their cries sharp against the wind. Buses rumble past, filled with people who have somewhere important to be. The last time I went into town, Penny Street was crowded with students whose energy made me feel ancient at thirty-five, displaced in my own city.

I close my eyes and hear my mother's voice, sharper now that she's gone: "Don't let people think you can't cope, Emma. There's no shame worse than that." But I can't cope, can I? I'm failing at the one thing women are supposed to do naturally, instinctively. Josh plays quietly beside me, and I wonder if he already knows his mother isn't enough.

Daniel's key turns in the front door at half past six, punctual as always. He appears in the doorway still wearing his suit jacket, his accountant's uniform. His gaze sweeps the living room, taking inventory: the scattered toys, Josh still in his pyjamas from this morning, me curled on the sofa with my laptop balanced on a cushion.

"Daddy!" Josh scrambles up and runs to him, arms outstretched.

Daniel scoops him up, planting a kiss on his head before setting him down. "Hello, trouble. Been good for Mummy?"

"Look, car!"

"That's great, son." He turns to me. "Busy day?" His tone is carefully neutral as he looks at me, but I catch the slight tightening around his eyes, the way his voice caught when he spoke to Josh.

"The usual chaos." I close the laptop, conscious of how little I've achieved. "How was work?"

"Fine. Good, actually. The Morrison account came through." He loosens his tie, running a hand through hair that's starting to thin at the crown. When he sits heavily in the armchair across from me, his shoulders sag. "Emma, we need to talk."

Something in his voice makes me straighten. "About what?"

"You can't keep doing this to yourself. To us." He glances at Josh, who's returned to his cars, then back at me. "You're drowning, love. Josh needs structure, routine. You need help."

The word 'help' lands like criticism. "I'm managing perfectly well."

"Are you? When did you last leave the house? When did we last have a proper conversation that wasn't about logistics or Josh's needs?"

Heat rises in my chest. "I'm doing my best, Daniel. I'm working, I'm looking after our son—"

"I know you are. But it's not sustainable." His voice softens, which somehow makes it worse. "Other families on this street have nannies, childminders. There's no shame in admitting you need support."

"I don't need—"

"Sarah Whitworth recommended someone. A lovely girl, apparently. Very experienced with early years."

A stranger in my house, judging my parenting, reorganising my chaos according to their superior methods. The thought makes my skin crawl.

"No," I say firmly. "Absolutely not."

Daniel's jaw tightens, but his voice stays gentle. "Then what's your solution? Because this isn't working, Emma. For any of us."

Josh has gone quiet during our exchange, sensing the tension that crackles between his parents. He clutches his toy car and watches us with wide, uncertain eyes.

"I'll sort it out," I say, my voice smaller than I intend. "I just need to get into a better routine."

Daniel nods, but I can see he doesn't believe me. Neither do I, really. But the alternative—admitting I can't cope, inviting scrutiny from some competent stranger who'll see through my pretence in minutes—feels impossible.

After he's gone upstairs to change, I sit in the gathering dusk with Josh curled against my side, his warm weight the only solid thing in a day that feels like it's dissolving around me. The rain has stopped, but the windows still weep with condensation.

Josh breathes softly against me, his curls damp with sweat, and I press my cheek to the top of his head. Whatever happens, he is mine. I am his.

I tell myself I don't need a stranger in my home, don't need someone else to love my child better than I can. I'm his mother, his first love, the person responsible for keeping him safe and whole.

I hold him tighter, as if love alone will be enough to keep us safe.

2.

Josh has managed to smear jam across the kitchen table, his school jumper, and somehow the wall behind his chair—his latest accidental artwork. I almost smile, but the clock on the microwave pulls me back to the rush.

Half-eaten toast lies abandoned on his *Thomas the Tank Engine* plate while he drags his book bag across the floor, leaving a trail of yesterday's worksheets in his wake.

"Josh, please. We need to leave in five minutes." I gulp lukewarm tea that tastes like defeat and try to coax life into my ancient printer. The hotel logo still needs finishing, and the client expects a sample by ten. The machine makes a grinding noise that suggests it has other plans.

"Mummy, where's my other shoe?"

I scan the chaos for a small blue trainer that could be anywhere in the house. Under the sofa, probably, or in the washing basket where shoes migrate for reasons I've never understood. The printer jams with a mechanical wheeze, and I resist the urge to give it a good shake.

"Check by the front door, love."

Josh disappears, leaving sticky fingerprints on the doorframe. I abandon the printer and grab his lunchbox from the counter—a piece of cheese, some crackers, an apple he won't eat. Not the elaborate bento boxes other mothers create, but it'll have to do.

The morning presses against us like an impatient hand.

We step out into Lancaster's grey embrace, the drizzle settling on everything with gentle persistence. Josh's hand is warm in mine as we navigate the narrow streets of Scotforth, past terraced houses that huddle together against the wind. Gulls call overhead, circling inland from Morecambe Bay with news of storms coming in from the Irish Sea.

Other parents emerge from their front doors like actors taking their cues, children bundled into waterproofs and hustled towards school. The pavements fill with the morning choreography of family life—pushchairs navigating puddles, toddlers dragging teddy bears, mothers calling after forgotten PE kits.

I feel like I'm running to catch up with a train that's already left the station.

We turn into the maze of snickets that shortcuts through the Victorian terraces, Josh's wellies splashing through every puddle he can find. The chatter of other families echoes off the brick walls, fragments of domestic organisation floating past: "...forgot his recorder again..." "...new teacher seems lovely..." "...nanny starts Monday, thank God..."

The world already moves faster than I can keep up with, everyone else equipped with energy I don't possess.

Dallas Road Primary appears ahead, its red-brick façade softened by the morning mist. The playground fills with the controlled chaos of drop-off—children racing towards their friends, parents clustered in small groups that shift and reform like murmurations of starlings.

I hover at the edge of it all, conscious of my hastily scraped-back ponytail and the coat that's seen better decades. Josh tugs my hand, eager to join his classmates, but I'm paralysed by the social geography of the school gates. The mothers arrange themselves in invisible hierarchies I can never quite navigate.

"Emma!" Gemma Harding waves from near the entrance, her blonde hair perfectly tousled despite the weather. She approaches with the confident stride of someone who's never doubted their place in the world. "How are you, love?"

"Fine, thanks. Bit of a mad morning." I attempt a smile that feels lopsided.

"Tell me about it." But Gemma looks anything but frazzled in her stylish mac and coordinated scarf. "I don't know how you do it, honestly. Working from home with Josh to look after as well. You're amazing managing it all."

There's admiration in her voice, but something else too—a kind of wonder that anyone would choose to live like this.

"We muddle through," I say, hating how defensive I sound.

"Well, you're doing brilliantly. Really." Gemma's smile is warm and pitying in equal measure. "Must be exhausting though."

I nod and make appropriate noises, but her words twist inside me like a knife. They all think I'm struggling. They can see it written across my face, probably smell it on my clothes—the desperation of a woman drowning in her own life.

Across the playground, I spot Sarah Whitworth emerging from her gleaming Range Rover. She moves with the unhurried grace of someone whose morning has gone exactly to plan, while a teenage girl—her au pair, presumably—unloads her three children like they're precious cargo.

The girl can't be more than nineteen, all long limbs and patient efficiency. She crouches to tie a shoelace, adjusts a coat collar, hands out water bottles with the kind of attention I wish I could give Josh but never seem to have time for. Sarah stands by, checking her phone, relaxed in the knowledge that someone else is handling the details.

Near the school gate, one boy howls as his mother peels him from her leg. Even Sarah Whitworth's au pair would struggle with that one.

Envy burns in my chest, sharp and unwelcome. They can afford help, and instead of being judged for it, they're admired. Sarah gets to be the elegant mother who delegates beautifully while I'm the one who's "amazing for managing"—a phrase that really means "what a shame she has to."

I imagine what it would feel like to hand Josh over to capable hands, to walk away knowing someone else would remember his PE kit and cut his sandwiches into triangles. The relief would be overwhelming, I think. Then the guilt crashes in: what kind of mother fantasises about abandoning her child?

"Mummy, look!" Josh tugs my sleeve, producing a crumpled drawing from his pocket. It's meant to be our house, I think—a wonky rectangle with windows like surprised eyes and smoke curling from a chimney. "I did it for you."

My heart swells. I crouch down to his level, smoothing his hair. "It's beautiful, sweetheart. I'm putting this on the fridge the second we get home."

His face lights up, and for a moment the playground chaos fades around us.

Miss Hardy, his teacher, appears at the classroom door with her practiced smile. "Come on then, Reception. Time to come in."

Josh releases my hand and runs towards his friends without a backward glance. I watch him disappear into the building, struck by how small he looks in his oversized jumper, how trusting he is that I'll be there when he comes out.

This is what's at stake. Not just my pride or my sanity, but his security. I want to protect him, to be everything he needs, but the fear gnaws at me daily: what if I'm not enough?

The other mothers begin to disperse, forming new clusters for the next part of their choreographed day. I catch fragments of conversation as they drift past.

"Coffee at mine? The new nanny can watch the little ones."

"She's been a godsend, honestly. Like family already."

"I don't know how I managed before her."

My chest tightens with a familiar blend of loneliness and resistance. They make it sound so easy, so natural to invite strangers into their homes, to trust their children to someone else's care. But the thought of opening our door to scrutiny, of having someone witness the full extent of my failures, makes my skin crawl.

I'm not invited to coffee. Haven't been for months, if I'm honest. I've become the cautionary tale they whisper about—the mother who's clearly not coping but too proud to admit it.

The playground empties around me like water draining from a bath. I pull my coat tighter and begin the walk back through Scotforth's maze of streets, past the houses where other families are settling into their well-ordered days.

The drizzle has intensified, turning the pavement slick beneath my feet. I think about Sarah Whitworth's au pair, about the way she handled those children with such natural competence. About the mothers who speak of their help like beloved family members rather than hired strangers.

Maybe Daniel was right. Maybe help wouldn't be weakness if it meant Josh could have the calm, patient mornings he deserves—the kind where I notice his jam artwork without my heart racing, where I have time to properly admire his drawings before the rush begins.

The thought lodges itself despite my resistance, taking root in the part of my mind that's exhausted from fighting.

3.

"Just meet her," Daniel says for the third time this morning, his voice carrying the patient tone he uses when he thinks I'm being unreasonable. "One conversation. If you don't like her, we'll look elsewhere."

I grip my coffee mug tighter, watching Josh colour in his dinosaur book at the kitchen table. "I don't want a stranger judging how we live, Daniel. Picking apart everything I do wrong."

"No one's judging you." But his eyes drift to the breakfast dishes still piled in the sink, the toys scattered across the floor. "Emma, we agreed to try this."

Did we? I remember him talking, me nodding because I was too tired to argue, but agreement feels like too strong a word for my surrender.

"Fine," I say, the word sharp. "One meeting. But I'm not promising anything."

Daniel's relief is palpable. "She's lovely, according to Sarah. Very experienced."

Sarah Whitworth's recommendation should reassure me, but it has the opposite effect. If Sophie's good enough for Sarah's immaculate household, she'll take one look at our chaos and run screaming.

The café on Penny Street buzzes with its usual mix of Lancaster life. Students cluster around laptops, their conversations a blend of academic jargon and weekend plans. Business types tap away at phones between meetings. Steam rises from the espresso machine while rain streaks the windows, turning the street outside into an impressionist painting.

I feel conspicuously out of place amongst the polished professionals and confident twenty-somethings. Josh fidgets in his chair, his legs swinging as he attacks a colouring sheet with fierce concentration. I've armed myself with crayons and snacks, hoping to keep him occupied long enough to get through this interview without embarrassment.

"Can I have the red one, Mummy?"

I pass him the crayon, my eyes scanning the café entrance. Part of me hopes Sophie won't show up, that I can tell Daniel we tried and go back to our messy but familiar routine.

Then she appears.

I recognise her immediately, though I'm not sure why. She's unremarkable in the best possible way—neat brown hair just touching her shoulders, sensible coat the colour of camel hair, a small leather satchel slung over her shoulder. Everything about her suggests competence without ostentation, warmth without desperation.

She spots us instantly, her smile lighting up her whole face as she approaches our table. For a second, I can't help but smile back, despite myself. "Emma? I'm Sophie. Thank you so much for meeting me."

Her handshake is firm, her voice soft with a Lancashire accent that's been smoothed by education. Daniel half-rises from his seat, clearly charmed by her punctuality and poise.

"Please, sit down," I say, gesturing to the empty chair. "Can I get you something? Coffee? Tea?"

"Tea would be lovely, thank you. Just milk, no sugar."

Daniel practically leaps up to fetch it, suddenly auditioning for Best Husband at the BAFTAs. I bite back a smile as he weaves through tables with exaggerated care, leaving me alone with this stranger who might become part of our daily lives.

Sophie settles gracefully, her attention immediately drawn to Josh's colouring.

"That's a brilliant stegosaurus," she says, leaning forward with genuine interest. "Is he your favourite dinosaur?"

Josh looks up shyly, then nods. "He's got spikes to protect him."

"Very wise. Protection's important, isn't it?"

Something in her tone makes me glance up sharply, but her expression remains perfectly pleasant. Daniel returns with her tea, and she wraps her hands around the cup with obvious gratitude.

"So," Daniel says, settling back into his chair, "perhaps you could tell Emma about your background?"

Sophie turns her full attention to me, as if Daniel's question is merely a prompt for the conversation she really wants to have. "Of course. I'm actually studying literature at Lancaster, but I've been working with families for several years now. There was a lovely family in Preston, two children aged four and six. I was with them for nearly two years."

"Why did you leave?" The question comes out more abruptly than I intended.

"The mother went back to work full-time, needed someone live-in. I couldn't commit to that level of availability so far from uni." Her smile doesn't waver. "Before that, I helped out with various families around Lancaster. Holiday cover, weekend babysitting, that sort of thing."

She reels off a list of references—names that sound plausible but generic, phone numbers she rattles off from memory. Daniel nods approvingly, but I notice he doesn't write them down. Neither do I, though I tell myself I'll ask for them again later.

"You've raised a wonderful boy," Sophie says, her gaze flicking to Josh, who's now drawing what might be a house or possibly a very angular dinosaur. "I can tell how much love and attention you've given him."

The words feel rehearsed, but I still tuck them away like a scrap of reassurance I'm starving for. It's exactly what a frazzled mother wants to hear, which makes me suspicious of its sincerity.

"What's your approach to discipline?" I ask, trying to sound like I know what I'm talking about. "Boundaries, routine, that sort of thing?"

Sophie's response is measured, thoughtful. She talks about consistency, positive reinforcement, the importance of clear expectations. All the right words delivered in the right tone, but something about it feels like she's giving the answers she knows I want to hear rather than expressing genuine philosophy.

Daniel leans forward, clearly impressed. "That sounds very sensible. Emma's quite firm about routines, aren't you, love?"

I am? Since when? But I nod anyway, feeling like a fraud discussing parenting strategies with someone who probably read about them in a textbook last week.

Sophie lifts her teacup and takes a delicate sip. As she sets it down, she hums softly under her breath—just a bar or two of melody, barely audible above the café's chatter. Something about the tune catches my attention, a familiar thread I can't quite grasp.

The moment passes so quickly I almost think I imagined it.

"The thing is," Sophie says, her voice drawing me back to the conversation, "I believe every child deserves to feel truly cherished. Secure in the knowledge that the adults in their life will always put their needs first."

The words are innocuous enough, but they land like criticism. Am I not cherishing Josh enough? Not putting his needs first? The guilt that's my constant companion flares bright and sharp.

Josh chooses that moment to knock over his beaker of squash. Orange liquid spreads across the table, dripping onto the floor with steady persistence. I lunge for napkins, my face burning with embarrassment.

"I'm so sorry, he's usually more careful—"

"Don't worry about it." She's already on her feet, producing tissues from her bag while simultaneously moving Josh's colouring sheet to safety. "Accidents happen."

But it's more than just help—she moves with the kind of fluid competence that makes me feel clumsy by comparison. Within seconds, she's mopped up the spill and settled Josh back into his chair with a fresh piece of paper.

"There we go," she says, crouching down to his level. "What shall we draw next?"

From her bag, she produces a small red toy car—the kind of thing any sensible childcare worker might carry. Josh's eyes light up as she rolls it across the table, making soft engine noises.

"Vroom! Look how fast it goes!" She guides the car in careful circles, and Josh giggles with delight.

His laugh makes my chest ache with love—and then, almost immediately, with fear. What if I can't make him laugh like that anymore?

"Can she come home with us, Mummy?" he asks, his small hand already reaching for the car. "Please?"

The ease of it stops me cold. Minutes ago, Josh was shy, clinging to my side. Now he's leaning towards this stranger like a flower turning towards the sun, his natural reserve completely dissolved.

Sophie straightens, but not before Josh's fingers close around the toy car. She doesn't take it back.

"That's up to your mummy and daddy," she says gently. "But I'd love to come and play with you again."

Daniel beams, clearly delighted by the instant connection. "Well, that seems to settle it. Josh certainly likes you."

I watch my son clutch the red car against his chest, his eyes bright with the particular joy that comes from unexpected gifts. Sophie has been with us less than an hour, and already she's won him over completely.

The rational part of my mind knows this is exactly what we want—someone who can connect with Josh, who understands children, who can step seamlessly into our lives without causing disruption.

So why does my stomach twist with unease as Josh slips his small hand into Sophie's without hesitation?

4.

The rain starts just as Sophie's taxi pulls up outside our house, the kind of fine Lancaster drizzle that seeps into everything without seeming to try. I watch from the front window as she pays the driver and retrieves a single small suitcase from the boot—navy blue with wheels, the sort of thing you'd take on a weekend break, not when moving into someone else's life.

"That's all she's brought?" I murmur to Daniel, who's already heading for the front door.

"She's travelling light. Sensible girl."

But it strikes me as odd, almost too little, as if she expects us to supply everything else she might need. Most people moving into a house, even temporarily, bring more than what fits in a weekend case.

Daniel opens the door before she can knock, his face bright with the enthusiasm of someone whose problems are finally being solved. "Sophie! Come in, come in. Let me take that for you."

She steps into our hallway with the grateful smile of someone accepting sanctuary. Her coat drips softly onto the Victorian tiles while she looks around with obvious appreciation.

"What a lovely home," she says, her eyes taking in the family photos on the wall, the coat hooks laden with our daily debris. "You can feel the warmth here."

Daniel practically glows. "Emma's done wonders with the place. Here, let me show you upstairs."

He's already lifting her suitcase, bounding up the stairs with more energy than I've seen from him in months. I follow, feeling like a guest in my own house.

The spare room looks smaller with Sophie in it. She sets her handbag carefully on the bed and turns in a slow circle, taking everything in with those observant eyes.

"This is perfect," she says, though her gaze lingers on the doorway—and beyond it, towards our bedroom down the landing. "Absolutely perfect."

Daniel smiles. "The bathroom's just there, and there's plenty of wardrobe space. Emma cleared it out specially."

She opens her suitcase, revealing neatly folded clothes and a small collection of personal items. Everything has its place, nothing wasted or superfluous. From the side pocket, she produces a silver-framed photograph—a couple in their fifties, standing in front of what looks like a Preston terraced house.

"My parents," she explains, setting it carefully on the bedside table. "They died when I was eighteen. Car accident."

The simple statement hangs in the air, and I feel churlish for my earlier suspicion. Of course she travels light—she has no family home to strip of belongings, no accumulation of a lifetime's possessions.

"I'm so sorry," I manage.

"Thank you. It was a long time ago now." Her smile is brave, practiced. "I've learned to make do with less, to find family where I can."

Something about the phrasing unsettles me, but Daniel's already moving on, pointing out the central heating controls and the quirks of the old sash windows.

Downstairs, Sophie surveys our kitchen with the assessing eye of someone planning a campaign. "Would you mind if I cooked tonight? I'd love to contribute somehow, and I noticed you've got mince in the fridge. I could do a shepherd's pie?"

Daniel lights up as if she's offered to solve world hunger. "That sounds wonderful. Doesn't it, Emma?"

I nod, though I'm already feeling displaced. The mince was for tomorrow's dinner, part of my carefully planned week of meals designed to stretch our budget. But objecting would make me sound petty, ungrateful for her offer to help.

Josh thunders down the stairs, drawn by the promise of new entertainment. Sophie crouches immediately to his level, her face bright with genuine pleasure.

"Hello again, Josh. Are you going to help me cook dinner?"

"Can I mash the potatoes?" His excitement is infectious, and despite everything, I can't help but smile at his eagerness.

"Of course you can. You'll be my sous chef."

I hover at the edge of my own kitchen, watching Sophie move through it with surprising familiarity. She finds the mixing bowls without asking, locates the potato masher in its drawer, sets Josh up at the counter with a tea towel tied around his waist like an apron.

"Mummy usually does dinner," Josh announces.

"Your mummy works very hard," Sophie says, glancing at me with a smile. "That's why I'm here—to help her have more time for the important things."

The important things. As if cooking for my family isn't one of them.

Daniel wanders through periodically, offering praise that he never gives my cooking. "Smells fantastic in here," he says, inhaling deeply. "Josh, you're being very helpful."

Not that my Tuesday night spag bol has ever drawn such applause.

By the time we sit down to eat, the kitchen has been transformed. Sophie has not only cooked but cleaned as she went, wiped surfaces, loaded the dishwasher. The shepherd's pie sits golden and perfect on the table, accompanied by vegetables I quickly steam while she's distracted with Josh.

Josh chatters throughout the meal, regaling Sophie with stories about his nursery friends, his favourite toys, the ducks we feed at the canal. She listens with the kind of focused attention I wish I could give him but rarely manage after a day of juggling work and domestic chaos.

His laughter bubbles through the house, and for a moment I forget the twist in my stomach, just glad to hear him so happy.

"And the big duck—his name is Gerald—he always gets the best bread because he's the bravest," Josh says through a mouthful of mince.

"Gerald sounds very important," Sophie agrees solemnly. "You'll have to introduce me to him soon."

"Can we go tomorrow? Please?"

"If your mummy says it's alright."

All eyes turn to me, and I feel the familiar weight of being the one who has to say no, set limits, be the practical parent while someone else gets to be fun.

"We'll see," I say, hating how it sounds. "You've got school tomorrow."

"But after school?"

Daniel catches my eye across the table. "It's nice to have some calm for once," he says, his tone carefully neutral but loaded with meaning.

After dinner, Sophie volunteers to help with Josh's bath. I tell myself I should be grateful for the assistance, that this is exactly what we hired her for. But as I listen to their laughter echoing from the bathroom, watch Josh splash happily while Sophie spins elaborate stories about his toy boats becoming pirate ships, I feel like an intruder peering into someone else's family life.

"Captain Josh needs to rescue the treasure from the evil octopus," Sophie says, making the rubber duck dance across the water.

Josh shrieks with delight, completely absorbed in her game. When did I last make bath time this entertaining? When did I stop seeing it as playtime and start treating it as just another chore to tick off the list?

I slip upstairs and retrieve Josh's favourite towel—the one with the dinosaur hood that he insists on after every bath. Sophie looks genuinely grateful when I hand it to her.

"Perfect timing," she says. "Thank you."

It's a small thing, but it reminds me that I still know my son's preferences, his routines, the tiny details that make him feel secure.

Bedtime brings another test. Josh, clean and pyjama-clad, looks between Sophie and me with the calculating expression of a child who knows he has options.

"Will Sophie read me a story tonight?"

"I always read your bedtime story, love." Bedtime was our ritual, the thread that tethered us together. I couldn't give that up without a fight.

"But Sophie tells them differently. With funny voices."

Sophie steps back gracefully. "I think tonight should be Mummy's turn," she says, but the damage is already done. Josh's face falls with disappointment, and I know that tomorrow he'll ask again, and the day after that.

Downstairs, Daniel pours himself a glass of wine and settles into his chair with visible relief. "She's a godsend," he says, not looking up from his paper. "Look at this place—it's actually tidy for once. And Josh ate everything on his plate without a single battle."

The criticism stings because it's accurate. Our house is tidier than it's been in months, the dishwasher is humming efficiently, and there's no pile of washing lurking in the corner.

The kitchen gleams in the overhead lights, every surface wiped clean, every dish in its proper place. Sophie has accomplished more in one evening than I usually manage in a week, and the efficiency of it makes my daily struggles look pathetic by comparison.

I pour myself tea and sit at the table where we ate her perfect meal, listening to the house settle around us. But the silence feels different now—charged with Sophie's presence, as if the very air has been rearranged to accommodate her.

"Emma?"

I turn to find Sophie in the doorway, her expression soft.

"I just wanted to say thank you again. For letting me be part of this." She gestures around the kitchen, taking in the domestic tableau we've created. "It already feels like home here."

Her gratitude is disarming. I nod, forcing a smile, and tell myself that if she truly makes life easier for Josh, maybe I can learn to live with the rest.

5.

The house exhales around me as Sophie's footsteps fade down the street, Josh's chatter dissolving into the November morning. For the first time in weeks, silence doesn't feel oppressive—it feels like freedom.

I climb the stairs to what we laughingly call my office, really just the box room with a desk wedged under the window. The drizzle taps against the glass with gentle persistence, but instead of making me feel trapped, it cocoons me in a bubble of rare tranquillity. No *Paw Patrol* theme tune, no demands for snacks or arbitration in disputes between toy cars, no guilt gnawing at me for ignoring my child while trying to work.

Just quiet.

I open my laptop and pull up the hotel logo that's been taunting me for days. The brief still makes my teeth ache—"fresh but timeless, modern but authentic"—but this morning, my mind feels clear enough to tackle the contradiction. My fingers move across the trackpad with something approaching confidence, adjusting curves, experimenting with typography.

When did I last feel capable? Professional? Like someone whose opinions might matter to people who aren't four years old?

The work flows in a way it hasn't for months. Ideas spark and connect, the design taking shape with each adjustment. I'm actually good at this, I remember with surprise. Before Josh, before the sleepless nights and constant interruption, I used to land decent clients, create things that mattered.

Before that day at the river when everything changed. The memory tries to surface—Josh's voice, water, that terrible frozen moment—but I push it down hard. Not now. Not when I'm finally feeling human again.

Maybe Daniel was right. Maybe Sophie isn't the threat I imagined but the solution I was too proud to accept.

[A soft knock interrupts my concentration. Sophie appears in the doorway carrying a mug of tea, steam curling from its surface like incense.

"I hope you don't mind," she says, setting it carefully beside my laptop. "You looked so focused, I didn't want to disturb you properly. But I thought you might need this."

The tea is perfect—strong but not bitter, just the right amount of milk. For once, I don't wonder if there's an ulterior motive—I just let myself enjoy it.

"Thank you," I say, meaning it. "That's very thoughtful."

"Josh was brilliant on the school walk," she says, perching on the edge of the chair opposite my desk. "Held my hand the whole way, chatted about his favourite books. He's such a bright little boy."

Pride swells in my chest. "He can be a handful sometimes."

"All the best children are." Her smile is warm, genuine. "It shows spirit, independence. You've raised him beautifully, Emma."

The compliment hits differently than yesterday's polished reassurances. This feels earned, observed, real. Maybe I've been unfair to her, projecting my own insecurities onto someone who's only trying to help.

"I should let you get back to work," Sophie says, rising gracefully. "But please, shout if you need anything. I'll be pottering about downstairs."

Alone again, I return to the logo with renewed energy. The design crystallises around a concept that's been eluding me for days—something that bridges old and new without compromising either.

By lunch time, I've produced something I'm genuinely proud of. I stare at the finished design, unable to resist a smile. For once, the work looks like the version in my head—clean, confident, exactly what the client wanted without knowing they wanted it.

The afternoon passes in a similar haze of productivity. Josh bounces through the front door full of stories about his day, brandishing a spelling test marked with gold stars. Sophie praises his achievement with the kind of focused enthusiasm I wish I could summon after my own long day of work.

"Look, Mummy! I got them all right!"

"That's wonderful, love." I scoop him into a hug, squeezing him so tight he squeals with laughter, and for that instant there's no room for guilt at all—just love. Just pride in this brilliant, funny little person I somehow helped create.

Daniel calls as we're finishing tea, his voice crackling through the speaker phone. "Running late again, I'm afraid. Client meeting ran over."

"No problem." Usually, his late calls trigger a cascade of anxiety—Josh still to bathe, bedtime routine to manage alone, another evening of single-handed domesticity stretching ahead.

"Everything under control?" he asks, and I can hear the relief in his voice when I confirm it is. "Glad Sophie's there to help. Makes all the difference, doesn't it?"

After tea, Josh disappears upstairs to play with his Lego while I savour the unusual peace downstairs. No toys scattered across the carpet, no sticky fingerprints on the coffee table, no debris trail marking his path through the house. Sophie has worked some domestic magic I can't fathom—not just cleaning, but somehow preventing the chaos from accumulating in the first place.

I wander into the living room, drawn by the novelty of having nowhere urgent to be, nothing pressing to do. Sophie moves quietly around the space, folding the throw from the sofa, straightening cushions with absent-minded efficiency. Even the way she folds a throw looks like an advert for domestic bliss. I half-expect her to start selling fabric conditioner on the side.

She's humming under her breath as she works, a low, tuneless melody that drifts through the room like smoke.

The song stops me dead.

My mother's lullaby. The one she used to sing when I was small and frightened, her voice soft and reassuring in the darkness of my childhood bedroom. Not a famous song or a nursery rhyme, but something from her own childhood, passed down through generations of women in her family.

Something she never wrote down, never recorded, never shared with anyone but me.

My pulse spikes as Sophie continues humming, oblivious to my presence in the doorway. The melody winds through the air, note-perfect, carrying memories I've kept locked away since my mother died five years ago. How can Sophie know it? How is it possible?

"Where did you learn that song?" The words escape before I can stop them.

Sophie looks up, startled, her hands still smoothing the throw. "Sorry?"

"The song. The one you were humming."

Her face goes blank for a moment, genuinely confused. "Was I humming? I wasn't aware..." She trails off, thinking. "Oh, you know how it is. Melodies get stuck in your head. I probably heard it on the radio or something."

But she didn't. I know she didn't, because that song was never on any radio, never recorded by any artist. It existed only in my mother's voice, in the secret space between mother and daughter that death should have sealed forever.

"It's just..." I struggle to find words that don't sound mad. "It reminded me of something my mother used to sing."

"How lovely." Sophie's smile is gentle, sympathetic. "She must have had excellent taste in music. It was haunting, whatever it was."

Her explanation sounds reasonable, natural, but every instinct I possess screams that she's lying. The song was exact, note-perfect, sung with the same rising inflection my mother used on the third phrase.

"I should check on Josh," I say, backing towards the doorway.

"Of course. I'll finish up down here."

Upstairs, I find Josh building an elaborate castle, Lego bricks scattered across his bedroom floor in organised chaos. He looks up when I enter, his face bright with architectural pride.

"Look, Mummy! It's got a moat and everything!"

I admire his construction with the appropriate enthusiasm, but my mind keeps returning to Sophie's humming, to the impossibility of that melody existing in her head. I must have imagined it, projected familiar notes onto an unfamiliar tune. Grief plays tricks like that sometimes, doesn't it? Makes you see patterns that aren't there, connections that exist only in your desperate desire for them to be real.

But as I help Josh sort his bricks by colour, the song plays in my head with crystalline clarity. Every note, every pause, every breath exactly as my mother sang it. Exactly as Sophie hummed it.

That night, I lie awake staring at the ceiling while Daniel sleeps peacefully beside me. The day had started so well, filled with the kind of domestic harmony I'd forgotten was possible. For the first time in months, I'd felt competent, creative, grateful for the help I'd been too proud to accept.

Now that sense of peace feels contaminated by something I can't name or explain.

6.

"I think I'll do the school run alone today," I announce over breakfast, trying to sound casual as I butter Josh's toast. "Give you a bit of a break."

Sophie looks up from where she's packing his book bag. "Oh, but Josh likes it when we both go, don't you, sweetheart?"

Josh nods enthusiastically, jam smeared across his chin. "Sophie knows all the best puddles on the way."

The logic is unassailable, the request reasonable. But something in me bristles at being outnumbered in my own kitchen, at having my parental decisions subjected to committee vote.

"Well," I say, forcing brightness into my voice, "I suppose we could all go together."

"Wonderful." Sophie's smile is warm, genuine, giving no hint that she's just manoeuvred me into doing exactly what she wanted. "It's such a lovely walk through Scotforth. I'm still getting to know the area properly."

Ten minutes later, we're threading through the terraced streets towards Dallas Road Primary, Josh skipping between us like a bridge connecting two shores. The November rain has turned the cobbles slick and gleaming, reflecting the grey sky in fractured pieces. Buses hiss past towards the university, their windows fogged with condensation and the breath of early commuters.

I watch Josh's small hand slip into Sophie's with the unconscious trust of childhood. His grin as he splashes through puddles is pure sunshine, and for a moment I can't begrudge him choosing Sophie's hand over mine. Still, my fingers curl, empty.

The school playground buzzes with its usual morning energy—children racing towards friends, parents clustered in the informal hierarchies that govern all social spaces. I usually hover at the edges of these groups, exchanging pleasantries but never quite belonging. Today, Sophie strides directly into the heart of it.

"Sophie, how's it going?" Sarah Whitworth asks, appearing at her elbow.

"Amazing. Thank you so much for the recommendation."

Within minutes, Sophie has inserted herself seamlessly into the social fabric of the school gates. She remembers names, asks appropriate questions about siblings and after-school clubs, laughs at the right moments. The other mothers gravitate towards her with the instinctive recognition of someone who belongs.

Part of me is grateful—the spotlight's finally off my shortcomings. But then I realise it isn't shining on me at all.

"She's a diamond," Gemma Harding murmurs to me, nodding towards Sophie as she crouches to tie another child's shoelace. "You're so lucky to have found her."

"Absolutely," agrees Helen Marsden, adjusting her designer handbag. "Wish I had someone like that. Makes life so much easier, doesn't it?"

Lucky to have found her? She practically materialised from Sarah's little black book of perfect nannies.

I smile and nod, making appropriate grateful noises, but inside something withers. They see Sophie as the capable one, the solution to my obvious inadequacy. Their compliments feel like backhanded sympathy—poor Emma, finally getting the help she so clearly needed.

The bell rings, and children begin the migration towards classrooms. Josh releases Sophie's hand reluctantly, then surprises me by throwing his arms around her legs in a fierce hug.

"See you after school, Sophie!"

"Have a wonderful day, darling." She smooths his hair with maternal tenderness that makes my chest tight. "Learn lots of exciting things to tell me about."

Miss Hardy, Josh's teacher, appears at my elbow with her professional smile. "He seems to have settled in wonderfully with the new nanny. Children are so adaptable, aren't they? He clearly adores her already."

The observation should please me—my child is happy, well-cared-for, forming healthy attachments. Instead, it stings like salt in an open wound.

After the bell, I expect the usual dispersal—parents hurrying off to jobs and coffee shops and the hundred small tasks that fill their days. But Sophie has become the centre of a small constellation, mothers orbiting around her with questions about childcare techniques and recommendations for local activities.

"The soft play centre on Bowerham Road is wonderful," she's saying to Helen Marsden. "Josh absolutely loves the climbing frames there."

When did she take Josh to soft play? How does she know about places I've never even heard of?

I hover at the edge of their circle, trying to find a way into the conversation, but Sophie's enthusiasm has captured their full attention. She discusses homework routines and healthy snack options with the authority of someone who's mastered the art of modern motherhood.

"What do you think about screen time limits?" asks Sarah, finger poised over her phone to record pearls of wisdom.

"Everything in moderation," Sophie replies smoothly. "I find if you engage with their programmes—watch together, ask questions—it becomes educational rather than just passive consumption."

The mothers nod sagely, as if she's revealed some profound secret rather than stating the obvious. But then, I've never managed to turn

CBeebies into a learning opportunity. Usually I'm just grateful for twenty minutes of peace while Josh zones out to *Bluey*.

The conversation drifts on without me, covering topics I should know about, strategies I should have mastered years ago. I stand slightly outside their circle, unheard when I try to contribute, dismissed when I suggest alternatives.

Finally, mercifully, the group begins to break up. Sophie says her goodbyes with the warm efficiency of a politician working a crowd, promising to share recipes and arrange playdates.

"Lovely to meet you all properly," she calls as we head towards the school gates. "See you tomorrow!"

We walk back through Scotforth in silence, my mind churning with frustration I can't articulate without sounding petty. At the corner of our street, I clear my throat.

"You know, I can handle the school run on my own. I've been doing it for months."

Sophie glances at me with surprise, her expression open and guileless. "Of course you can. You're a wonderful mother, Emma. But I don't mind helping—it's nice to feel part of things, to get to know Josh's world properly."

The response is so reasonable, so sweetly grateful, that objecting would make me sound churlish. She's offering help, integration, community—all the things I've been struggling to build for myself. How can I complain about someone solving problems I've failed to address?

"I suppose," I say, hating how ungracious I sound.

"The other parents seem lovely," Sophie says, apparently oblivious to my discomfort. "Helen mentioned a book club that meets monthly. And Gemma said something about a mums' night out next week. It's wonderful that Josh is part of such a warm community."

A community I've never felt truly part of, despite living here for years. A warmth I've never accessed, despite countless attempts at small talk and coffee invitations that never quite materialise.

In one morning, Sophie has achieved the social integration I've been pursuing for months.

That evening, Daniel arrives home in uncommonly good spirits. He kisses my cheek and ruffles Josh's hair before settling into his chair with obvious satisfaction.

"Ran into Tom Marsden at lunch," he announces, loosening his tie. "He said Helen was singing Sophie's praises after the school drop-off this morning. Apparently all the mothers think she's wonderful."

"Do they?" I keep my voice carefully neutral.

"Said she fitted right in, had all sorts of useful tips about childcare. Tom thinks we're lucky to have found her." Daniel's eyes find mine across the living room. "Everyone thinks Sophie's wonderful. We're lucky, Em."

If Sophie's so wonderful, where does that leave me? More importantly—where does that leave Josh, if I fade into the background?

I smile, because that's what wives do when their husbands share good news about domestic arrangements. But as I watch Sophie's edges creep into every corner of my life, I promise myself I won't disappear quietly.

7.

The house settles around us with an unfamiliar peace. Tea plates disappear into the dishwasher without my intervention, toys migrate back to their proper homes, surfaces gleam with the kind of cleanliness I've forgotten was possible. Sophie moves through our domestic chaos like a conductor orchestrating a symphony, each gesture purposeful, each result effortless.

I should feel grateful. This is what I wanted, wasn't it? Order from chaos, breathing space, the luxury of sitting with a cup of tea while someone else manages the endless details of family life.

Instead, I feel displaced. The peace gnaws at me because I didn't create it, can't sustain it, had no hand in achieving it. Our home feels more like home than it has in years, but somehow less mine.

"Bath time, Josh!" Sophie calls, her voice carrying the kind of cheerful authority that makes compliance seem like a privilege rather than a chore.

Josh thunders up the stairs without the usual negotiations about five more minutes or one more game. I follow, expecting to reclaim some territory in our evening routine, but find myself surplus to requirements.

"Look, Sophie!" Josh brandishes his dinosaur toothbrush with the pride of someone showing off a prized possession. "It's got a T-Rex head!"

"How brilliant!" Sophie examines the brush with the serious attention it deserves. "Bet he'll make sure all the plaque dinosaurs get scared
away from your teeth."

Josh giggles, transforming tooth-brushing from daily battle into
imaginative play. He opens his mouth wide, making dinosaur roars
while Sophie guides the brush with patience. Two minutes pass without tears, threats, or the exhausting negotiations that usually mark this
part of our day.

"Excellent brushing," Sophie says. "T-Rex would be very proud."

I hover in the bathroom doorway, offering unnecessary reminders
about rinsing thoroughly and wiping his face, corrections no one needs
for a process that's running more smoothly without my intervention.

In his bedroom, Josh changes into his space-themed pyjamas while
Sophie straightens his duvet with the kind of casual competence that
makes everything look effortless. The room, usually a disaster zone of
scattered books and abandoned toys, has somehow been restored to order without Josh even noticing.

I retrieve his favourite teddy from where it's fallen behind the
bed—the worn brown bear he can't sleep without. Sophie looks genuinely grateful when I tuck it under his arm.

"Story time!" Josh announces, bouncing onto his bed with anticipation.

I step forward, ready to reclaim this sacred part of our routine.

"Sophie, will you read to me tonight?"

It stings that he wants Sophie, but part of me is glad he's so eager
for stories at all, so alive to words and voices. The request still hits like a
physical blow, though I keep my expression carefully neutral. "I always
read your bedtime story, love."

"But Sophie does funny voices," Josh says. "And she knows all the
best bits."

I've tried voices before, but Josh always complains that my Gruffalo
sounds like I've got a bad tummy.

Sophie glances between us, sensing the undercurrent of tension. "Perhaps Mummy should read tonight. I wouldn't want to interfere with your special time together."

Josh's face falls with disappointment, and I know that insisting will only make me the villain in his story—the mother who denies him the bedtime reader he actually wants.

"It's fine," I say, hating how the words taste. "Sophie can read tonight."

Josh's face lights up as he selects *The Gruffalo* from his bookshelf, climbing into Sophie's lap without hesitation. She settles back against his pillows, adjusting his weight with the natural ease of someone who's done this countless times before.

I watch from the doorway as she opens the book, her voice taking on the different characters with theatrical flair that makes Josh giggle with delight. The mouse squeaks, the fox growls, the Gruffalo booms—each voice distinct and perfectly pitched.

Josh cuddles deeper into Sophie's chest, his eyelids growing heavy as the familiar story unfolds. He looks utterly content, utterly safe, surrounded by the kind of unconditional love I thought was mine alone to provide.

The knot in my chest tightens with each passing page. This is what I wanted for him—security, happiness, the feeling of being cherished. But I'd imagined providing it myself, not watching someone else give him what I'd been failing to deliver.

"The End," Sophie whispers, closing the book gently.

Josh's breathing has evened out, his small body relaxed against hers in complete trust. She eases him down onto his pillow with care, pulling his duvet up to his chin without waking him.

I step forward and press a soft kiss to his forehead, breathing in the sweet scent of his hair. He stirs slightly, murmuring something unintelligible, and I smooth his fringe with gentle fingers.

"Sweet dreams, my love," I whisper.

Downstairs, Daniel looks up from his newspaper with visible satisfaction as Sophie and I enter the living room.

"All settled?" he asks, though Josh's peaceful capitulation was audible throughout the house.

"Like an angel," Sophie says. "He's such a good little boy."

"Makes a change from the usual bedtime battles." Daniel's eyes find mine across the room. "She's good for him, Em. Good for all of us."

I nod, because agreement is expected, but the words sit heavy in my stomach. Of course she's good for us. That's exactly the problem.

Later, I lie awake listening to the house settle around us. Daniel sleeps peacefully beside me, his breathing deep and untroubled. Through the thin walls, I can hear the occasional creak of floorboards, the distant hum of the boiler, all the familiar sounds of our home at rest.

But something feels different. The rhythm has changed, reorganised itself around Sophie's presence in ways I can't quite articulate. Even the silence feels like hers now.

I replay the evening's events, trying to pinpoint the moment everything shifted. Josh choosing Sophie's lap over mine. His easy surrender to sleep in her arms. The way he looked at her with uncomplicated adoration while I stood forgotten in the doorway.

Is this how it starts? The gradual erosion of the mother-child bond, replaced by something newer, shinier, more competent? What if he forgets I'm the one who stayed up through the fevers, who held him after every nightmare? Will I become redundant in my own child's life?

The thoughts circle like vultures, feeding on every insecurity I've tried to bury. Maybe this is what I deserve for being an inadequate mother, for struggling when others seem to find it effortless. Maybe Josh deserves better than what I've been giving him.

Just as sleep begins to claim me, a sound drifts through the walls—faint humming from Sophie's room. The melody is soft, barely audible, but unmistakably familiar.

My mother's lullaby.

The tune threads through the walls with haunting clarity, each note perfect, each pause exactly where my mother used to breathe. It's impossible, inexplicable, but there's no mistaking the song that should exist only in my memory.

I lie rigid in the darkness, every nerve alert. Part of me aches to hear my mother's voice again, but all I hear is Sophie's—and that makes it unbearable.

8.

I tuck Josh's duvet around his shoulders, smoothing the fabric with hands that still shake slightly from the evening's small defeats. Sophie has already handled bath time with her effortless competence, turning what's usually a battlefield into a playground of imaginative games and willing cooperation.

"One more story, Mummy?" Josh's voice carries the hopeful wheedle of a child testing boundaries. "Sophie said she knows a really good one about a dragon who lives in a castle."

"Tomorrow, love," I say, trying to keep my voice gentle. "It's already past bedtime."

Josh's face clouds with disappointment, but he doesn't argue. Even his protests have become more reasonable since Sophie's arrival, as if her presence has taught him better ways to navigate disappointment.

I lean down and breathe in the warm, milky scent of his hair, wishing I could press pause, keep him this small and safe forever. His lashes flutter against his cheeks as sleep tugs at him, and my chest aches with the fierce tenderness that still catches me off guard sometimes.

"Sweet dreams, my love."

"Night, Mummy."

I kiss his forehead and switch off the overhead light, leaving only his night light glowing soft and blue against the wall.

Downstairs, I pour myself a generous glass of wine—Sauvignon Blanc from a bottle Daniel opened last weekend and promptly forgot about. The living room feels larger without Josh's toys scattered across every surface, but also emptier somehow. I settle onto the sofa with my sketchbook, hoping to lose myself in work.

The hotel logo still needs refinements, subtle adjustments to the kerning that only I would notice but that matter more than I can explain. My pencil moves across the paper in half-hearted gestures, but concentration won't come. Every line feels forced, every curve wrong.

A creak from upstairs breaks the evening quiet. Probably Josh, getting up for water or the toilet. I wait for the sound of his feet on the landing, the whispered "Mummy" that usually follows these late night expeditions.

Nothing.

Another creak, longer this time, like someone moving carefully across floorboards. Josh sometimes gets disoriented in the dark, confused about which door leads to the bathroom.

I set down my wine and climb the stairs quietly. The landing lies in shadow, Josh's door standing slightly ajar as I left it. Through the gap, I can see his small form curled beneath his duvet, breathing deep and steady.

But the door to our bedroom stands wide open.

Sophie stands beside our dresser, her back to the doorway, holding something in her hands. The light from the street lamp outside catches the silver of the frame she's examining—the photograph of my childhood home in Skerton, the terraced house where I lived until I was sixteen.

What is she doing in our bedroom? What possible reason could she have for being there, for touching our personal belongings?

I clear my throat softly. "Sophie?"

She turns with a startled gasp, her hand flying to her chest. But she recovers quickly, her face settling into an expression of mild embarrassment.

"Emma! I'm so sorry, I was just dusting—I didn't want to disturb you earlier when you were working." She holds up the photograph as evidence of innocent intentions. "I thought I'd tidy up a bit while you were relaxing."

Dusting without a cloth—now there's a trick I'd like to learn.

"You don't need to dust our bedroom," I say, my voice sharper than I intended. "That's not what we're paying you for."

"Of course not. I just wanted to help." Sophie steps closer, still holding the frame, her eyes drawn back to the image. "It's a beautiful house. You must have loved living there."

The comment stops me cold. I've never mentioned my childhood home to Sophie, never talked about Skerton or the terraced street where I grew up. The photo sits on our dresser along with others—our wedding, Josh as a baby, holidays from happier times. But how would she know which house was mine?

"How did you—" I begin, then catch myself. She's looking at a photograph. Obviously she can see it's a house. The comment could be innocent, general, the kind of thing anyone might say.

"It must have been lovely," Sophie says, her thumb tracing the edge of the frame. "Growing up in a proper family home like that. So much character in those old terraces."

Unease rises in my chest. She's studying the photograph too intently, holding it too carefully, as if memorising details rather than simply dusting.

I hold out my hand. "I'll take that."

My fingers tighten on the frame when she passes it to me—not because it's silver, but because that house was where my mother sang me to sleep, where I learned who I was. Sophie's intrusion feels like a violation of something deeper than privacy. ·

For a moment, Sophie doesn't move. Her eyes meet mine across the dimly lit bedroom, and I see something flicker in their depths—calculation, perhaps, or challenge. The silence stretches between us, loaded with meanings I can't quite grasp.

Then she smiles, warm and apologetic. "Of course. Sorry, I was just admiring it. Such a lovely family photograph."

But as she extends the frame towards me, she hesitates just a beat too long. Her fingers linger on the silver edge, reluctant to let go. Our eyes lock in what feels like a quiet standoff, each of us measuring the other's intentions.

"Thank you," I say, taking the photograph with hands that aren't quite steady.

"Goodnight, Emma." Sophie's voice carries a softness that could be genuine affection or perfect performance. "Sleep well."

She slips past me in the doorway, her movement graceful and silent. I listen to her footsteps fade down the hall towards her own room, each soft sound marking her retreat from territory she had no right to enter.

Alone in our bedroom, I set the photograph back in its usual place on the dresser. But my hands are shaking now, and the frame feels different somehow—heavier, charged with the memory of Sophie's lingering touch.

She wasn't dusting. There was no cloth in her hands, no cleaning supplies, no evidence of any domestic activity. She was studying the photograph, absorbing details from my past with the focused attention of someone gathering intelligence.

But why? What could she possibly want with an image of my childhood home, a place she's never been, a life she wasn't part of?

I sink onto the edge of our bed, the wine from earlier now sitting like acid in my stomach. Everything about Sophie's presence in our room feels wrong—the invasion of privacy, the smoothness of her excuse, the way she'd held that photograph like it meant something to her.

Maybe Daniel would call it paranoia. But as I sit in the half-dark with my childhood staring back from the photo frame, I feel a hollow ache for the one person who'd know what to make of this—my mother. She'd have seen through Sophie's excuses, would have known what questions to ask.

She would have known what to do.

9.

I sit at the kitchen table. My hands shake as I lift the glass. The Sauvignon Blanc burns my throat, but I barely notice. All I can think about is the way Sophie had hesitated before returning the frame, as if she was reluctant to let go of whatever secrets it held.

The front door clicks open, followed by Daniel's familiar footsteps in the hallway. He appears in the kitchen still wearing his work clothes, his tie loosened but not removed. The sight of him—solid, practical, oblivious to the undercurrents swirling through his own home—makes my chest tight with frustration.

"Good day?" I ask, though the words come out sharper than intended.

"Long." He pulls out a chair and sits heavily, rubbing his eyes with the heel of his palm. "Morrison account is becoming a nightmare. Three meetings and we're still nowhere near—"

"Sophie was in our bedroom tonight."

The words interrupt his tired recounting, hanging in the air between us like an accusation. Daniel looks up, his expression shifting from exhaustion to mild confusion. "What?"

"I found her in our bedroom, going through our things. She was holding that photograph of my childhood home, the one from Skerton."

Daniel's frown deepens. "She was tidying, wasn't she? That's what she does—helps around the house."

"It wasn't tidying, Daniel. She didn't have any cleaning supplies, no cloth, nothing. She was studying the photograph, holding it like..." I struggle to find words that don't sound mad. "Like it meant something to her."

That familiar paralysis creeps through my limbs, the same feeling that comes when I need to act but can't. When Josh needs me to move, to decide, to be the mother who saves rather than watches.

I shake off the thought, but the memory of frozen moments clings like river weed.

"Emma." His voice carries the patient tone he uses when he thinks I'm being unreasonable. "You've been on edge for weeks. Maybe you're reading too much into—"

"I'm not reading anything into it! She knew about the house, Daniel. She made comments about it being beautiful, about me loving it there. How could she know that?"

Daniel rubs his forehead, deep lines creasing his brow. "Because it's a photograph, Emma. Anyone can see it's a house. Anyone might comment that it looks nice."

The reasonable explanation should satisfy me, but it doesn't. It can't, because it ignores the feeling I had standing in that doorway, watching Sophie's fingers linger on something that was mine.

"You weren't there," I say, my voice smaller now, defensive. "You didn't see the way she was looking at it."

"No, I wasn't there because I was at work. Trying to keep us afloat financially while you..." He stops himself, but the unfinished sentence hangs between us.

"While I what?"

Daniel sighs, suddenly looking older than his thirty-seven years. "While you project your stress onto someone who's trying to help us. Sophie's been nothing but wonderful, Emma. Look at Josh—he's eating better, sleeping through the night, actually excited about school.

The house is tidy, the washing's done, you've got time to work on your designs without constant interruption."

He's right, and that's what makes it worse. Sophie has transformed our chaotic household into something approaching domestic bliss, and here I am complaining about it.

"Yes, she's been good for him," I say, forcing myself to be fair. "I can see that. But that doesn't explain why she was in our room. If she's crossing boundaries with our things, what's to stop her crossing them with Josh?"

"She lives here, Emma. Of course she moves through the house." Daniel's patience is wearing thin, his voice taking on the edge it gets when he's tired of a conversation. "What do you want her to do, tiptoe around like a ghost?"

"I want her to respect boundaries. I want her to ask before she goes into our private spaces."

"She was tidying!"

We both glance towards the ceiling, conscious of Josh sleeping above us.

"She was trying to help, and you're turning it into some kind of violation."

The word stings because it's accurate. It was a violation, regardless of Sophie's stated intentions. But I can't make Daniel understand that without sounding paranoid, possessive, ungrateful for the miracle she's wrought in our lives.

"She's good for him," Daniel says, his voice gentle now, trying to bridge the gulf that's opened between us. "Good for all of us. You should be grateful we found her."

"I am grateful," I lie, the words scraping my throat raw. "I just think we need some boundaries, some—"

"You need to relax." Daniel reaches across the table and covers my hand with his.

I want to lean into his reassurance, let myself believe it. But the memory of Sophie's lingering fingers won't let me.

"You're tired, stressed from work. Sophie's helping, and you're looking for reasons to push her away because accepting help feels like admitting defeat."

His analysis is delivered with the certainty of someone who's solved a complex equation. Emma equals stress plus pride equals irrational suspicion of helpful nanny. The formula is neat, logical, and completely wrong.

"Maybe," I say, because arguing further will only make me look more unstable.

Daniel squeezes my hand and stands, his crisis management complete. "Get some sleep, love. Things will look better in the morning."

He heads for the stairs, leaving me alone in the kitchen with my wine and my doubts.

Daniel disappears upstairs, and the silence folds in around me. I grip my glass, staring at the photograph on the dresser in my mind, and wish my mother were here. She'd know if I was imagining things. She'd know how to keep Josh safe.

10.

"I'll do Josh's bath tonight," I say as Sophie begins clearing the tea plates with her usual efficient grace.

She pauses, a stack of dishes balanced in her hands. "Of course. I was just going to run it for you—get the temperature right."

"I can manage." I need this—one small part of our evening routine that belongs to me alone.

Sophie's smile doesn't waver. "Absolutely. He loves his bath time with Mummy."

Twenty minutes later, I kneel beside the bathtub watching Josh arrange his plastic boats in battle formation, steam rising from the warm water. The bathroom feels smaller with just the two of us, more intimate than it has in weeks.

"The yellow boat's called Gerald," Josh announces, making it bob across the water. "Like the duck at the canal."

"Gerald the boat and Gerald the duck," I say, laughing despite everything. His logic makes no sense and perfect sense all at once. I soak in the sound of his voice, the way he makes connections that only a four-year-old could see.

"Sophie says coincidences are just the universe being tidy."

Even here, even in this reclaimed moment, she intrudes. But I push the irritation away, focusing on my son's warm presence, the way the bathroom light catches the gold in his hair.

"Arms up, love. Let's get you washed."

Josh stands obediently, water streaming from his small body as I reach for his flannel. That's when I see it—a purplish mark on his upper arm, just below his shoulder. Not large, barely the size of a ten pence coin, but unmistakably a bruise.

My stomach drops. Bruises are normal at his age, I know. But the thought of him hurt—even in some silly playground accident—makes my chest ache. "Josh, what happened to your arm?"

He glances down at the mark with the casual indifference of childhood, already losing interest. "What?"

"This bruise, sweetheart. Did you fall? Bump into something?"

Josh shrugs, his attention drifting back to his boats. "Don't remember."

Children bruise easily—I know this. They fall, they bump into things, they collect marks and scrapes like badges of honour. But something about this one makes my chest tight with unease. The placement, perhaps, too high up his arm to be from a typical playground tumble.

"Are you sure you don't remember? Maybe at school, or—"

"Everything alright in here?" Sophie appears in the doorway carrying fresh towels. Her eyes find the bruise, as if drawn by some magnetic force.

"Josh has a bruise," I say, my voice carefully neutral. "I was just asking how it happened."

Sophie's expression shifts to gentle concern. "Oh, that's from earlier today. We went for a walk by the Millennium Bridge after nursery, and he tripped near the playground. Went down quite hard, poor thing."

Her explanation flows smoothly, each detail perfectly reasonable.

"You didn't mention it when I got home."

"Didn't I? He seemed fine afterwards, and you know how resilient children are. I put some ice on it straight away." Sophie steps into the bathroom, her presence somehow filling all the available space. "It looked much worse this afternoon—already healing beautifully."

Josh splashes happily, oblivious to the tension. His easy contentment should reassure me, but instead it deepens my unease. Wouldn't he remember a fall hard enough to leave a bruise? Wouldn't he have mentioned it, sought comfort?

"Come on then, little man," Sophie says, holding out a towel. "Let's get you dry."

Josh stands without protest, reaching automatically for Sophie's outstretched arms. The movement is so natural, so trusting, that it makes my throat close with something that might be grief.

Later, after Josh is tucked into bed with one of Sophie's elaborate bedtime stories ringing in his ears, I corner Daniel in our bedroom. He's already changed into his pyjamas, the day's stress visibly lifting from his shoulders now that he's home.

"Did you see Josh's bruise?"

"Sophie mentioned it." He shrugs one shoulder. "Kids bruise, Em. He's four—practically held together with plasters and good intentions."

"Sophie said he fell, but he doesn't remember it. Doesn't that seem odd?"

Daniel sits heavily on the edge of our bed, running his hands through his hair. "Emma, please. We've been through this."

"Through what?"

"Your suspicions about Sophie. Your need to find fault with everything she does." His voice carries the weariness of someone who's had this conversation too many times. "She told you what happened. It was an accident. Kids fall."

"But the placement of the bruise—"

"Is exactly where you'd expect from a tumble." Daniel's tone grows firmer, more definitive. "She handled it properly, Em. What more do you want?"

What do I want? For him to share my unease, to question Sophie's too-perfect explanations, to wonder why our son trusts her more than he trusts me. But I can't say any of that without sounding mad.

"I just want us to be careful. To pay attention."

"We are paying attention. Sophie's been nothing but responsible." Daniel reaches over and squeezes my shoulder. "You're tired, love. Stressed. Maybe you should consider talking to someone—"

"I don't need to talk to someone." The suggestion stings more than it should. "I need my husband to take my concerns seriously."

"I do take them seriously. That's why I'm worried about you." His voice softens with what he probably thinks is kindness. "This fixation on Sophie isn't healthy, Em. She's helping our family, and you're turning every small thing into evidence of some grand conspiracy."

The word 'fixation' hits like a slap. Part of me knows how it sounds—paranoid, picking at nothing. But another part can't let go of the unease, the feeling that something's not right beneath Sophie's perfect surface.

"Maybe you're right," I lie, because fighting further will only cement his belief that I'm losing perspective.

Daniel kisses my forehead and heads for the bathroom, our conversation closed by his satisfaction that he's provided the reasonable perspective I clearly lack.

Alone, I pad down the hallway to Josh's room. He's already fast asleep, his small form curled beneath his dinosaur duvet. In the soft glow of his night light, the bruise on his arm looks darker, more deliberate.

I perch on the edge of his bed, careful not to disturb his sleep, and study the mark more closely. It's definitely finger-shaped. Too precise to be from a fall, too specific to be accidental.

But even as the thought forms, doubt creeps in. I'm tired, stressed, looking for patterns that might not exist. Children bruise in all sorts of ways, don't they? And Josh shows no fear of Sophie, no reluctance to be alone with her. Surely a child would instinctively pull away from some-one who hurt them?

"Sophie makes the best swings," Josh murmurs in his sleep, a smile playing at the corners of his mouth.

He's dreaming of her, finding comfort in memories of their shared adventures while I sit here cataloguing imaginary injuries.

I lean down and kiss his forehead, breathing in his familiar scent of soap and innocence. "Sweet dreams, my love."

In the hallway, I stand for a long moment staring at his closed door. The house settles around me with its familiar creaks and sighs, but something feels different. Charged. As if the very air has shifted to ac-commodate possibilities I don't want to consider.

The bruise was small, barely a shadow—but it spread through me like a warning.

What if I'm wrong?

Worse—what if I'm right, and I'm the only one who sees it?

11.

I push my trolley through the automatic doors of Booths, breathing in the familiar scent of fresh bread and floor cleaner. For the first time in weeks I feel like myself again—someone capable, someone in control. No Sophie with her carefully considered meal plans, no helpful suggestions about organic vegetables or Josh's dietary preferences. Just me, a trolley, and the mundane satisfaction of crossing items off a list I wrote myself.

The supermarket hums with its usual Saturday morning energy. Families navigate the aisles with varying degrees of chaos, pensioners study price labels with forensic attention, students grab essentials. I feel anonymous here, invisible in the best possible way.

Until I hear her laugh.

The sound carries across the fruit and vegetable section, bright and musical above the general chatter. I know that laugh by now—have heard it echoing through my house for weeks, charming my son, impressing my husband, apparently delighting everyone it touches.

I round the corner by the organic carrots and there she is. Sophie stands by the apple display, a wire basket hooked over one arm, leaning in close to Mrs Hopkins from two doors down. They look for all the world like old friends sharing secrets, their heads bent together in animated conversation.

My grip tightens on the trolley handle until my knuckles show white. When did Sophie become friends with my neighbour? Mrs

Hopkins barely nods when I pass her in the street, but here she is chatting to Sophie like they've known each other for years.

Sophie touches Mrs Hopkins' arm as she speaks, the casual intimacy of the gesture making my stomach clench. She has a gift for physical connection, I realise—the light touches that make people feel special, chosen, included in something warm and exclusive.

"Emma!" Sophie's voice cuts across the produce section as she spots me hovering by the bananas. She waves brightly, her face lighting up with apparent delight. "We were just talking about you!"

Nothing good ever follows that phrase, but I force my feet to carry me over to their little gathering. Mrs Hopkins looks up with the slightly glassy expression of someone who's been thoroughly charmed.

"Your Sophie's a treasure," she announces without preamble. "You're so lucky, Emma. Not many people get this kind of help."

The words hit like familiar punches. Lucky Emma, who clearly couldn't cope without assistance. Poor Emma, finally getting the support she so obviously needs.

"She's been wonderful," I agree, because what else can I say?

"I was just telling Mrs Hopkins about the lovely walks we take with Josh," Sophie says, her voice warm with maternal pride. "He's such a curious little boy—wants to know the name of every bird, every flower."

It's true he's always asking questions, always tugging at the world to understand it. That's my boy, even if Sophie gets the credit for noticing. When do they take these walks? And since when does Josh care about flora and fauna beyond the ducks at the canal?

Mrs Hopkins turns to Sophie with renewed interest. "Have you tried the nature trail by the river? Lovely for children, that is."

"Oh yes, Josh adores it there. Don't you think so, Emma?"

I nod because they're both looking at me expectantly, but I have no idea what nature trail they're discussing. Another piece of Josh's life that's happening without my knowledge, guided by someone else's enthusiasm.

The conversation flows around me. They discuss local events I haven't heard about, PTA meetings I wasn't invited to, community initiatives that somehow never reached my attention. Sophie nods and asks thoughtful questions, demonstrating the kind of neighbourhood engagement I've never managed.

Funny how I lived here three years without a tea invitation, but Sophie cracks the code in three weeks. Perhaps she's part nanny, part magician.

"Daniel works so hard, doesn't he?" Sophie says during a lull in the conversation, her tone carrying just the right note of admiring concern. "Emma's lucky to have such a dedicated husband."

Mrs Hopkins nods approvingly. "Not many men put in those hours. Shows real commitment to providing for his family."

The comment should be complimentary, but it lands wrong. As if Daniel's long hours are an admirable sacrifice rather than a convenient escape. As if my struggles at home are the inevitable result of being left to cope alone, rather than evidence of my own inadequacy.

"Sophie helps me manage everything beautifully," I hear myself saying, the words tasting like sawdust. "I don't know what we'd do without her."

"That's what community's for," Mrs Hopkins declares with satisfaction. "Looking after each other, stepping in when needed."

But Sophie isn't community—she's a stranger who appeared three weeks ago and somehow inserted herself into every aspect of our lives. Yet standing here watching her chat easily with my neighbour, she looks more rooted, more connected than I feel in my own hometown.

The conversation drifts to weekend plans, local market stalls, the kind of social fabric I've never managed to weave myself into. Sophie's contributions are thoughtful, engaged, demonstrating an investment in Lancaster life that puts my own detachment to shame.

I watch Mrs Hopkins' face transform as Sophie speaks, the polite tolerance she usually shows me replaced by genuine warmth. When did my neighbour start looking at someone else with the expression I've been hoping to see for years?

"Well, I should let you get on," Mrs Hopkins says eventually, though she seems reluctant to end the conversation. "Lovely to see you both. Sophie, do pop round for tea sometime—I'd love to hear more about those nature walks."

The invitation is extended to Sophie, not to me. I stand there holding my shopping list like a prop in someone else's play, watching my neighbour's social energy focus entirely on the woman who's supposed to be working for me.

After Mrs Hopkins wanders off towards the dairy aisle, Sophie turns to me with that warm smile that's fooled everyone else.

"Wasn't that lovely? She's such a sweet woman. Josh would adore her garden—she's got bird feeders everywhere."

Another detail about my neighbourhood I didn't know, another connection Sophie's made in weeks that I've failed to build in years.

"I should finish the shopping."

"Of course. I'll leave you to it."

But as I push my trolley towards the meat counter, I catch a glimpse of Sophie selecting vegetables with the focused attention of someone who knows exactly what she's looking for. Her basket already contains ingredients for what looks like a substantial meal—planned, purposeful, domestic.

She's shopping for our family dinner. While I'm here playing at being the competent housewife, Sophie's already planned the evening meal, knows what we need, has everything under control.

I abandon my trolley in the breakfast cereal aisle and walk out into the November drizzle, my cheeks burning. I wanted so badly to bring home fish fingers and smiley-face waffles, to be the one who made Josh's eyes light up. Instead, I walked away, carrying only the ache of being left out of my own story.

The walk home takes twenty minutes through Scotforth's wet streets, past terraced houses where other families are settling into their Saturday routines. I pass windows glowing with domestic contentment—children's drawings stuck to glass, families gathered around kitchen tables, the ordinary happiness I've been chasing for years.

By the time I reach our front door, I can already hear Josh's laughter from inside. Through the kitchen window, I see Sophie unpacking shopping bags while he sits at the table, chattering away about something that's captured his complete attention.

She's bought everything we need and more, I realise. The shopping I abandoned, the meal I failed to plan, the domestic competence I can't seem to master—it's all here, handled with the effortless grace that makes everyone think she's a miracle.

Josh looks up as I enter, his face bright with the particular joy that comes from undivided adult attention.

"Sophie bought fish fingers!" he says. "And the waffles with the smiley faces!"

"How lovely," I manage, hanging my coat on the hook Sophie's somehow trained everyone to use.

By the time I step through the door, it feels like her shop, her kitchen, her smile lighting up my son's face. I kiss the top of his head anyway, clinging to the hope that some part of him will always know I'm his mother.

12.

Daniel's footsteps thunder up the stairs, Josh's delighted squeals echoing through the house as bath time transforms into some elaborate game involving pirate ships and sea monsters. I should feel grateful for the domestic harmony, for the way Sophie has made our evening routine effortless rather than exhausting.

Instead, I stand in the hallway folding Josh's school jumpers with hands that won't stop shaking, the memory of this afternoon's humiliation at Booths still fresh. The cotton still smells faintly of bubble bath and crayons—my boy's scent clinging to the fabric. My hands shake anyway. The way Mrs Hopkins had looked at Sophie—with warmth, respect, genuine affection—while barely acknowledging my presence.

The sound of water splashing upstairs makes my stomach clench unexpectedly. Josh laughing in the bath should bring joy, but instead I feel that familiar tightness in my chest, the way my feet seem to grow roots into the floor. There was another time, another laugh that turned to something else—but the memory slips away like water through fingers before I can grasp it properly.

The house settles around me with its familiar creaks and sighs, but something feels different. As if the very air holds secrets I'm not supposed to know.

That's when I hear it.

A voice from the kitchen, low and careful, the kind of tone people use when they don't want to be overheard. Sophie's voice, though I can't make out the words from where I stand.

I set down the washing and creep closer, my bare feet silent on the Victorian tiles. The kitchen door stands slightly ajar, and through the gap, I can see Sophie with her back to me, mobile phone pressed to her ear.

"...she doesn't suspect anything yet," Sophie says, her voice barely above a whisper.

It could be about anyone, I tell myself. A friend hiding a pregnancy, a colleague planning a surprise party. But the words lodge in my chest like hooks.

"Just a matter of time," she says, shifting position so I catch her profile. Her expression is focused, businesslike—nothing like the warm, helpful woman who's been charming my family for weeks.

I press myself against the wall, hardly daring to breathe. Upstairs, Daniel's voice carries through the floorboards as he negotiates with Josh about getting out of the bath, but down here the world has narrowed to Sophie's careful whispers.

"I'll keep close to her," she says into the phone. "Make sure she doesn't cause any problems."

The pronouns are maddeningly vague—she could be talking about anyone. A difficult employer in a previous job, a friend going through a divorce, a relative with mental health issues. But every instinct I possess screams that she's talking about me.

"Don't worry," Sophie's voice carries a note of confidence. "I know exactly what I'm doing."

The call ends with a soft click, and I freeze. Through the gap in the door, I see Sophie slip her phone into her pocket and run her hands through her hair, someone collecting themselves after a difficult conversation.

I should retreat, pretend I never heard anything, file this away as another paranoid fantasy to discuss with no one. But my feet won't move, rooted to the floor by the terrible certainty that I've just over-heard something I was never meant to hear.

Sophie turns towards the door, and for a heart-stopping moment our eyes meet through the gap. Her expression shifts—surprise, then something sharper. The mask of helpful competence slips for just an in-stant, revealing something underneath that makes my chest tight.

Then she's moving towards me, her face already rearranging itself into its familiar warm smile.

"Emma!" Her voice carries just the right note of cheerful surprise. "I didn't see you there."

"I was just..." I gesture vaguely at the washing basket, my voice catching in my throat. "Sorting laundry."

"Of course." Sophie's smile doesn't waver, but something in her eyes remains watchful, alert. "Sorry if I was being loud. That was my cousin—she's having terrible boyfriend trouble. You know how it is with family drama."

Convenient cousin. There always is one when excuses are needed.

A cousin with boyfriend problems would explain the hushed tones, the careful phrasing, the note of weary competence in her voice.

But it doesn't explain the chill that ran down my spine when she said those words: *she doesn't suspect.*

"Family can be complicated," I manage, my voice steadier than I feel.

"Exactly. She always calls when she needs someone to listen, and you can't really say no, can you?" Sophie laughs lightly, waving away the minor inconvenience of other people's problems. "I should proba-bly get upstairs and help Daniel with Josh. Bath time can be quite the adventure."

Before I can respond, the sound of running feet announces Josh's escape from the bathroom. He appears at the top of the stairs wrapped in a towel, his hair plastered to his head and his face bright with the particular joy of a successful bath-time game.

"Sophie! Daniel says you know a story about underwater pirates!"

"Do I indeed?" Sophie's voice transforms instantly, taking on the theatrical warmth she reserves for Josh. "Well, we'll have to see about that, won't we?"

His laughter echoes upstairs, bright and pure, and I want to bottle it, guard it. Keep it safe from whatever Sophie was whispering about.

Daniel appears behind Josh, his shirt damp and his expression carrying the satisfied tiredness of a father who's successfully managed bath time without tears or tantrums.

"She's a miracle worker," he says, grinning at Sophie. "Usually it takes an hour and several battles to get him clean."

"It's all about finding the right game," Sophie says, already climbing the stairs towards Josh. "Isn't that right, captain?"

Josh giggles with delight as Sophie scoops him up, towel and all, spinning him gently before heading towards his bedroom. Daniel follows, leaving me alone in the hallway with the echo of normal family life ringing in my ears.

But nothing feels normal anymore.

Later, after Josh has been tucked into bed with one of Sophie's elaborate stories, I lie in our bed staring at the ceiling while my mind churns with fragments of overheard conversation.

She doesn't suspect anything yet.

Just a matter of time.

I'll keep close to her.

The words circle endlessly, each repetition adding weight to my growing certainty that Sophie isn't who she pretends to be. But what proof do I have? A phone call that could have been about anyone, explanations that sound perfectly reasonable, the word of a woman who's made our chaotic household function like clockwork.

Daniel sleeps peacefully beside me, his breathing deep and undisturbed. In the morning, he'll wake refreshed and grateful for another day of domestic harmony courtesy of our miraculous nanny. He'll see Josh eating his breakfast without fuss, the house tidy, his wife finally getting the help she so clearly needs.

He won't see the calculation behind Sophie's warm smiles, won't hear the careful precision in her voice when she thinks no one's listening. He'll dismiss my concerns as stress, paranoia, the inevitable result of someone who's forgotten how to accept help gracefully.

But I heard what I heard.

13.

The kitchen radio murmurs with local news about roadworks on the A6 and delays at Lancaster station while Josh sits at the table eating his way through a slice of perfectly buttered toast. The butter reaches all the way to the crusts—something I never manage in my morning rush—and Josh shows none of his usual breakfast resistance.

Sophie stands at the counter preparing his lunch box with the kind of methodical care that makes every sandwich look like a work of art. Her sandwiches look like something from a Waitrose advert. She's already dressed for the day in neat jeans and a cream jumper, while I'm still in my pyjamas clutching a mug of tea like a lifeline.

"Sleep well, sweetheart?" I ask Josh, ruffling his hair as I pass.

He nods through his mouthful of toast, swinging his legs contentedly. Everything about the scene should please me—my son eating without fuss, the kitchen tidy, the morning running smoothly. Instead, I feel like an intruder.

Sophie moves around the space with the confidence of someone who belongs here, who's earned her place through competence and care. When did my kitchen become hers? When did Josh start looking to her first for guidance, comfort, the small attentions that mark a child's allegiances?

After breakfast, Josh sprawls on the living room floor with his collection of toy cars, arranging them in elaborate patterns that follow some logic I can't fathom. The intensity on his face is pure Josh, as if nothing else in the world matters but lining up those cars just so. I settle onto the sofa with my laptop, hoping to catch up on emails before the school run.

"Mummy," Josh says suddenly, looking up from his cars with the solemn expression he reserves for important pronouncements. "Family is who looks after you."

He looks so serious, so certain, that my heart aches with pride. Then the words register, and the pride curdles.

"Where did you hear that, love?" I ask, keeping my voice light.

Josh shrugs, already losing interest in the conversation. "Sophie says it."

From the kitchen comes the sound of running water as Sophie tackles the washing up. She doesn't turn around when she speaks, but her voice carries clearly.

"Oh, just something I told him. It's nice for him to know he's loved, isn't it?"

The explanation sounds reasonable, even touching. But something about the phrasing bothers me—the deliberate way Josh repeated it, as if he'd been coached to remember those exact words.

Family is who looks after you. Not who loves you, not who gave birth to you, not who's been there since the beginning. Who looks after you. As if love is transactional, earned through daily services rather than given unconditionally.

"Of course," I say, but my voice sounds thin, uncertain.

Sophie appears in the doorway, tea towel in hand, her smile warm with the satisfaction of someone who's provided wisdom as well as practical help.

"I think it's important for children to understand different kinds of family. Blood relations aren't everything, are they? Sometimes the people who choose to love you matter more than the people who have to."

The observation sounds profound, even enlightened. But delivered in my living room, about my son, it feels like a threat disguised as philosophy.

Josh has already moved on, making vrooming noises as he crashes two cars together in some epic collision. But Sophie's words echo in the sudden quiet, reshaping something fundamental about the ground we all stand on.

The walk to school passes in a blur of morning drizzle and domestic chatter, but Josh's phrase keeps circling in my head like a stuck record.

Family is who looks after you.

The more I replay it, the more sinister it sounds—not wisdom but indoctrination, preparing Josh to accept a new definition of belonging that doesn't necessarily include me.

After drop-off, I find myself taking the long way home through Scotforth's maze of terraced streets. The repetitive rhythm of walking usually calms me, but this morning my mind churns with unwelcome possibilities.

What if Sophie is deliberately teaching Josh to see our relationship in transactional terms? If he grows up believing family is whoever looks after you, what happens the day Sophie leaves? What happens to him when she's gone, when he's learned to measure love by daily services that can be withdrawn without warning?

The paranoia feels familiar now, the constant second-guessing of my own perceptions. But Josh's solemn repetition of Sophie's phrase suggests something more deliberate than casual influence.

That evening, Daniel arrives home to find Josh building an elaborate Lego fortress while Sophie cooks something that smells of herbs and domestic competence. The picture of family harmony should warm me, but instead it makes my chest tight with unspoken dread.

"Sophie taught Josh about families today," I say as Daniel loosens his tie and settles into his chair.

"Did she? What sort of thing?"

"That family is who looks after you. Not who loves you or who you're related to, but who provides care."

Daniel glances at Josh, who's absorbed in his construction project, then back at me with mild confusion. "What's wrong with that? She's probably just trying to teach him values. Help him understand that love comes in different forms."

The casual dismissal stings more than it should. "Don't you think it's a bit...calculating? Teaching a four-year-old to judge relationships based on services provided?"

"Emma." Daniel lets out a long sigh. "She's helping him feel secure, letting him know he's cared for. What's the problem with that?"

I want to explain the problem—that Sophie is systematically redefining Josh's understanding of family in ways that position her as essential and me as expendable. But saying it aloud would only reinforce Daniel's belief that I'm projecting paranoid fantasies onto innocent interactions.

Bedtime brings another small defeat. When I move towards Josh's room to begin our usual routine, he looks past me to where Sophie stands in the doorway.

"Sophie tuck me in tonight?" he asks with the guileless directness of childhood.

"I always tuck you in, love," I say, trying to keep my voice steady.

"But Sophie looks after me." Josh's logic is unassailable in the way only children's can be. "She's family."

The words hit hard. Not that he loves Sophie, not that he wants her involved, but that she's family while I'm...what? The biological accident who happened to give birth to him?

Sophie steps back gracefully. "Perhaps Mummy should tuck you in tonight."

Josh's face clouds with disappointment, and I know that tomorrow he'll ask again, and the next day, until I'm the one who feels like an intruder in his bedtime routine.

After Daniel kisses Josh goodnight and heads downstairs to his evening paper, I linger in our bedroom staring at the framed photograph of my childhood home. The same photo Sophie had held with such careful attention, studying it like she was memorising details from a life that had nothing to do with her.

Now I understand what she was doing. Not just snooping, but researching. Learning about my past so she could better understand how to dismantle my present.

The phrase she taught Josh isn't random philosophy—it's preparation, laying groundwork for a world where biology matters less than daily services, where the woman who's been here three weeks can claim equal footing with the mother who's been here from the beginning.

Sophie isn't just helping with Josh. She's carefully replacing me, piece by piece, using my son's natural affection as a weapon against the bond I thought was unbreakable.

Josh's words echo long after the lights go out—family is who looks after you—and I know, with a chill I can't shake, that he isn't talking about me anymore.

14.

The dishes sit in neat stacks beside the sink. Josh sleeps peacefully upstairs, lulled by one of Sophie's elaborate bedtime stories, while rain patters against the kitchen windows with gentle persistence. The house feels smaller in the lamplight, more intimate, but also more oppressive—as if the walls are closing in around secrets I can't name.

I steel myself for what needs to be said. No more hints or careful suggestions. No more allowing Daniel to brush aside my concerns with reasonable explanations that explain nothing. Tonight, I'm going to make him listen.

Daniel sits at the kitchen table with his laptop open, squinting at spreadsheets. The mortgage, the car payment, the utility bills—all the domestic mathematics that keep our middle-class existence afloat.

"We need to talk about Sophie," I say, settling into the chair across from him.

He doesn't look up immediately, his fingers still moving across the keyboard. "What about her?"

"Something's not right. The way she moves through this house like she owns it, the things she says to Josh, the boundaries she crosses." The words pour out faster than I intended, fuelled by weeks of accumulated unease. "She was in our bedroom going through our things. She teaches Josh that family is defined by who provides care rather than who loves him. There was that bruise—"

"Emma." Daniel's voice cuts through my grievances. "Stop."

"You're not listening—"

"I am listening. That's the problem." He closes the laptop with more force than necessary and finally meets my eyes. "You're being irrational, Em. She's helping. Why can't you see that?"

"It isn't about me, Daniel. I just want to know that Josh still sees me as his mum, that he doesn't get confused about who's supposed to love him unconditionally."

Daniel's jaw tightens. "She's doing her job. The job we hired her to do because you couldn't cope."

The words hang in the air between us, brutal in their honesty. Because you couldn't cope. As if my struggles with work-life balance, my exhaustion, my occasional failures at domestic perfection are character flaws rather than the normal challenges of modern parenting.

"I was coping."

"Were you?" Daniel's tone shifts. "Because I remember a lot of tears, a lot of complaints about being overwhelmed, a lot of evenings when I came home to chaos and takeaway containers."

Heat rises in my cheeks. "So I wasn't perfect. So I struggled sometimes. That doesn't mean—"

"It means Sophie is exactly what we needed." He gestures around the tidy kitchen, the evidence of domestic harmony surrounding us. "Look at this place, Emma. Look at Josh. She's turned everything around for us."

"Yes, she's good at all of that," I concede, trying to keep my voice level. "But that doesn't mean I should be pushed out of Josh's life."

"She's giving him stability. Structure. Things he wasn't getting before."

The accusation stings because it's not entirely unfair. My own parenting has been inconsistent, reactive, shaped more by burnout than philosophy. But that doesn't make Sophie's influence benign.

"What about the money?" Daniel continues, warming to his theme. "Your freelance work is unpredictable, Emma. One month you're busy, the next you're scrambling for clients. Sophie gives us breathing room, takes the pressure off."

He gestures towards the stack of bills on the counter—council tax, electricity, the endless parade of domestic expenses that arrive with clockwork regularity. "We can't afford for you to fall apart because you're jealous of someone who's trying to help us."

"I'm not jealous," I say, but my voice cracks on the word.

Jealous of a nanny? Maybe I am. But not in the way he thinks.

"Aren't you?" Daniel leans back in his chair, his expression shifting from frustration to something that might be pity. "She's competent, calm, everything seems effortless for her. She connects with Josh in ways that come naturally, while you...struggle."

The observation cuts deeper than any shout could. He sees my failures as clearly as I do—the moments when patience deserts me, when I choose efficiency over engagement, when I feel like I'm drowning in the shallow end of motherhood.

"She's been here three weeks, Daniel. Three weeks, and you're ready to hand our family over to her."

"I'm not handing anything over. I'm grateful for help when it's offered." His voice rises slightly. "I can't keep doing this, Emma. I can't keep coming home to conspiracy theories and accusations. She's helping our family, and you're looking for reasons to push her away because accepting help feels like admitting defeat."

I wanted him to believe me, to tell me I wasn't imagining things. Instead, I feel like a child scolded for making a fuss.

The conversation dies there, smothered by the weight of his certainty and my inability to articulate the wrongness I feel. Daniel pours himself a measure of whisky—not his first of the evening, I notice—and settles back into his chair with the air of someone who considers the matter closed.

"I'm going to bed," I say to the silence.

"Good idea. Things always look better in the morning."

But as I climb the stairs, nothing feels better. The house settles around us with its familiar creaks and sighs, but the sound that follows me upstairs isn't architectural—it's Sophie's voice, humming softly from Josh's room.

The melody drifts through the darkness. The tune my mother used to sing, the one that should exist only in my memory. Sophie's voice weaves through the air, as if she's sung it a thousand times before.

I pause on the landing, listening to the impossible familiarity of the song. Josh must be asleep by now, but Sophie continues humming, the sound carrying through the thin walls like a territorial claim.

In our bedroom, I can hear Daniel moving about downstairs—the clink of glass, the rustle of newspaper, the comfortable sounds of a man whose domestic world has been restored to order. He can't see what I see, can't hear the calculation beneath Sophie's warmth. To him, she's a miracle worker who's solved problems he was tired of witnessing.

The lullaby threads through the walls, that same song my mother sang to me. I press my fist to my mouth, wishing she were here to tell me I'm not losing Josh, that I'm not losing myself.

15.

I wake to silence. Not the usual chaos of Josh bouncing on his bed demanding breakfast, or the sound of cereal bowls clattering in the kitchen. Just quiet.

The clock reads half past eight. School starts in twenty minutes.

I throw on my dressing gown and hurry downstairs. The kitchen stands empty, breakfast dishes already washed and stacked beside the sink. Josh's school bag is gone from its hook by the door.

A note on the counter, written in Sophie's neat handwriting: Gone to school. Thought you could use the sleep. S x

For a moment, I picture Josh at the breakfast table earlier—his legs swinging happily under the table, his face sticky with butter. The sight would have made me smile before the ache crept in. The relief hits first—blessed silence, an extra hour of rest I desperately needed. Then comes the sting of displacement. She didn't ask. Didn't check if I wanted to take Josh myself, if I had planned to use the walk for some rare mother-son time. She simply decided, as if Josh's routine was hers to re-organise.

I pour coffee with hands that shake slightly. When did the school run become Sophie's domain? When did my permission become optional?

By lunch time, I've managed to lose myself in work—a new logo for a boutique in Keswick that actually seems pleased with my initial concepts. The house feels different without Josh's constant chatter, more like the workspace I've been trying to create for months.

That's when I hear Sophie's voice from the kitchen, bright and authoritative as she speaks into her phone.

"Tuesday afternoon would be perfect," she's saying. "Josh loves playing with Oliver. Shall I pick him up from school, or would you prefer to drop him round?"

I freeze at my desk. A playdate. Sophie is arranging a playdate for my son, speaking with the casual authority of someone who makes these decisions regularly.

"Wonderful. I'll make sure to have some of those biscuits he likes. Three-thirty, then."

The call ends with friendly goodbyes, and I sit staring at my laptop screen while fury builds in my chest. Who gave her permission to make social arrangements for Josh? When did she become his social secretary?

But even as anger rises, a small voice whispers that this is helpful, isn't it? One less thing for me to organise, one less awkward conversation with other mothers who always seem more competent than I feel.

The conflict between gratitude and resentment makes my stomach clench.

Later, walking back from the corner shop, I encounter Mrs Daniels wrestling with her wheelie bin at the kerb.

"Afternoon, Emma," she calls, straightening with obvious relief. "Lovely to see you."

"Afternoon, Mrs Daniels."

"Saw your Sophie walking Josh home yesterday," she says, her tone carrying warm approval. "Such a reliable girl. Always has time for a chat, always cheerful. You're very lucky."

Lucky Emma, whose life has been rescued by Sophie's competence. Poor Emma, who clearly needed the intervention.

"Yes, she's very helpful," I manage.

"And so good with Josh. You can see how much he adores her. Like having a big sister, really."

Big sister. Not nanny, not helper, but family. The casual reclassification makes my chest tight with something that might be grief.

Back home, I find Sophie in the kitchen preparing Josh's afternoon snack with the methodical care she brings to everything. Even her apple slices look smug, lined up like soldiers in his lunch box. Her presence fills the space, making it feel smaller, less mine.

"Sophie," I say, my voice steadier than I feel. "I'd prefer if you asked before making plans for Josh. The playdate with Oliver—I should have been consulted."

She looks up from the apple she's slicing into neat segments, her expression shifting to gentle surprise.

"Of course. I'm so sorry—I didn't think you'd mind. His mother mentioned it at school, and it seemed like such a lovely opportunity for Josh to socialise."

Her apology sounds genuine, but something flickers behind her eyes—irritation, perhaps, or calculation. The expression passes so quickly I might have imagined it.

"Just for future reference," I say, trying to soften the criticism.

"Absolutely. I'll make sure to check with you first."

But twenty minutes later, as I pass Josh's room, I hear Sophie's voice through the half-open door.

"Don't worry, darling," she's saying, her tone warm with reassurance. "I'll always take care of you. That's what family does."

If he grows up believing that, what happens when she leaves? When she decides she's done with us? Where does that leave him, having learned to trust promises that were never meant to be permanent?

I retreat to my workspace, seeking refuge in the only space that still feels entirely mine. The small box room where I keep my laptop, my sketches, the diary I've been keeping since Sophie arrived—my attempt to make sense of the changes transforming our household.

I flip through recent entries, reading my own handwriting with the strange detachment that comes from reviewing private thoughts. Complaints about Sophie's increasing control. Worries about Josh's shifting loyalties. Fears about Daniel's dismissive attitude.

Maybe I was overreacting, cataloguing slights where there were none. But then I saw it.

An entry I don't remember writing, in handwriting that isn't quite mine.

Remember you're lucky.

The words are written in Sophie's neat script, inserted between my own messy paragraphs like a correction, a reminder, a threat. The ink is the same, the paper unmarked, but the hand is unmistakably hers.

My diary. My private thoughts, my safe space for processing the chaos she's created in our lives. She's been in here, reading my most vulnerable observations, then adding her own commentary like a teacher marking homework.

The violation hits like ice water. Not just the physical intrusion—entering my room, touching my possessions—but the psychological invasion. She's read my fears, my doubts, my desperate attempts to understand what's happening to my family.

And she's responded with a message designed to silence them.

Remember you're lucky.

The words pulse with quiet menace. Lucky to have her help. Lucky she's solved our domestic problems. Lucky she hasn't done something worse.

My hands shake as I close the diary, my safe space now contaminated by her presence. How long has she been reading my thoughts? What else has she seen, catalogued, filed away for future use?

The idea of her copying my voice, slipping into my role, even invading my inner world makes me feel stripped bare. Nothing is private anymore. Nothing is mine.

That evening, Josh bounces between Sophie and me with the easy affection of childhood, unaware of the undercurrents swirling around him. He chatters about his day, his upcoming playdate, the story Sophie promised to tell at bedtime.

Daniel arrives home to find dinner ready, the house tidy, our son happy and well-cared-for. He kisses my cheek and ruffles Josh's hair, his satisfaction obvious. Problems solved, domestic harmony restored, wife finally getting the help she needed.

He can't see what I see.

After Josh is tucked into bed with one of Sophie's elaborate stories, I listen to her moving through our house. Her footsteps in the hallway, her voice humming that impossible lullaby, her presence filling every corner of our domestic space.

She doesn't knock on my door to apologise for reading my diary. Doesn't acknowledge the violation or offer explanation. She simply continues her routine as if nothing has happened, as if my privacy was always hers to breach.

16.

The cursor blinks accusingly at me from my laptop screen, a digital metronome marking time I'm not using productively. Around me, Lancaster Library café hums with its usual afternoon energy—students hunched over textbooks, the hiss of the cappuccino machine, elderly locals reading newspapers with the concentrated attention of people who have nowhere else to be.

I should be working on the Keswick boutique logo, but every time I try to focus on typography or colour schemes, my mind drifts back to Sophie moving through my house, humming that impossible lullaby, rearranging our lives to suit her vision of domestic perfection.

Rain streaks the tall windows, turning the view of Castle Hill into an impressionist blur. I feel conspicuously out of place among the students with their easy confidence and endless possibilities. When did I become the older woman nursing a single coffee for too long, staring at nothing while her life unravels at home?

The diary entry haunts me. *Remember you're lucky.* Written in Sophie's neat handwriting, inserted between my own desperate attempts to make sense of what's happening to my family. The violation feels fresh every time I think about it—not just the physical intrusion of entering my workspace, but the psychological invasion of reading my private thoughts and responding to them.

She's been inside my head, cataloguing my fears, and she's left me a message designed to silence them.

I close the laptop. The pretence of productivity isn't fooling anyone, least of all myself. My chest feels tight with something that might be panic or fury—I can't tell the difference anymore.

The walk home should calm me, but instead it feeds the dread building behind my ribs. Every step brings me closer to whatever Sophie has orchestrated in my absence. Will Josh greet me with another of her philosophies? Will I find more evidence of her expanding influence?

I tell myself I'm being ridiculous. She's probably reading to him, or helping with puzzles, or any of the dozen constructive activities that make her such a treasure in Daniel's eyes. Normal, helpful nanny behaviour that only looks sinister through the lens of my exhausted paranoia.

But the violation of my diary proves I'm not imagining things. The boundary crossings, the calculated charm, the way she studies our family like we're specimens in her personal laboratory—it's all real.

I let myself into the house quietly, keys turning with barely a whisper in the lock. Voices drift from the living room—Sophie's warm encouragement and Josh's concentrated breathing that means he's working hard at something.

I pause in the doorway, taking in the scene before they notice me.

Josh sits at the coffee table with crayons scattered around him, his tongue poking out in concentration as he grips a red crayon with his whole fist. Sophie kneels beside him, one hand gently guiding his as he forms letters on lined paper.

Large, uneven letters that spell out the words: *Mummy Sophie.*

The letters blur because my eyes sting. That word is mine—his word for me—and seeing it attached to someone else feels like a theft of the deepest kind.

"What are you doing?"

Both of them look up, startled. Josh's face lights up with pride at his handiwork, while Sophie's expression shifts from surprise to something more guarded.

"Emma! You're back early." She recovers quickly, her voice carrying its usual warmth. "We were just practising writing, weren't we, Josh?"

"Look, Mummy!" Josh holds up the paper with obvious pride. "I wrote Sophie's name!"

But it doesn't say Sophie. It says Mummy Sophie, the letters wobbly but unmistakable, declaring a relationship that doesn't exist, shouldn't exist, can never exist.

"It was just a game," Sophie says, her tone light and dismissive. "Children experiment with words, don't they? He thought it was funny."

Josh giggles nervously. "Sophie helped me with the letters."

My hands clench at my sides. "You taught him to write that."

"Don't be silly." Sophie holds up the paper as if it's evidence of innocent play rather than calculated manipulation. "Children say all sorts of things. You know how imaginative they are at this age."

Her calmness makes me feel shrill, unreasonable, the hysterical mother overreacting to harmless child's play. But nothing about this feels harmless.

I kneel down to Josh's level, keeping my voice soft. "Sweetheart, listen. I'll always be your mummy. That's who I am. That's who I'll always be."

Josh's face scrunches with confusion. He looks between us. "But Sophie said she looks after me. And family is who looks after you."

There it is again. Sophie's phrase, her redefinition of family bonds that positions her as essential while reducing me to biological accident. She's been coaching him, preparing him, teaching him.

"Sophie is not your family," I say gently. "She's our helper. I'm your mummy."

"But she lives here," Josh says. "And she makes me sandwiches. And she knows the best stories."

He's right. She does make the sandwiches, tell the stories, keep the house ticking. But none of that changes the fact that I'm his mother.

Each observation still hits like a small knife—evidence of competence I can't match, affection I'm losing, daily presence that matters more than biology.

"Shall we put this away?" Sophie asks brightly, reaching for the crayons with brisk efficiency. "Time for Josh's snack, I think."

Of course she's humming again as she begins clearing the table. If domestic competence doesn't win me over, perhaps a folk soundtrack will.

The melody fills the room with its impossible familiarity.

Josh watches her with the easy affection of childhood, already moving on from the tension he doesn't understand. But I can't move on. Can't pretend that seeing those words—Mummy Sophie—hasn't changed something fundamental.

"I don't want him writing things like that," I say, my voice smaller now.

Sophie glances up from the crayons she's arranging. "Of course not. I understand completely. We'll stick to proper letters from now on."

Her agreement sounds reasonable, conciliatory, designed to make me feel petty for objecting to a child's innocent game. But the paper lies crumpled in the wastepaper basket like evidence of a crime I can't quite name.

Later, after Sophie has served Josh his snack and settled him in front of CBeebies, I retrieve the paper from the bin. The letters stare up at me, wobbly but definitive: *Mummy Sophie.*

Not Auntie Sophie or Friend Sophie or even just Sophie. Mummy. The most sacred word in Josh's vocabulary, the title I've carried since the moment he drew breath. Now it's been attached to someone else, written in his own hand, coached by the woman who's systematically dismantling every boundary in our home.

I fold the paper and slip it into my pocket. My son's hand wrote those letters, but the word belongs to me. And I don't know how to stop Sophie from taking it.

17.

Sophie appears in the kitchen doorway, pulling on her coat. "I'm just popping out for a walk," she says, adjusting her scarf. "Need some fresh air before bed."

I look up from the design sketches I'm pretending to work on. "A walk? It's nearly nine o'clock."

"I know it's late, but I've been cooped up inside all day. Won't be long." Her smile is warm, apologetic, designed to deflect further questions. "Daniel's got Josh sorted upstairs."

She's gone before I can respond, the front door clicking shut behind her. Through the kitchen window, I watch her silhouette disappear into the drizzle, her stride purposeful rather than leisurely.

The silence in the kitchen feels too heavy. I can't face another evening alone with my thoughts, trapped between my laptop and the growing certainty that something fundamental is wrong with our lives. Before I can second-guess myself, I grab my coat and follow.

The streets glisten under the streetlamps, wet cobbles reflecting amber light in fractured patterns. Sophie moves ahead of me with confident steps, her dark coat making her difficult to track in the shadows between pools of light. I keep my distance, pulling my hood up against the drizzle and the possibility of being seen.

If anyone saw me skulking like this, they'd think I was the one up to no good.

She passes the corner shop, the bus stop where students cluster during term time, the Victorian terraces that huddle together against the weather. Her route seems random at first, but there's purpose in her movement, destination in her stride.

The city centre opens ahead of us, quieter at this hour but still alive with the glow of pub windows and the distant sound of laughter spilling from doorways. The castle looms against the sky like a medieval warning, its ancient stones dark against the low clouds.

Sophie doesn't pause to admire the architecture or duck into any of the welcoming pubs. She heads straight for the Millennium Bridge, her footsteps echoing on the wet pavement.

The bridge spans the River Lune in an elegant arc of steel and glass. Below, the river runs black and silent, carrying the reflections of street lights towards Morecambe Bay. During the day, it's a pleasant walk with views across the water to the hills beyond. At night, it feels exposed, windswept, menacing.

Sophie crosses without hesitation, her figure small against the bridge's soaring lines. I follow at a careful distance. What could she possibly want on the other side? The suburbs there are residential, unremarkable, nothing that would draw a casual evening walker.

The other side of the bridge opens onto Skerton—older than Scotforth, rougher around the edges, the kind of neighbourhood that Lancaster's tourism brochures don't feature. Terraced streets climb the hill in neat rows, their Victorian brick facades weathered by decades of northern rain.

These streets hold the geography of my childhood. The bus stop where I waited each morning for the grammar school service, watching other kids walk to the local comprehensive while I clutched my blazer against the wind. The parade of shops where my mother sent me for emergency milk or bread, always with strict instructions to come straight home.

Sophie moves through them with the confidence of someone who belongs here, who knows these streets as well as I once did. She doesn't hesitate at junctions or pause to check street names. She walks like she's coming home.

My breath catches as she turns into Chatsworth Road, the street where I lived until I was sixteen. Nothing has changed much—the same terraced houses with their pocket-handkerchief front gardens, the same uneven pavement where I learned to ride my bike under my mother's watchful eye.

Sophie stops outside number thirty-seven.

My childhood home.

The shock hits like ice water. It feels like Mum has been stolen from me all over again—her kettle, her songs, her quiet endurance—claimed by someone who has no right to them.

My legs nearly buckle. I grip a lamppost for support, rainwater soaking through my coat as I watch Sophie fish a key from her pocket—a key that unlocks the front door to my past.

She slips inside as if she belongs there, as if this isn't the most profound violation yet in a campaign of systematic intrusion. Light appears in the front window, warm and welcoming, turning the house into a beacon in the night.

How does she have a key? How does she know this address? I've never mentioned Chatsworth Road to her, never spoken of my childhood home or the memories it holds. The house appears in one photograph on our dresser, but that image shows only the exterior—nothing that would reveal its interior layout or significance.

Yet Sophie has walked straight to it, unlocked it, claimed it.

The rain intensifies, drumming against the pavement with growing insistence. I stand frozen in the shadow of the lamppost, watching light move behind familiar curtains. Someone else is living in my mother's house, sleeping in bedrooms that once echoed with family arguments and whispered reconciliations.

But Sophie isn't just visiting. She has a key. She belongs there now, somehow, as if she's inherited not just my present life but my past as well.

Childhood memories flood back with brutal clarity. My mother at the kitchen table, hands wrapped around a mug of tea, her face drawn with the particular exhaustion that comes from loving someone who keeps breaking your heart. The narrow stairs where I used to sit listening to my parents' muffled arguments through thin walls. The back garden where she taught me the names of flowers while my father stayed inside, hidden behind his newspaper.

The house where I learned that families could fracture along invisible fault lines, that love wasn't always enough to hold things together, that sometimes the people you trust most are the ones who hurt you deepest.

Now Sophie has claimed that too.

I stumble backwards, my chest tight with something that might be panic or rage. Every assumption I've made about Sophie's motivations crumbles as the truth crystallises with sickening clarity. This isn't coincidence. It isn't even simple manipulation.

Sophie has been planning this.

The pieces fall into place with terrible logic. She knows this city, these streets, this house. She knows me in ways I never authorised, never suspected.

I force my feet to carry me away from Chatsworth Road, back through the maze of terraced streets towards the bridge. But Sophie's light continues to burn in that window, marking territory I thought was safely buried in my past.

18.

Early December has leached the warmth from Lancaster, leaving behind brittle air that stings the lungs. The sun hangs low even at half past three, casting long shadows that stretch across the playground of Dallas Road Primary.

I huddle against the school railings wrapped in my heaviest coat, scarf pulled up to my nose, watching Sophie emerge from the building with Josh bouncing beside her. His school bag swings wildly as he chatters about something that's captured his imagination, gesturing with the exaggerated enthusiasm that makes other parents smile.

Sophie listens with the focused attention she brings to everything, nodding and asking questions that make Josh beam. They make such a perfect picture—devoted carer and happy child—that my chest tightens with something that might be envy or grief.

I expect them to turn towards home, following our usual route through Scotforth's familiar streets. Instead, Sophie takes Josh's mittened hand and heads in the opposite direction, past the corner shops and terraced houses, towards the outskirts where Lancaster begins to fray at the edges.

Something sharp moves through me—part curiosity, part dread. Without quite deciding to, I begin following.

They move through side streets I barely know, past allotments where winter vegetables struggle in the hard ground and bare-branched trees reach towards the grey sky. Suburban comfort gives way to something rawer, more industrial, the kind of Lancaster the tourists never see.

Sophie keeps up her cheerful conversation with Josh, pointing out interesting shapes in the clouds. To anyone observing, they're simply on a pleasant afternoon walk. Am I the one making this sinister? Am I losing my grip on reality?

We emerge onto the footpath that runs alongside the River Lune, near the sprawl of the Marsh estate. The area stretches ahead in shades of brown and grey—mud underfoot, concrete barriers marked with graffiti, the sullen water reflecting nothing but emptiness. Gulls cry overhead, wheeling and diving for scraps.

It's a bleak place, especially in winter. Not somewhere you'd bring a small child for entertainment.

Yet Sophie leads Josh confidently along the path as if this were the most natural destination in the world.

"Look, darling," she says, pointing towards a patch of muddy grass where a few hardy ducks paddle in the shallows. "Shall we see if they're hungry?"

Josh breaks free and runs ahead, his wellies splashing through puddles. His cheeks flush pink from the cold, and for a second I almost smile. Then I see whose hand he was reaching for when he stumbled.

Sophie settles onto a weathered bench, pulling a packet of stale bread from her bag. She watches Josh with obvious affection, her expression soft in the failing light.

I step out from behind the concrete pillar I've been using for cover. "Sophie."

She turns without surprise, her expression almost expectant, as if she's been waiting for this moment.

"Emma." Her smile carries warmth that doesn't quite reach her eyes. "I wondered when you'd appear."

The casual tone stops me short. As if she knew I was following. Planned for this confrontation.

"Why are you living in my old house?" The words tumble out before I can stop them.

Sophie tilts her head slightly. "Which house would that be?"

"You know which house. Thirty-seven Chatsworth Road. My childhood home. I saw you there—you have a key."

"Ah." Sophie nods as if I've solved a simple puzzle. "What a coincidence. Lancaster's a small place, isn't it? When I saw it was available to rent, it felt...familiar. Sometimes you just know when somewhere is right for you."

The explanation sounds reasonable. But the coincidence stretches credibility past breaking point.

"You've been in my bedroom," I say, my voice growing stronger. "You've read my diary. You knew that house mattered to me."

Sophie's smile doesn't waver. "You're imagining things, Emma. I dust your room sometimes—it's part of helping out. As for your diary..." She shrugs delicately. "I've never read anyone's diary. That would be a terrible invasion of privacy."

The denial comes so smoothly, so convincingly, that for a moment I doubt what I saw. Every word feels like a blade disguised as kindness, slicing away at my certainty. She has an answer for everything, explanations that sound perfectly reasonable while explaining nothing.

"Then how do you know my mother's lullaby?" I ask, desperate to anchor myself to something concrete. "The song you hum—it's not recorded anywhere. It only existed in our family."

"Lullaby?" Sophie's brow furrows with apparent confusion. "I hum all sorts of things, Emma. Tunes get stuck in your head, don't they? From the radio, from films. Maybe it's more common than you think."

I realise with growing horror that I'm the one who looks desperate here, standing in this desolate place making wild accusations while Sophie remains calm, concerned, slightly pitying. She's managed to position me as the unstable party.

Josh runs back towards us, clutching a muddy stick. His eyes are bright with simple pleasure, his mitten soggy from the river. "Sophie, look what I found! It looks like a sword!"

"How wonderful," she says, examining his discovery with serious attention. "A proper knight's sword."

Josh giggles, reaching automatically for Sophie's hand. The gesture cuts through me like cold steel. My son, seeking comfort from someone who's systematically dismantling our family.

"We're going home," I say, extending my own hand towards Josh. "Come on, love. It's getting dark."

Josh's face falls slightly, but he obeys. The three of us stand there for a moment in an awkward triangle, connected by a child who doesn't understand the adult currents swirling around him.

"Of course," Sophie says, rising gracefully. "I'll catch up in a few minutes. Just want to enjoy the peace a bit longer."

She settles back onto the bench with the contentment of someone exactly where they want to be. As if this desolate riverbank offers something she can't find elsewhere.

I lead Josh away along the muddy path, adjusting his mitten where it's slipped loose. Behind us, Sophie remains seated, a still figure against the grey landscape.

At the edge of the footpath, I glance back once. Sophie hasn't moved. She's still watching us go, her posture relaxed, almost meditative.

She doesn't look caught. She doesn't look defensive or guilty.

She looks content—as though everything is proceeding exactly according to plan.

19.

The bay window weeps with drizzle while fairy lights begin to twinkle in neighbours' houses. Christmas creeps closer with its promise of family harmony I can't imagine achieving. I sit at the kitchen table, hands wrapped around a mug of tea gone cold, rehearsing words that sound more desperate each time I practise them.

Daniel will be home soon from another late meeting, another crisis that keeps him at the office while Sophie orchestrates our domestic life with increasing confidence.

Tonight, I need him to listen. Really listen, not just provide the reasonable explanations that dismiss every concern I raise.

The key in the lock announces his arrival, followed by the familiar sounds of coat hanging, briefcase setting down, the small rituals of a man transitioning from work to home.

He appears in the kitchen doorway looking tired but satisfied, the expression of someone whose professional problems have clear solutions.

"Good day?" I ask, though my voice carries none of its usual lightness.

"Productive. Morrison account is finally sorted." He kisses my cheek absently, his attention already drifting towards the neat pile of post Sophie has arranged on the counter. "Smells good in here. What did Sophie make?"

Always Sophie. Never what did we have for dinner, never did you cook. The assumption that our domestic contentment flows from her efforts rather than mine cuts deeper each time.

"Shepherd's pie," I say. "Daniel, I need to tell you something."

Something in my tone makes him look up properly, his tired satisfaction replaced by wariness. "What is it now?"

The words tumble out in a rush, as if speaking quickly might make them more convincing. I tell him about following Sophie after school, about the route across the Millennium Bridge, about watching her unlock the door to thirty-seven Chatsworth Road with a key that shouldn't exist.

"She's living in my childhood home," I say, my voice shaking with urgency. "Not renting nearby, not staying with friends. Living in the actual house where I grew up. She has a key, Daniel. She belongs there somehow."

Daniel listens with the patient attention he gives to Josh's elaborate bedtime stories, nodding at appropriate intervals but with an expression that suggests he's waiting for the punchline.

When I finish, he chuckles softly. "Coincidence, Em. Lancaster's small—half the people we know live in houses you've walked past before. Remember when we discovered Gemma's mum used to live three doors down from your nan? These things happen in places like this."

His reasonable tone makes my account sound hysterical by comparison. The urgency I felt, the cold dread of discovery, all of it evaporates under his casual dismissal.

"It's not coincidence. She's been planning this."

"Planning what, exactly? Moving to Lancaster? Renting an available house?" Daniel sits heavily in his chair, rubbing his eyes with the gesture of a man dealing with more stress than he can handle. "Emma, you've been under enormous pressure. Work deadlines, Josh's needs, managing everything here. Could be the burnout. Maybe this is grief bubbling up—your mum's death, memories of that house. It's natural to read significance into coincidences when you're emotionally vulnerable."

Grief bubbling up. Emotionally vulnerable. As if my legitimate concerns are symptoms of unprocessed trauma rather than rational responses to threatening behaviour.

"She hummed my mother's lullaby. She's been in our bedroom, read my diary. These aren't coincidences, they're violations."

Daniel reaches across the table and covers my hand with his, the gesture meant to comfort but feeling condescending instead. "Love, you're making connections that aren't there. Sophie's been nothing but helpful. She's transformed our lives—look at Josh, look at this house, look at how much calmer everything is."

"You always take her side." The accusation escapes before I can stop it, raw with weeks of accumulated resentment.

Daniel's expression hardens. "I don't take sides, Emma. I look at evidence. Sophie hasn't given me a reason not to trust her. She cooks, she cleans, she helps with Josh—exactly what we hired her to do. You're the one making wild accusations based on coincidences and paranoid interpretations."

The word paranoid hangs between us like a blade. Not concerned or worried or protective—paranoid. As if my maternal instincts, my growing unease about our family's safety, are symptoms of mental instability rather than legitimate warnings.

"She's dismantling our family piece by piece," I say, my voice smaller now, defeated. "Can't you see it?"

"What I see is a woman who's helped us when we needed it most, and a wife who's determined to find fault with that help because accepting it feels like admitting failure." Daniel's voice carries the particular edge that means he's tired of the conversation. "Maybe you should talk to someone professional about this, Em. These fixations aren't healthy."

In Daniel's mind, I'm not a woman protecting her family from a genuine threat. I'm a patient who needs therapeutic intervention.

The conversation dies there, smothered by his certainty and my inability to provide evidence he'll accept. Daniel retreats to the living room with his laptop, surrounding himself with the comfortable logic of spreadsheets and tax returns while I clear the dinner dishes.

Upstairs, I listen to Sophie reading Josh his bedtime story, her voice carrying the theatrical warmth that makes him giggle with delight. The sound should comfort me—my son happy, safe, loved. Instead, it feels like another small defeat in a war I'm losing without understanding the rules.

Later, alone in our bedroom while Daniel works downstairs, I replay his words with the obsessive attention of someone picking at a wound. Maybe he's right. Maybe I am paranoid, seeing patterns that don't exist, connections that live only in my stressed imagination.

But the image won't leave me—Sophie's key sliding smoothly into the lock of my childhood home, her expression of calm satisfaction as she disappeared inside. The certainty in her movements, the familiarity with which she navigated those remembered streets.

That wasn't coincidence. That was ownership.

The floorboards creak softly as Sophie moves across the landing from Josh's room to her own, her footsteps light but somehow possessive. She's claimed not just Josh's bedtime routine but the very rhythms of our house, the domestic choreography that should belong to me.

Daniel's laughter still rings in my ears—not because it soothed me, but because it proved I was utterly alone in this fight.

20.

The tinsel draped around Lancaster Library's café counter catches the afternoon light, but I feel no seasonal cheer as I pack my laptop away. Around me, students chatter about Christmas plans while elderly locals discuss family visits with the mixture of anticipation and dread that marks December conversations.

I should share their festive energy. Christmas shopping, mince pies, the promise of family time that everyone pretends to want. Instead, I dread the walk home through streets bright with fairy lights and the cheerful chaos of holiday shoppers spilling from Penny Street's boutiques.

The December air bites at my cheeks as I navigate Lancaster's crowded pavements, dodging couples laden with shopping bags and families herding excited children between toy shops and sweet stalls. The city has dressed itself for celebration—garlands strung between lamp posts, windows glowing with seasonal displays, the scent of mulled wine drifting from pub doorways.

It all feels like theatre I'm watching from the outside, unable to find my way onto the stage.

I pause at the corner where the path splits—one way leads past the canal, the other through the city centre. The canal route is shorter, but my feet won't turn that direction. They never do anymore, not since that day when the water moved too fast and I moved too slow.

The memory tries to surface—Josh's voice high with panic, my legs like stone—but I shake my head hard, choosing the longer route through crowds that don't know what kind of mother I really am.

The key turns in our front door with its familiar scrape, but the warmth that greets me isn't just from the central heating. Light spills from the living room in shades of gold and crimson, accompanied by Josh's delighted laughter and the rustle of tinsel.

I step into the doorway and freeze.

Our Christmas tree stands in the bay window, fully decorated and glowing with fairy lights. Not the sparse, lopsided effort we usually manage after an evening of bickering about bauble placement and tangled wires, but a picture-perfect creation that belongs in a John Lewis window. Every ornament hangs at precisely the right height, the lights distributed with mathematical precision, the tinsel draped with professional competence.

Sophie kneels beside the tree helping Josh position the star on the topmost branch, her hands steady on his small waist as he stretches upward. The tableau is achingly perfect—devoted carer and happy child sharing a moment of seasonal magic.

Daniel beams from the sofa, his face bright with satisfaction. "Look what they did together! Isn't it wonderful?"

What they did together. Not what we did as a family, not what Josh and I accomplished while waiting for Daddy to come home. What Sophie and Josh created while I was elsewhere, excluded from our own family traditions.

"It's lovely," I manage, though my voice sounds thin, forced.

Decorating the Christmas tree has been our ritual since Josh was old enough to hold a bauble without dropping it. The annual battle to untangle lights that have somehow formed complex knots during eleven months of storage. The arguments about whether the star or the angel should crown the top. The inevitable disaster when Josh tries to help and sends ornaments crashing to the floor.

It's messy, chaotic, often frustrating—but it's ours. Was ours.

Now Sophie has transformed our domestic shambles into something worthy of a Christmas card, complete with Josh's rapt attention and Daniel's grateful approval.

"Perhaps we could take it down and do it together," I suggest, my voice carefully casual. "As a family tradition."

Daniel's smile falters while Sophie looks up from adjusting a lower branch, her expression gently confused.

"But Josh loved doing it this way," she says, her tone carrying just the right note of concern for a child's feelings. "Didn't you, sweetheart? We had such fun choosing where everything should go."

Josh nods eagerly, his face glowing with pride in their shared achievement. "Sophie let me put all the red ones on myself! And we made the lights go in a spiral!"

His enthusiasm cuts through me. This is what I wanted—my son excited about Christmas, engaged in family traditions, creating happy memories. But I'd imagined being part of those memories, not watching them unfold from the sidelines.

"It's just," I begin, then falter. How do I explain that this perfect tree represents another piece of our family life that's been optimised without my consent? Another tradition I've been edited out of?

"She's taking over, Daniel." The words escape before I can stop them, raw with frustration. "Can't you see it? She's systematically replacing me in every aspect of our family life."

Daniel's face hardens with the particular expression he wears when he thinks I'm being unreasonable. "Emma, for God's sake. She spent her afternoon making Christmas magical for our son while you were at the library. How is that taking over?"

"Because decorating the tree is our tradition. Something we do together, as a family."

"We are doing it as a family," Daniel snaps. "Sophie is part of this household. She lives here, she looks after Josh, she contributes more to this family's happiness than—"

He stops himself, but the unfinished comparison hangs between us.

Sophie rises from her position by the tree, smoothing her jumper. "Perhaps I should check on dinner," she says quietly. "Let you two talk."

Her tactical withdrawal is perfectly timed, leaving Daniel and me facing each other across the glowing tree while Josh continues arranging ornaments with oblivious contentment. She's made herself absent from the conflict while ensuring her handiwork remains as evidence of her domestic competence.

"This is what I mean," I say desperately. "She orchestrates everything. Creates these perfect moments, then disappears when there's conflict, leaving us to fight about whether we should be grateful or concerned."

"What exactly are we supposed to be concerned about, Emma? That our son is happy? That our house is clean? That someone cares enough to make Christmas special without being asked?"

"That's not—"

"That she's holding the family together while you obsess over imaginary problems and isolate yourself from the people trying to help you." His voice rises, then drops as he glances at Josh playing nearby. "You're jealous of her. Just admit it."

The accusation lands hard. "I'm not jealous—"

"Aren't you? She's competent, calm, everything seems effortless for her. She connects with Josh naturally while you struggle with basic parenting tasks. She makes our home feel like a home instead of a disaster zone."

Each word hits with surgical precision, finding every insecurity I've tried to bury. He's right, isn't he? Sophie does make everything look effortless. She does connect with Josh in ways that seem natural while

I fumble through motherhood like someone playing a role I haven't learned properly.

But that doesn't make her infiltration acceptable. That doesn't give her the right to claim our family traditions as her own.

"She's erasing me," I say, but the words come out jumbled, desperate, feeding his perception of my instability. "Piece by piece, she's taking everything that makes me Josh's mother, your wife, the centre of this family."

Daniel's expression shifts from anger to something that might be pity. "Emma, listen to yourself. You're talking like someone's trying to murder you, not help you."

He gathers Josh from beside the tree, lifting him with the easy strength of fatherhood. "Come on, mate. Let's run you a bath."

They disappear upstairs, leaving me alone with Sophie's perfect Christmas tree. The fairy lights blink cheerfully, cycling through their programmed sequence of colours. Red, gold, green, white—each hue reflecting off the baubles.

I sink onto the sofa Daniel has vacated, staring at the tree that should represent family joy but feels like evidence of my redundancy. Every ornament tells the story of an afternoon I wasn't part of, a tradition that's been claimed by someone who has no right to our family history.

The house settles around me with its familiar creaks and sighs, but the sounds feel different now. Sophie's presence has changed the very acoustics of our home, made it ring with her efficiency rather than our chaos.

From upstairs comes the sound of bath time—Daniel's deep voice mixing with Josh's higher tones and the splash of water. Normal family sounds, except I'm not part of them. I'm the audience to their domestic harmony, watching from the cheap seats.

21.

The café on King Street glows with Christmas warmth—fairy lights strung around the windows, a holly wreath on the door. I arrive early, choosing a table by the window where I can watch Lancaster's festive bustle while rehearsing words I've practised all morning.

Gemma will understand. She has to. She's known me since we were teenagers navigating the social minefield of Lancaster Girls' Grammar, sharing secrets and ambitions over cheap bottles of wine. If anyone can see past Sophie's perfect facade to the manipulation beneath, it's my oldest friend.

Gemma arrives in a flurry of scarves and shopping bags, her cheeks flushed from the December cold. She settles across from me with obvious relief, shrugging off her coat to reveal the kind of effortlessly stylish outfit that makes teaching look glamorous.

"You look tired," she says, studying my face with the frank assessment of long friendship. "Everything alright?"

Over lattes that smell of cinnamon and false comfort, I spill everything. Sophie's boundary violations, her systematic takeover of our family traditions, the way Josh has started calling her family while treating me like a supporting character in his own life. The words pour out in a desperate rush, my voice wavering between anger and something that might be grief.

"She's replacing me," I finish, my hands wrapped around my mug for warmth it can't provide. "Piece by piece, she's becoming Josh's mother while I become irrelevant."

"Em," she says gently, "it sounds like Sophie's been a blessing for your family. Maybe you're too close to the situation to see it clearly."

The response hits like cold water. "What do you mean?"

"You've been under enormous pressure since Josh was born. The burnout, the money worries, trying to be everything to everyone." Gemma's voice carries the patient tone of someone explaining something obvious. "Maybe your grief about your mum, your stress about work—maybe it's colouring how you see Sophie's help."

Each word lands, building a wall of reasonable doubt around my legitimate concerns. Gemma sees my struggles, my failures, my obvious need for the intervention Sophie represents.

"But she's not just helping. She's taking over. Josh prefers her stories to mine, Daniel takes her side in every argument, she's living in my childhood home—"

"Your childhood home?" Gemma's eyebrows rise slightly. "That does sound like a coincidence. But Em, think about the positives. Josh is thriving, isn't he? Daniel seems less strained when I see him. Your work has picked up because you have the time to focus properly."

The rational assessment makes my fears sound hysterical by comparison. Gemma catalogues the benefits of Sophie's presence with the precision of someone grading an essay, finding my paranoid interpretations wanting.

"Maybe it's okay to accept the help," Gemma says. "You don't have to fight everything, Em. Sometimes the universe sends exactly what we need, even if we're too proud to admit we need it."

The philosophy stings because it echoes everyone else's response to my concerns. Daniel, the neighbours, now Gemma—all of them see Sophie as salvation while I'm cast as the ungrateful recipient of miraculous intervention.

"She's not what she seems," I say, but even to my own ears the protest sounds weak, unsubstantiated.

"Maybe not. Maybe she's human, flawed, a bit eager to please." Gemma reaches across the table and covers my hand with hers, the gesture meant to comfort but feeling patronizing instead. "But maybe she's also exactly what your family needs. I just don't want you to make yourself ill fighting something that might actually be good for you."

The concern in her voice cuts deeper than anger would have. She's treating me like a fragile thing, someone whose judgement can't be trusted, whose instincts need to be gently corrected by more rational minds.

I try to argue further, to explain about the diary entry, the phone calls, the calculated way Sophie positions herself at the centre of every family moment. But the words come out shrill, desperate, feeding Gemma's obvious belief that I'm the problem rather than Sophie.

The café buzzes around us with seasonal contentment—couples sharing mince pies, families planning Christmas visits, the comfortable chaos of people whose lives make sense. I feel conspicuous in my distress, the woman having a breakdown in public while her friend provides damage control.

"I should head back," Gemma says eventually, gathering her shopping bags. She kisses my cheek before leaving, her perfume a reminder of the confident, capable woman she's become while I've been drowning in domestic quicksand.

Walking back through Lancaster's Christmas-dressed streets, I feel ghostlike among the shoppers laden with bags and good intentions.

Everyone else belongs to this festive tableau while I drift through it like a spirit haunting scenes of contentment I can't access. Even Gemma doesn't believe me. My oldest friend, the person who should know me well enough to trust my instincts, has dismissed my concerns with the gentle patronization reserved for people whose grip on reality needs adjustment.

The castle looms ahead, its medieval stones dark against the December sky. For centuries, it housed people who'd been judged dangerous to society's order—criminals, political prisoners, those whose version of truth didn't align with official narratives. Now it's a tourist attraction, its dark history sanitized for family consumption.

But standing in its shadow, I understand how easily someone can become the designated problem while the real threat operates with everyone's blessing. Sophie has positioned herself as the solution while I've been cast as the woman who can't accept help gracefully, whose paranoid fears threaten the domestic harmony she's created.

The bells toll five o'clock. Time for normal families to be heading home to warmth and dinner and the comfortable routines that mark the end of ordinary days.

I should go home too, to the house where Sophie will be preparing something delicious while Josh chatters about his day and Daniel counts the hours until bedtime. The perfect domestic scene I should be grateful to witness rather than resentful about being excluded from.

I'd come seeking comfort, but left with only one certainty—if even Gemma thought Sophie was a blessing, then maybe the madness was mine after all.

22.

The house settles around me as Sophie's footsteps fade down the street, her voice carrying back through the December air—something about errands in town, leaving me alone with the silence I've been craving for weeks.

My hands tremble as I climb the stairs, each step creaking like an accusation. Sophie's room stands at the end of the landing, its door slightly ajar as always, as if she has nothing to hide.

I shouldn't be doing this. I know I shouldn't. But the alternative—never knowing—is unbearable.

The room greets me with its usual unsettling perfection. The bed is made with hospital corners, not a wrinkle in the duvet cover. Her desk stands clear except for a neat stack of university textbooks and a single pen. Clothes hang in the wardrobe arranged by colour, each garment spaced precisely the same distance from its neighbours.

It feels staged, like a showroom designed to suggest domestic harmony without revealing anything personal. No photos beyond the single frame of her parents, no clutter, no mess—nothing to prove a life actually being lived here.

I start with the obvious places. Dresser drawers: folded jumpers in perfect stacks, underwear organised by type and colour. Desk drawers: notebooks filled with neat, careful handwriting, highlighters arranged in rainbow order. Nothing to suggest the chaos of ordinary life.

Who lives like this? Who maintains such rigid order unless they're hiding something behind it?

I push aside the wardrobe hangers with growing desperation, running my hands along the back where fabric meets wood. My fingers brush against something out of place—a hard edge jutting slightly beyond the smooth line of the panels. I tug, and a slim card folder slides free from where it's been wedged flat against the back wall, hidden behind the hanging clothes.

The folder is plain, brown, the kind an office might discard without thought.

Inside, there's a neat bundle of papers held with an elastic band. My breath catches as I lift them out with shaking hands.

My name stares back at me in bold letters across the top page.

Emma Hartwell.

My maiden name. Not Cartwright. Hartwell. The name that belonged to the girl I used to be, the girl from Skerton. Beneath it: a list of addresses spanning decades. Chatsworth Road. The flat near the university. The bedsit in town. Every place I'd lived, traced with methodical attention.

Other documents follow—photocopied certificates, brittle letters, fragments of records that feel like they've been handled too many times.

And at the bottom, a photograph.

My father. Younger than I remember him, smiling with the careless confidence of the 1980s. Across his face, one word scrawled in red ink: *LIAR.*

The room tilts. My legs buckle and I sink onto her bed, clutching the photo.

This isn't about Daniel, or Josh, or domestic order. Sophie's obsession isn't with my present—it's with my past. With my family. With him.

The word LIAR burns across my father's smile like an accusation, like a threat.

What did he do? What could he have hidden that would bring Sophie here?

I think of her humming my mother's lullaby. Of the way she walked Skerton's streets as if they were her own. Of how easily she slipped into our lives, as though she'd been rehearsing the role for years.

Because she has been rehearsing.

A sound jolts me back—someone laughing in the street outside, a passing voice carried thinly through the December air. Not Sophie. Not yet.

My pulse hammers as I gather the papers, stacking them carefully and slipping them back into the card folder.

I wedge it against the wardrobe's back wall, behind the neat row of clothes, sliding the hangers forward until they fall in perfect symmetry once more.

The bed looks untouched. The desk remains immaculate. The photograph, though—it burns against my palm, heavier than paper should ever be.

When I step back, the room looks as pristine as it did when I entered, as if I've never been here at all.

But the knowledge won't go back.

As I close the door, the house feels altered, charged with new meaning.

Sophie isn't saving us. She isn't even competing with me for Daniel or Josh.

She's come for me.

23.

Light fades outside our bay window while I pace the living room. Rain streaks the glass in patterns that blur the street beyond, turning the familiar Scotforth terraces into smudges of brick and light.

My nerves buzz.

The photograph sits heavy in my pocket, my father's face branded with that single devastating word: *LIAR*.

Every few minutes I touch it through the fabric, reassuring myself it's real, that I haven't imagined the evidence of Sophie's obsession with my family.

Finally, I have proof.

Something concrete that even Daniel can't dismiss as paranoid fantasy. Sophie has been researching my past, collecting documents about my family, preparing for something that goes far deeper than simple domestic manipulation.

But knowing the truth and convincing others of it are different challenges entirely.

Daniel has spent weeks, months seeing me as the unstable party while Sophie glows with helpful competence. How do I shatter that narrative without looking even more unhinged?

The front door opens with its familiar scrape, followed by Sophie's light footsteps in the hallway. She hums softly as she shakes off her coat—that damned folk tune again, my mother's lullaby that shouldn't exist in her memory.

Shopping bag in hand, cheeks pink from the December cold, she moves through our hallway with the easy confidence of someone who belongs here. More than belongs—owns. Every gesture speaks of proprietorial comfort, as if she's the mistress of this house while I'm merely a tolerated guest.

"Sophie." My voice comes out sharper than intended.

She looks up with that warm smile that's fooled everyone else, her eyes bright with apparent pleasure at seeing me. "Emma! How was your afternoon? I found those lovely apples you like at the market—thought I'd make a crumble for after dinner."

"I know what you're doing," I say, the words tumbling out before I can rehearse them properly. "I know you've been digging into my family. I found the documents. I found the photo."

For just a moment, Sophie freezes. Her smile falters, and something flickers behind her eyes. But she recovers so quickly I might have imagined the crack in her facade.

"Emma." Her voice carries wounded innocence, hurt confusion. "What are you talking about?"

"Don't." I pull the photograph from my pocket, holding it up like evidence in a courtroom. "My father's picture. With 'LIAR' written across his face in your handwriting. Hidden in a secret drawer behind your wardrobe."

Sophie's eyes widen as she takes in the photograph, her expression shifting through shock, hurt, and something that might be betrayal. "Why are you so threatened by me, Emma? I'm just trying to help your family."

The response catches me off guard. Not denial, not explanation, but a question that turns my accusation back on me. As if I'm the problem for discovering her deception rather than her being the problem for perpetrating it.

"You've been researching my past, my family, living in my childhood home—"

"Because I care about you!" Sophie's voice trembles with emotion, her eyes filling with tears. "I've done everything for you, for Josh, for this family. And you repay me by sneaking into my room like a common thief?"

Her tears look genuine, her hurt authentic, and for a horrible moment I doubt my own perceptions.

"But the photo—" I begin, but Sophie's sobs cut through my protest.

"I can't believe you'd do this to me," she whispers, clutching her chest as if my accusations have physically wounded her. "After everything I've sacrificed to help your family."

The front door slams, followed by the heavy tread of Daniel's shoes on the hallway tiles.

"What's going on?" he demands, taking in the scene—me holding the photograph like a weapon, Sophie weeping by the door.

Sophie turns to him with tear-brightened eyes, her voice breaking with hurt. "She was in my room, Daniel. Going through my things. She's accusing me of awful things, making up stories."

"You searched her room? What the hell, Em?"

The condemnation in his tone stops my breath. Not concern for my obvious distress, not curiosity about what I might have found, but immediate judgement that I'm the villain in this scenario.

"Look at this!" I thrust the photograph towards him, desperate for him to see what I see. "She's obsessed with my family. She has documents, research, evidence that she's been planning this for years."

Daniel barely glances at the photograph before his attention returns to Sophie's tear-stained face. "You're paranoid, Emma. Sophie is here because you couldn't cope, and now you're punishing her for stepping up when you failed."

"But why would she have a photo of my father?" I ask. "Why would she write 'liar' across his face?"

Daniel's nostrils flare. "Maybe it's not your father! Maybe it's someone else entirely, and you're so desperate to find conspiracy that you're seeing connections that don't exist."

The possibility hadn't occurred to me, and for a moment doubt creeps in. Could I have misidentified the photograph? Could my stress-addled brain be creating patterns from coincidence?

But no. I know my father's face, know the way his smile tilted slightly to the left, know the scar above his eyebrow from a childhood accident. That photograph is definitely him, definitely marked with Sophie's condemnation.

"I should leave," Sophie whispers, her voice barely audible through her tears. "I don't want to cause trouble for your family. Maybe it would be better if I go."

"Don't be silly, Sophie," Daniel says, his voice warm with reassurance. "You've been amazing for us. Don't let Emma's...difficulties drive you away."

Her difficulties. As if my legitimate concerns about manipulation and deception are character flaws rather than rational responses to threatening behaviour.

Sophie lifts her head to meet Daniel's eyes, her expression brave despite her tears. "I just wanted to help. To give Josh the stability he deserves, to support Emma when she's struggling. But if my presence is causing this much conflict..."

"Your presence isn't the problem," Daniel says firmly, his gaze finding mine across the room. "The problem is Emma."

Sophie's gaze flicks to me over Daniel's shoulder as he continues reassuring her, and for just a moment her mask slips. The tears stop, her expression clears, and she looks at me with calm satisfaction.

Her eyes say what her lips don't: I'd lost.

24.

I wake to silence and the grey light of mid-morning streaming through curtains. The house feels unnaturally quiet, as if someone has wrapped it in cotton wool while I slept. My phone shows half past nine—Daniel will have already taken Josh to school, probably with Sophie chattering beside them about the day's plans.

The argument from last night crashes back with sickening clarity. Daniel's fury when he found me holding the photograph, his immediate assumption that I was the villain while Sophie played the wounded victim. The way he dismissed my evidence without examination, as if my word carried no weight against her tears.

I drag myself downstairs to find the kitchen gleaming. Breakfast dishes washed and stacked, surfaces wiped to showroom standard, the morning's chaos erased as if it never existed. Even the argument feels sanitised by her domestic competence, reduced to an unfortunate episode in an otherwise well-managed household.

The photograph lies on my bedside table where I left it, my father's face staring up at me with that familiar lopsided smile. The word *LIAR* burns across his features in careful handwriting, an accusation that feels both devastating and meaningless without context.

What did he lie about? What secrets from decades past could have motivated Sophie's elaborate infiltration of our family? I trace the letters with my fingertip, as if the ink might reveal its secrets through touch alone.

My mind spirals through possibilities, each more disturbing than the last.

The uncertainty makes me physically sick.

My hands shake as I make coffee, the mundane task requiring more concentration than it should. Nothing feels solid anymore—not my marriage, not my family, not even my own perceptions of reality.

To escape the house and my churning thoughts, I walk into Lancaster's city centre through streets slick with December drizzle. The cobbles on Penny Street gleam like oil beneath the grey sky, reflecting the Christmas lights strung between lamp posts in fractured rainbows.

Dalton Square opens ahead of me, transformed by the seasonal market into something from a Christmas card. Wooden stalls sell mulled wine and roasted chestnuts while families browse handmade crafts and children's faces glow with excitement at the carousel spinning near the Town Hall. The enormous Christmas tree dominates the square, its lights twinkling against the sky.

The festive cheer feels like mockery.

I'm buying coffee from a cheerful vendor when I see her.

Through the crowd of shoppers and tourists, Sophie stands at the edge of the square talking to a tall man I don't recognise. Their heads are bent close together, their body language suggesting conspiracy rather than casual conversation. Even at this distance, something about their intimacy makes my pulse spike with alarm.

Who is he? Another player in whatever game Sophie is orchestrating? Someone else with secrets about my family, about my father's mysterious crimes?

I push through the crowd, dodging pushchairs and shopping bags, trying to get closer without being seen. But a group of carol singers chooses that moment to launch into 'Silent Night' directly in my path, their voices rising in harmony while their collecting buckets block my view.

When they finally move on, Sophie has vanished.

I scan the square frantically, searching every face in the crowd. The tall man is gone too, as if they've melted into the Christmas shoppers like smoke. Market stalls that should provide hiding places reveal nothing when I check behind them. The carousel continues its cheerful rotation, children shrieking with delight while their parents wave from the sidelines.

No trace of Sophie or her mysterious companion.

I sink onto a bench beside the Christmas tree, my legs suddenly unreliable. Was she really there? The conversation had looked urgent, secretive, significant—but now I can't summon the details with any clarity. What did the man look like? How old was he? What were they discussing with such apparent intensity?

The harder I try to focus on the memory, the more it slips away like water through my fingers.

Shoppers flow past in endless streams, their arms laden with bags and their faces bright with seasonal purpose. A brass band strikes up 'Jingle Bells' near the Town Hall while children dance to the familiar rhythm. Everything pulses with the kind of communal joy that makes my isolation feel acute.

Gemma's words echo in my head with growing insistence: *Maybe your grief and stress are colouring how you see Sophie's help. Maybe the universe sends exactly what we need, even if we're too proud to admit we need it.*

Daniel's furious dismissal follows: *You're paranoid. She's here because you couldn't cope, and now you're punishing her for helping.*

What if they're right? What if my desperate need to find conspiracy has created patterns from coincidence, threats from kindness, enemies from allies? What if Sophie really is just a young woman trying to help a struggling family, while I've constructed an elaborate mythology around innocent gestures?

The photograph in my pocket feels less like evidence now and more like symptom—proof not of Sophie's deception but of my own deteriorating grip on reality. Maybe I misidentified the face, projected my father's features onto a stranger because I needed the connection to exist.

Maybe the man in the square was never with Sophie at all, just another Christmas shopper whose conversation I've transformed into conspiracy through the lens of my paranoid fantasies.

The possibility terrifies me more than Sophie herself. If I can't trust my own perceptions, if my instincts have become symptoms rather than warnings, then I'm truly alone in ways I hadn't imagined.

The Christmas lights blur as tears I didn't know I was crying catch the coloured glow. Around me, Lancaster celebrates the season with traditional English determination—stoic in the face of December weather, finding joy in community rituals that stretch back generations.

But I sit separate from it all, unable to distinguish between threat and salvation, between reality and the elaborate fictions my stressed mind might be creating to explain away my failures as wife, mother, woman.

I can't tell if Sophie's haunting me—or if I am haunting myself.

25.

The kitchen feels smaller this morning, compressed by silence that sits between Daniel and me.

He eats his toast methodically, eyes fixed on his phone screen, scrolling through emails with the focused attention of someone avoiding conversation. The sounds of breakfast—cutlery on ceramic, coffee brewing, the gentle percussion of rain—fill the space where words should be.

I clear my throat. "Sleep well?"

"Fine." He doesn't look up.

"Josh seemed excited about the nativity rehearsal yesterday. Did Miss Hardy say how it went?"

Daniel shrugs, still reading. "Sophie already filled me in. Apparently he's a very convincing shepherd."

The casual dismissal stings more than it should. Even our conversations about our son are pre-empted by Sophie's reports, as if she's become the primary source of information about Josh's life while I'm relegated to asking for updates like a distant relative.

"I thought I might pop in to watch the actual performance," I say, trying to sound casual rather than desperate for inclusion.

"Sophie's already organised tickets. Front row, apparently." Daniel finally looks up, but his expression carries mild irritation rather than warmth. "She mentioned it to you yesterday, didn't she?"

She hadn't, but I nod anyway. Another conversation that happened without me, another family event orchestrated around my absence.

The morning limps on in similar fashion—Daniel's responses growing shorter, his attention consistently elsewhere. By the time I settle down for work, I feel like we've had an entire conversation conducted in semaphore, all surface gestures hiding deeper currents I can't navigate.

The day passes in a blur of attempted productivity. I try to work on a logo design for an art gallery in Windermere, but concentration slips away. Every few minutes, I find myself staring out at the grey December afternoon, wondering when my marriage became this careful dance around subjects we can't discuss.

It's late afternoon when I hear their voices drifting from the kitchen—Daniel's deeper tones mixing with Sophie's lighter ones in the kind of easy conversation that's become impossible between us. Something about their rhythm draws me from my desk, and I find myself lingering in the hallway, straining to catch their words.

"She's under enormous pressure," Sophie is saying, her voice warm with understanding. "Grief does that to people—makes them see threats where there aren't any."

"I don't know how to reach her anymore," Daniel says, and the defeat in his voice makes my chest tight. "Everything I say seems to make things worse. She looks at me like I'm the enemy."

"You're not the enemy. You're just trying to hold everything together while she works through whatever this is." Sophie's tone carries the patient wisdom of someone older than her years. "It must be so difficult for you."

The sympathy in her voice makes my skin crawl. She's positioning herself as Daniel's emotional confidante while I'm cast as the problem that requires management, the unstable wife whose behaviour needs explaining to concerned observers.

"I keep thinking about counselling," Daniel says, his voice dropping to barely above a whisper. "Marriage guidance, maybe. But I'm afraid she'd see it as another attack on her sanity."

"You can't set yourself on fire to keep someone else warm," Sophie says, and I can hear the gentle smile in her voice. "You have to protect yourself too. And Josh."

The conversation continues, but I can't listen anymore. My legs carry me upstairs on autopilot while their voices fade behind me, their easy intimacy a counterpoint to the silence that's grown between Daniel and me.

In our bedroom, I sink onto the edge of the bed we've shared for eight years and stare at the framed wedding photograph on the dresser. Young faces beam back at me—Daniel in his hired morning suit, me in ivory silk that cost more than our monthly grocery budget. We look deliriously happy, convinced we're embarking on an adventure that will only grow sweeter with time.

Now that photograph feels like evidence from someone else's life. The woman in the ivory dress believed her husband would always choose her side, would always believe her word over a stranger's. She thought their bond was unshakeable, that marriage meant facing the world as allies rather than competitors for domestic harmony.

She was naive in ways that make my chest ache with loss.

That evening, I venture back downstairs to find dinner already prepared—something elaborate involving herbs I can't identify and vegetables arranged with artistic precision. Sophie moves around our kitchen while I sit at the table feeling like a guest in my own home.

"This looks wonderful," Daniel says, his voice carrying warmth it hasn't held for me in weeks. "You've outdone yourself, Sophie."

"Just something simple," she replies with the modest pleasure of someone whose efforts are properly appreciated. "I thought we could all use a treat after the stress of recent days."

The stress of recent days. My paranoid accusations, my unreasonable behaviour, my inability to accept help graciously. All framed as unfortunate weather that's passed over their domestic tranquillity.

Throughout dinner, Daniel directs his conversation mainly to Sophie—asking about her university course, her thoughts on Christmas plans, her opinion on Josh's progress at school. I contribute when directly addressed, but increasingly I feel like the awkward third wheel in a conversation that flows more naturally without my participation.

After we eat, Sophie clears the table while Daniel thanks her with genuine gratitude. He helps carry plates to the kitchen, their movements around each other comfortable and coordinated. When did they develop this easy domestic choreography? When did I become the observer rather than the participant in my own family's rhythms?

Later, alone in our bedroom, the house settles around me with its familiar creaks and sighs, but the sounds feel different now.

Through the floorboards, I can hear the murmur of voices from downstairs—Daniel and Sophie sharing one of their increasingly frequent conversations. Their tones carry the easy intimacy of people who understand each other, who share concerns about the unstable woman upstairs who used to be the centre of this household.

26.

The client meeting runs later than expected, leaving me to navigate Lancaster's damp streets well past nine o'clock. Christmas lights twinkle in windows while the distant sound of carols drifts from The Three Mariners.

The festive warmth of other people's homes makes my own destination feel cold by comparison.

The terraced streets narrow as I approach our neighbourhood. A few houses still show signs of life—the blue flicker of televisions through drawn curtains, porch lights left burning for late arrivals. Most have settled into evening quiet, their occupants secure in the kind of family routines I used to take for granted.

I pass the corner where the old footpath leads down to the river, my steps automatically quickening despite the darkness. Even at night, even when I can't see the water, I know it's there—moving with that relentless current that carries things away before you can reach them.

My hands clench involuntarily, remembering the feeling of being unable to grasp what was slipping away, unable to make my body obey when it mattered most.

Our house appears ahead, its bay window glowing with the warm light that should signal sanctuary. But as I approach the front gate, something white catches my attention against the dark paint of our door.

A folded sheet of paper, taped neatly in place like a formal announcement.

I fumble with the gate latch, then hurry up the short path to examine what someone has left for us.

I unfold it under the porch light and read the words written in careful block letters:

He lied to you both.

My hands begin to shake. The message is unsigned, undated, offering no clue about its author or intended recipient. But the word 'both' confirms that I'm not the only person caught in whatever web of deception surrounds my family.

Both. Sophie and me. Two women, connected by lies told by the same man.

But which man? My father, whose photograph bears Sophie's angry accusation? Daniel, whose recent distance might conceal more than marital frustration? Or someone else entirely?

I scan the street, searching for whoever might have delivered this cryptic warning. Nothing moves except the occasional car passing towards the main road, their headlights sweeping across wet tarmac before disappearing into the night. The sound of dripping gutters provides steady percussion, accompanied by the distant hum of Lancaster's evening traffic.

No one lingers in doorways or behind parked cars. No figure retreats into shadows. If someone wanted to watch my reaction to their message, they've hidden themselves well.

Should I show it to Daniel? Confront Sophie about what she might know? Or does displaying it publicly serve someone else's agenda, forcing revelations before I'm prepared for their consequences?

I stuff the paper into my coat pocket and fumble for my keys, desperate to escape the vulnerable exposure of the porch light. But as the key slides into the lock, a sound behind me makes me freeze.

The scrape of plastic against concrete. One of our recycling bins shifting position.

I turn slowly, and see Sophie emerging from the shadows beside our house. She moves with casual ease.

"Just sorting the recycling," she says, her voice carrying the same warm friendliness she brings to everything. "You're home late."

The note crackles in my pocket as I stare at her, trying to read meaning in her expression..

But something about her positioning bothers me. She's standing exactly where someone would wait if they wanted to observe my reaction to finding that message. Close enough to watch, far enough to claim innocent purpose if discovered.

"Client meeting ran over," I manage, my voice steadier than I feel.

"Those can be tricky. Always best to give them your full attention, though—that's how you build lasting relationships." Sophie brushes her hands together, removing imaginary dust from her recycling duties. "Everything go well?"

The question could be purely polite, but it lands differently after finding that note. Does she know about the message? Did she write it herself, another move in whatever psychological game she's been playing? Or is she as surprised by it as I am, another victim of the same mysterious truth-teller?

"Fine," I say, turning back to the door. "Just tired."

"Of course. It's been a long day for everyone."

I twist the key and push inside, grateful for the warm air that greets me. The house smells of Sophie's cooking—something involving rosemary and garlic that makes my empty stomach clench with hunger. Normal domestic scents that should comfort rather than unnerve.

"Daniel's upstairs with Josh," Sophie says, following me into the hallway. "Story time ran a bit long tonight. I think they're finally finished."

"I'll just pop up and say goodnight," I say, moving towards the stairs.

"Of course. I'm sure Josh would love to see you before bed."

The phrasing stings—as if my presence is a treat rather than a given, a special occasion rather than parental right. But I don't respond, too conscious of the paper in my pocket and Sophie's watchful presence behind me.

At the bottom of the stairs, I glance back. Sophie hasn't moved from the hallway, her position giving her a clear view of both the front door and my ascent.

She smiles when our eyes meet—a smile that says she's never surprised, only waiting for me to catch up.

27.

My hands still tremble as I climb the stairs. Josh's laughter echoes from his bedroom—pure, uncomplicated joy that cuts through my churning thoughts.

I pause on the landing, pressing my palm against the wall until my breathing steadies.

Whatever web of lies surrounds our family, whatever Sophie knows or doesn't know, Josh deserves his bedtime routine untainted by adult poison.

I paste on a smile that feels like paper stretched over broken glass, then push open his door.

Daniel sits cross-legged on Josh's bed, holding a picture book about pirates at an angle that catches the lamplight. His voice takes on exaggerated gruffness as he reads about buried treasure and high seas adventures, making Josh giggle with each theatrical flourish.

"Ahoy there, me hearty!" Daniel bellows, pointing at an illustration of a parrot. "Have ye seen me golden doubloons?"

"Pirates don't talk to parrots, Daddy," Josh corrects with four-year-old authority. "Parrots talk to pirates."

"Quite right, Captain Josh. My mistake."

I settle onto the edge of the bed, letting their familiar banter wash over me. For a moment, the note in my pocket feels less urgent, less threatening.

This is real—Daniel's gentle voice, Josh's sleepy contentment, the warm circle of lamplight holding us all.

Maybe everything else is shadow and paranoia, tricks my exhausted mind plays when love should be enough.

"Mummy! Daddy's reading about treasure."

"I can hear that, sweetheart. Very exciting."

Daniel wrestles Josh into his space-themed pyjamas while I arrange tomorrow's clothes on the chair. Josh chatters about his day between yawns—something about finger painting and how Oliver brought dinosaur biscuits for snack time.

In the bathroom, we squeeze around the small sink. Daniel holds Josh steady while I brush his teeth, and Josh makes faces in the mirror that dissolve us both into laughter. The domesticity feels almost violent in its normalcy.

I want desperately to lean into Daniel's shoulder, to whisper about the note burning in my pocket. But the words lodge in my throat. He'll dismiss it as paranoia. Or worse—he'll show it to Sophie, ask her opinion, seek her reassurance about his wife's deteriorating mental state.

Back in his bedroom, Josh climbs into bed and arranges his stuffed dinosaur with careful attention to positioning. Daniel pulls the duvet up to his chin while I smooth his fringe away from his forehead.

"Night, Mummy. Night, Daddy," Josh whispers, his eyelids already heavy.

"Sweet dreams, my love," I say, pressing a kiss to his warm cheek.

Daniel ruffles his hair gently. "See you in the morning, me heartie."

The moment stretches, tender and perfect—until I notice Sophie's cream scarf draped over the back of Josh's chair. She's been here tonight, in his room, part of his routine. The scarf seems to pulse with quiet claim: *I belong here too.*

I bite my tongue, refusing to spoil the calm. Josh deserves this peace, even if it's built on foundations I can't trust.

Downstairs, Daniel pours himself a measure of whisky and settles into his chair with the weary satisfaction of another day survived. The house feels different with Josh asleep—smaller, more charged with unspoken tensions.

"I've been thinking," he says, swirling the amber liquid. "About everything you've been going through. The stress, the suspicions about Sophie."

I tense, expecting another lecture about paranoia and burnout.

Instead, he reaches into his trouser pocket and produces a folded scrap of paper. "I've been doing some research. There's a local counsellor, highly recommended. He specialises in postnatal anxiety, family adjustment issues."

He leans forward, pressing the paper into my hand. His fingers are warm against mine, but the gesture feels like surrender wrapped in kindness.

I bristle, ready to argue that I don't need fixing, that the problem isn't my mental state but Sophie's manipulation. But Daniel cuts me off before I can speak.

"Just...call him. Please." His voice is desperate, pleading. "For Josh's sake. For us."

Not a suggestion but a requirement. Not concern but ultimatum dressed as care. Call the counsellor, admit you're the problem, stop making waves about Sophie.

I stare down at the paper in my palm, seeing not a therapist's contact details but evidence of how completely I've lost the narrative of my own life.

In Daniel's version, I'm the one who needs help. Sophie is the miracle worker keeping us functional while his wife slowly unravels.

"Emma? Will you call him?"

I want to scream the truth—about the note in my pocket, about Sophie's lies. But instead I nod, because what else can I do?

28.

After a sleepless night turning both the note and Daniel's ultimatum over in my mind, I resolve to end this charade once and for all. The therapist's number sits folded on my bedside table like evidence of my husband's verdict: Emma has lost her grip on reality. Emma needs professional help. Emma is the problem that requires fixing.

The bitter irony cuts deep—just as I'm closest to uncovering the truth, Daniel's positioned me as the unreliable narrator of my own life. If I'm going to prove my sanity, I need concrete evidence. Hard facts that even Daniel can't dismiss as the paranoid fantasies of an overwrought mother.

No more confrontations in our house where Sophie can manipulate the scene, no more arguments where Daniel automatically takes her side. This time, I'll corner her somewhere public, neutral ground where her theatrical tears won't have an audience that matters.

Caton Road retail park on a Saturday afternoon—bustling with Christmas shoppers, car parks crammed with families loading bags into boots, the Salvation Army band playing carols near the entrance to Marks & Spencer. Open space, witnesses, escape routes. Somewhere Sophie can't orchestrate the narrative or paint me as the unhinged woman attacking an innocent guest.

I text Sophie about meeting for errands, my hands shaking as I type the casual message. The therapist's number burns in my mind. Daniel's gentle ultimatum echoes: *For Josh's sake. For us.* As if love can be conditional on compliance with his version of reality.

She responds immediately with her usual warmth—of course she'd be happy to help with shopping, always eager to be useful.

The chill air bites at my cheeks as I wait outside M&S, watching families stream past with their arms full of seasonal purchases.

Sophie appears through the crowd with her characteristic grace, handbag slung over her shoulder, that warm smile lighting her features. She looks like any other young woman running weekend errands, nothing to suggest the calculated intrusion she's perpetrated on our family.

"Emma!" She approaches with genuine-seeming pleasure. "What a lovely idea. I've been meaning to pick up a few things myself."

Her casual friendliness makes what I'm about to say feel surreal, inappropriate. But the note in my pocket—*He lied to you both*—gives me strength I wouldn't have found alone.

"I know what you're doing," I say without preamble, my voice steadier than I feel. "I know you've been digging into my family. I know you've been researching my past."

Sophie tilts her head with that familiar gesture of mild interest, as if I've made an observation about the weather.

"Have I?" she says, her voice carrying none of its usual defensiveness.

"The photograph. The documents. My father's face with 'LIAR' written across it." The words pour out in a desperate rush. "You're obsessed with my family, with our history. Why?"

Sophie's lips curve into a slow smile that transforms her face completely.

"Because..." Her voice carries a different quality now—steady, deliberate, stripped of its usual careful warmth. "I'm your half-sister."

The retail park spins around me—cars, shoppers, Christmas lights blurring into impressionist streaks. My legs nearly buckle under the weight of what she's just claimed.

Half-sister. The word rewrites every interaction we've had, every moment of unease I've felt watching her move through my house with such proprietary ease. Daniel thinks I need therapy, but this—this validates every instinct I've had about her wrongness, her calculated intrusion into our lives.

"That's not—you can't be—"

"Can't I?" Sophie steps closer, her presence suddenly predatory rather than helpful. "Think about it, Emma. Really think. Your father's absences when you were growing up. The arguments you heard through bedroom walls."

Each observation lands with sickening accuracy. Memories I'd buried surface like corpses in flood water—Dad's mysterious business trips, Mum's red-rimmed eyes after certain phone calls, the tension that crackled through our Chatsworth Road house during my teenage years.

"He gave you everything," Sophie says, her voice low but sharp enough to cut through the ambient noise of Saturday shopping. "The house. The family name. The respectable life. Christmas mornings, birthday parties, bedtime stories. Everything a daughter should have."

Shoppers stream past us with their bags and seasonal plans. Their normalcy feels like mockery now.

"He gave me nothing," Sophie's voice drops to barely above a whisper. "A monthly envelope with cash. Instructions to never contact his 'real' family. Promises that someday he'd acknowledge me properly—lies that kept my mother hoping until the day she died."

The annotated photograph flashes through my mind with new significance. Not random obsession but personal condemnation. *LIAR* written across the face of the man who gave her life but withheld recognition, love, belonging.

"You're lying," I say, but the protest sounds hollow even to me.

"Am I? Then why does your childhood lullaby sound so familiar when I hum it? Why did I spend years watching from across the river while you grew up in the life that should have been mine?"

Each question strips away another layer of comfortable assumptions.

The crowd surges around us. Their laughter sounds distant, muffled, as if I'm hearing it underwater. Reality has tilted off its axis, leaving me grasping for purchase on shifting ground.

"The house in Skerton," I whisper. "You're living there because—"

"Because it should have been mine too. Because every memory you made in those rooms was built on his lies, his careful compartmentalisation of the family he acknowledged and the daughter he denied." Sophie leans closer, her breath warm against my ear. "I belong there more than you ever did."

The words cut deeper than any physical violence could. Not just claiming a place in our current life but asserting prior ownership of my entire past. Every Christmas morning, every birthday celebration, every moment of childhood security—all of it tainted by the knowledge that somewhere across Lancaster, another daughter was being denied the same privileges.

Daniel's voice echoes in my memory: *For Josh's sake. For us. Call the counsellor.* He thinks I'm losing my mind, but here's the proof I've been sane all along. Sophie's obsession with my family, her impossible knowledge of our history, her systematic replacement of me—it wasn't paranoia. It was recognition of a threat I couldn't yet name.

"I don't believe you," I say, but my voice cracks on the lie.

Sophie's smile widens. "You don't have to believe me, Emma. The truth doesn't need your permission to exist."

She steps back, adjusting her handbag as if we've just discussed Christmas dinner plans rather than the complete destruction of everything I thought I knew about my family.

"I should head back," she says, her voice returning to its usual helpful warmth. "Our Josh will be wondering where we are."

Our Josh. Our family. Our home that she's claimed piece by piece while I stood by and watched.

29.

Frost clings to the railings around Dallas Road Primary, catching the weak sunlight and throwing it back in sharp fragments. The air tastes of winter mornings and car exhaust, bitter on the tongue as I walk Josh through the school gates with hands that won't stop trembling.

The playground buzzes with its usual morning energy, but today the chatter feels different. More urgent, more seasonal. Fragments of conversation drift past about nativity rehearsals and Christmas shopping lists, about turkey orders and visiting in-laws. The comfortable complaints of parents whose biggest concern is whether to buy the extended warranty on their child's new bicycle.

I try to arrange my face into something approaching normalcy, but Sophie's revelation from yesterday sits in my chest.

Half-sister.

The word tastes foreign, impossible, even as part of me recognises its terrible logic.

All those years of Dad's mysterious absences, the arguments that stopped when I entered rooms, the tension that permeated our Chatsworth Road house.

Josh tugs my hand, eager to join his friends by the climbing frame. His mittened fingers are warm through my gloves, solid and real in a world that feels increasingly unstable.

"Can I play with Oliver before the bell?" he asks, his breath making small clouds in the December air.

"Course you can, love."

I watch him bound towards the group of Reception children, his school bag bouncing against his back. For a moment, his easy joy cuts through my anxiety. Whatever secrets are unravelling around us, Josh remains untouched, innocent, protected by the particular grace of being four years old.

Then I see her.

Sophie stands near the gate in a small knot of mothers. She's dressed in that camel coat again, the one that makes her look effortlessly put-together while I feel perpetually dishevelled. Her laugh carries across the playground, warm and musical above the general chatter.

I hover at the edge of the playground, clutching my tote bag like a shield. The space between Sophie's group and where I stand feels vast, unbridgeable. When did I become the outsider at my own son's school? When did the other parents start looking past me to the woman who's claimed my domestic territory?

Gemma isn't here this morning—probably dealing with her own school's Christmas chaos. Without her familiar face, I feel adrift amongst the casual alliances that govern playground politics. These women know each other's coffee preferences, share childcare emergencies, form the kind of supportive network I've always struggled to penetrate.

The wind shifts, carrying fragments of conversation in my direction. I step closer, drawn by some masochistic need to understand how completely she's integrated into the community I've never quite managed to join.

"Emma's been quite fragile since the breakdown." Sophie's voice drifts across the playground, pitched low but not so low that I can't hear every word. "It's been hard for her. We just do what we can to support her."

The other mothers nod with sage understanding. Their faces show the particular blend of sympathy and relief that comes from observing someone else's crisis while feeling grateful for your own stability.

"Sometimes trauma surfaces when you least expect it," Sophie says. "The death of her mother probably triggered something that was already there."

If I protest Sophie's account, I'll only confirm her assessment. If I argue that I'm not fragile, not broken, it will sound exactly like the desperate protests of someone who is.

In a community as small as ours, reputations matter. Whispers spread through school gates and coffee mornings with the efficiency of wildfire.

Sarah Whitworth catches sight of me hovering nearby and offers a smile that doesn't reach her eyes—the careful expression reserved for people who might be unstable, unpredictable. "Morning, Emma. How are you holding up?"

Holding up. As if I'm enduring some terrible ordeal rather than simply existing as a mother and wife.

"I'm fine," I say, but even to my own ears the protest sounds hollow, defensive.

"Course you are, love." Helen pats my arm with gentle condescension. "It must be hard, though. Bless you."

Hard. What exactly is hard? Being married, having a child, managing a household like thousands of other women? But her tone suggests she's referring to some specific challenge, some particular burden I'm courageously bearing.

Sophie has painted me as a tragic figure without explicitly stating any accusations. The perfect manipulation—sympathy rather than condemnation, concern rather than criticism.

I open my mouth to correct their assumptions, to explain that I'm not fragile or struggling or in need of the special handling they're offering. But Sophie steps closer, her hand finding my elbow with familiar ease.

"She pushes herself too hard," Sophie says, her voice warm with affectionate concern. "Always has. I keep telling her to take more time for herself, but you know how mothers are."

I swallow the protest that rises in my throat, tasting bile and defeat in equal measure.

The bell rings. Children race towards their classroom doors while parents begin the usual migration back to cars and coffee shops and the comfortable routines of their well-ordered lives.

Sophie moves through the crowd with easy grace, accepting thanks and compliments like she's receiving her due.

I walk back through Scotforth's familiar streets alone, my footsteps echoing off wet cobbles while my mind churns with the implications of what I've witnessed. Sophie isn't just manipulating my family anymore—she's systematically dismantling my reputation in the wider community.

By Christmas, everyone will have heard whispers about poor Emma Cartwright, struggling through a mental breakdown, lucky to have such devoted help. The narrative will spread through coffee mornings and book clubs, through chance encounters at the supermarket and conversations at the gym.

I'll become the cautionary tale mothers share when they want to feel grateful for their own mental health. The woman who couldn't cope, whose obvious inadequacies required intervention by a stranger wise enough to see what needed doing.

The worst part is how reasonable it all sounds. A woman under pressure, grieving her mother's death, struggling with work-life balance while trying to manage a demanding child and an increasingly distant marriage.

Of course she might become fragile. Of course she might need support she's too proud to request directly.

Sophie has crafted the perfect explanation for my behaviour that casts her as a saviour while positioning me as the problem requiring a solution.

Any evidence I present of her manipulation will be filtered through their new understanding of my compromised mental state.

Terraced houses blur past in shades of brick and slate, their windows glowing with the warm light of families getting on with their ordinary Tuesday morning routines. Behind those windows, people are making breakfast, checking school bags, arguing about whose turn it is to put the bins out. Normal domestic chaos that suddenly seems precious in its simplicity.

Sophie has stolen that from me.

Not just the easy competence that makes daily life manageable, but the right to be seen as capable, stable, worthy of basic respect from other parents.

She wasn't stealing my life in secret anymore. She was rewriting it in front of everyone.

30.

I sit at the kitchen table with my phone clutched between my hands, thumb hovering over Gemma's contact. After yesterday's humiliation at the school gates, I need someone who knew me before Sophie arrived to reshape everyone's perceptions. Someone who remembers that I used to be competent, stable, worthy of basic respect.

The message takes three attempts to compose, each version sounding more desperate than the last. Finally, I settle on something approaching casual: *Coffee at The Gregson this afternoon? Need to catch up properly.*

Gemma's reply comes within minutes: *Perfect! 2pm? Could use the break from marking.*

Finally, a conversation where I won't have to navigate Sophie's careful manipulations or Daniel's increasing impatience with my concerns. Just two old friends sharing coffee and honesty.

I spend the morning planning what I'll say, rehearsing explanations that don't sound mad. How do you tell someone their friend has been systematically dismantled by a woman claiming to be her half-sister? How do you describe manipulation so subtle it feels like gaslighting yourself?

But Gemma will listen. She has to. We've been friends since school, shared secrets and anxieties through teenage heartbreak and university stress. If anyone can see past Sophie's perfect facade to the calculation underneath, it's the person who's known me longest.

The Gregson sits at the heart of Lancaster's social geography, its Victorian bulk dominating the junction where students, locals, and professionals intersect over pints and conversation. During the day, it transforms from student drinking hole to respectable meeting place for people who want decent coffee without paying city prices.

I arrive early, claiming a table by the window where I can watch for Gemma's familiar figure amongst the afternoon shoppers. Rain patters against the glass while inside, conversations flow around topics I can't quite catch—work stress and Christmas plans, the comfortable complaints of people whose biggest concerns are manageable.

My phone buzzes. A text from Gemma: *Sorry, swamped with work. Rain check?*

I stare at the message, trying to parse the subtext. Gemma's always busy during term time, marking endless essays and planning lessons that stretch far beyond school hours. The cancellation makes perfect sense.

But the timing feels cruel. Just when I need her most, when isolation threatens to drown me completely, she pulls away.

I should go home. Should accept that today won't bring the relief I'd been counting on, that I'll have to navigate Sophie's evening manipulations without the comfort of having been heard and believed by someone who matters.

Instead, I find myself walking through Lancaster's city centre, drawn by the need to delay returning to a house that no longer feels like mine.

The Christmas market sprawls across Dalton Square, wooden stalls selling mulled wine and handmade crafts while children queue for rides on the carousel. The scents of cinnamon and roasted almonds drift through the December air.

I drift through the crowds, anonymous amongst the families and couples who move with shared purpose. Everyone else seems to inhabit a world where December means celebration, where Christmas markets represent joy rather than reminders of social connections I can't access.

The weight of isolation presses against my ribs. Since Sophie's arrival, every social interaction has become a performance where I'm always slightly off-script.

Near the Town Hall, I pause to watch a group of carol singers. Their faces glow with the particular satisfaction that comes from community participation, from belonging to something larger than individual concerns.

When did I last feel that sense of belonging? When did my world shrink to the boundaries of my own anxiety?

The answer comes with uncomfortable clarity: when Sophie arrived and began isolating me from every source of support and validation I'd relied on.

I'm turning back towards Penny Street when I see them.

Through the steamed windows of The Hall café, two figures sit opposite each other at a small table near the back. One blonde head bent towards one brunette, coffee cups between them, the comfortable intimacy of people deep in conversation.

Gemma. And Sophie.

Gemma's face is animated, her hands gesturing as she speaks. She leans forward with the focused attention she brings to conversations that matter, the expression I'd been hoping to see directed at me this afternoon.

Sophie sits opposite her, nodding with that warm understanding she brings to every interaction. Her posture suggests active listening, genuine engagement, the kind of sympathetic presence that makes people feel heard and valued.

They look like old friends catching up, like women who've found unexpected connection in the comfortable chaos of Lancaster life.

The betrayal hits hard. Gemma chose Sophie over me. Chose the woman who's systematically destroying my family over the friend she's known for twenty years.

I step back from the window, a pulse hammering in my skull. Around me, Penny Street continues its afternoon rhythm—shoppers browsing windows, couples sharing umbrellas, the ordinary commerce of people whose lives make sense. But I feel ghostlike amongst them, untethered from the social fabric I'd thought I belonged to.

What has Sophie told her? What carefully crafted narrative has she spun to explain away my concerns, my accusations, my desperate attempts to protect what's left of my family?

The same story she told the school mothers, probably. Poor Emma, struggling with a mental breakdown. Emma, whose grip on reality has become unreliable since her mother's death. Emma, who needs gentle management rather than direct confrontation.

Sophie has positioned herself as the reasonable voice while painting me as the problem requiring a solution. And Gemma—Gemma who's known me since we were teenagers, who should recognise manipulation when she sees it—has apparently bought the narrative completely.

Through the café window, I watch Sophie pat Gemma's arm with familiar affection. The gesture looks natural, earned, as if they've shared confidences that bond women together. Gemma's expression shows the particular warmth reserved for people who understand, who provide perspective on difficult situations.

My chest tightens with something that might be grief. Not just for the friendship I'm losing, but for the version of myself that existed before Sophie's arrival. The woman who had allies, who could count on support when life became overwhelming, who belonged to networks of care and concern that made isolation impossible.

That woman is disappearing as thoroughly as Sophie erases every trace of my authority in my own home.

I turn away from the window, unable to watch their easy intimacy any longer.

31.

The December afternoon presses against Dallas Road Primary as condensation rises from children's breath in small clouds. I pull my coat tighter against the chill, joining the cluster of parents who huddle near the playground gates with their faces pinched by cold and the particular exhaustion that comes from surviving another day of domestic logistics.

Around me, mothers stamp their feet and check phones while fathers glance at watches, all of us united by the shared desire to collect our offspring and retreat to heated cars. The playground beyond the railings buzzes with the controlled chaos of afternoon play, children's voices sharp against the winter air.

When the bell rings, they pour out like released pressure—Reception children clutching book bags and water bottles while their older siblings race past. I scan the familiar faces, looking for Josh's untidy hair and the *Thomas the Tank Engine* coat he insists on wearing despite its increasingly battered state.

He appears through the crowd with his face lit up like Christmas morning, waving something above his head with the particular pride that comes from creating art worthy of public display. His cheeks are flushed from playground cold, his school jumper slightly askew, everything about him radiating the uncomplicated joy of being four years old.

"Mummy! Look what I made!" He crashes into my legs, thrusting a crumpled piece of paper towards my face. "Miss Hardy said it's the best one in the class!"

The drawing unfolds in my hands. Coloured pencils on cream paper, the familiar wobbly lines that mark Josh's artistic development, stick figures arranged beneath what appears to be our house.

Three figures stand in front of the familiar rectangle with its triangle roof and square windows. Daniel's form is recognisably tall, his smile a wonky line beneath the brown scribbles that represent his hair. Josh has drawn himself small but proud between the two adult figures, his arms stretched wide to hold their hands.

The third figure wears a skirt, has long brown hair, and stands protectively beside Josh with what appears to be a maternal expression drawn in careful crayon strokes.

I scan the paper desperately, looking for the fourth figure that should complete our family portrait. But there's nothing. No mother lurking at the edges, no Emma relegated to background status.

"That's me and Daddy," Josh says, bouncing on his toes. "And that's Mummy Sophie!"

Not Sophie. Not Nanny Sophie or Helper Sophie or any of the careful distinctions I've tried to maintain.

Mummy Sophie.

He's drawn his ideal family, and I'm not in it.

"It's lovely, sweetheart," I manage, my voice sounding thin and strange. "Very colourful."

A gentle touch on my shoulder makes me turn. Miss Hardy crouches beside us, her expression carrying the careful concern teachers perfect for difficult conversations with parents.

"Might I have a quick word?" she asks, her voice pitched low to avoid interested ears.

Josh immediately loses interest in our adult conversation, spotting his friend Oliver across the playground and racing off to share some urgent four-year-old intelligence. Miss Hardy watches him go with the fond expression all his teachers develop—he's bright, cheerful, easy to love. Everything a Reception child should be.

"He's been a bit confused lately about family structures," she says gently, her eyes flicking to the drawing in my hands. "Yesterday he told the class about his two mummies. Today he's drawn what appears to be his preferred configuration."

Heat rises in my cheeks. Around us, other parents collect their children with the efficient choreography of school runs, their conversations focused on packed lunches and piano lessons rather than the psychological architecture of domestic arrangements.

"I'll talk to him."

"Of course. Children go through phases of attachment, especially when family circumstances change." Miss Hardy's smile is kind but carries the professional distance of someone who's navigated these conversations before. "It's quite normal for them to become confused about roles when new people enter their lives."

New people. As if Sophie is just another babysitter rather than the woman who's claimed my son's deepest loyalties while I stood by and watched it happen.

"He's very fond of Sophie," Miss Hardy says. "Talks about her constantly. The games she plays, the stories she tells, the special meals she cooks. It's lovely that he has such a positive relationship with his carer."

Carer. Not nanny, not helper, but carer. The professional term that encompasses everything from nursing home attendants to foster parents, suggesting a depth of responsibility that goes far beyond temporary assistance.

"Yes," I say, because any other response would require explanations I can't provide without sounding unhinged. "She's been very helpful."

The understatement burns my throat..

Miss Hardy straightens. "I'm sure you'll sort it out. Children are wonderfully resilient—they adapt to whatever family structure works best."

The observation should comfort me, but instead it feels like another small defeat. Josh is adapting beautifully to a family structure where Sophie occupies the primary maternal role while I've become an irrelevant peripheral figure.

The walk home passes in a blur of December drizzle and domestic dread. Josh skips ahead, clutching his drawing like a treasure, pausing periodically to point out interesting puddles or remarkably shaped clouds. His cheerful chatter provides a soundtrack to my growing horror at what he's revealed through innocent artistic expression.

"Why did you draw Sophie as your mummy?" I ask, trying to keep my voice light, conversational, the kind of curious inquiry any parent might make about their child's creative choices.

Josh shrugs, his attention already drifting to a particularly promising stick he's spotted beside the pavement. "Because she looks after me."

The simplicity of his logic cuts deeper than any elaborate explanation could have. Sophie feeds him, bathes him, reads him stories, plays imaginative games that make ordinary afternoons feel magical. Therefore, Sophie is Mummy.

I am relegated to some undefined category—not quite family, not quite stranger, occupying the uncomfortable space reserved for people whose role can't be easily explained.

"But I'm your mummy," I say, hating how desperate the protest sounds.

"You're Mummy Emma," Josh says with the patience of someone explaining something obvious to a slow adult. "Sophie is Mummy Sophie. Like Oliver has Mummy Sarah and Daddy Tim."

The casual comparison to his friend's parents makes my chest tighten. Oliver's parents are divorced, sharing custody with the kind of civilised arrangement modern families navigate when love fails but responsibility remains. In Josh's mind, I'm not his primary mother but one of two maternal figures who happen to share caregiving duties.

Sophie has achieved this transformation without open conflict or dramatic scenes. She's simply been present, competent, reliable while I've struggled with the basic mechanics of domestic life. Her claim to Josh's affections has been earned through daily service rather than seized through manipulation.

Which makes it infinitely harder to fight.

At home, Josh bounds upstairs to play with his Lego while I remain in the kitchen, staring at his drawing spread across the counter. The three stick figures beam up at me with their crayon smiles, their arrangement suggesting the kind of family harmony that should make any mother proud.

But I'm not in it.

The absent fourth figure haunts the composition more powerfully than any presence could have. Josh has edited me out of his ideal family with the unconscious cruelty of childhood, creating a domestic tableau where Sophie occupies the central maternal role I thought was mine by right.

My hands shake as I trace the careful lines of Sophie's stick-figure face. Even rendered in wobbly crayon strokes, she looks competent, necessary, beloved. The kind of mother children dream about rather than endure.

The front door opens, followed by Sophie's light footsteps and Daniel's heavier tread. Their voices carry from the hallway—something about Josh's progress at school, about Christmas plans that seem to involve elaborate preparations I haven't been consulted about. The comfortable exchange between partners who share responsibilities rather than the careful politeness of employer and employee.

I fold Josh's drawing quickly, stuffing it into my handbag before they can see the evidence of how completely Sophie has replaced me in our son's imagination.

32.

Drizzle streaks the tall sash windows of our Victorian terrace, turning the view of Scotforth into smudges of brick and slate. I walk through the long hallway while the central heating hums its familiar protest against the Lancashire cold. The draught still finds its way through gaps in the old frames, making the house feel perpetually chilled despite our best efforts.

From upstairs comes Josh's laughter—bright, uncomplicated, the sound of a child secure in his bedtime routine. Daniel's deeper voice mingles with his lighter tones, something about pirates and treasure and the elaborate stories that make going to sleep feel like an adventure rather than a chore.

I breathe properly for the first time today. The hallway feels empty of Sophie's presence, quiet except for the domestic sounds that should comfort rather than remind me of everything I'm failing to provide. My tote bag sits heavy on my shoulder, weighted with Josh's hidden drawing and the cryptic note someone left on our door. Evidence of secrets I can't begin to unravel.

The radiator beneath the window clanks its familiar rhythm while fairy lights from neighbours' houses glow faintly through the streaming glass. Other families settling into their evening routines, their windows glowing with the warm light of homes that work.

Footsteps on the stairs signal Daniel's descent from successful bedtime negotiations. He appears at the bottom, phone in hand, his expression carrying the particular tension that means he's been dealing with something while I've been hiding downstairs.

"Gemma's been messaging," he says without preamble, his frown deepening as he scrolls through what appears to be a lengthy conversation. "She's worried about you."

My stomach drops. Of course she is. After seeing her cosied up with Sophie in that café, laughing over coffee while I waited for a meeting that was never going to happen, I should have expected the concerned friend routine to follow.

"She says you've been acting strangely lately," Daniel continues, his eyes not leaving his phone screen. "Paranoid. Making accusations that don't add up."

"I'm fine," I say quickly, my voice pitched higher than intended. "Honestly, it's nothing."

Daniel looks up from his phone, studying my face with the kind of quiet disappointment that cuts deeper than anger. As if I'm confirming exactly what Gemma's been telling him, providing evidence for whatever narrative they've constructed about my deteriorating mental state.

"Are you?" His voice carries doubt wrapped in weariness. "Because according to Gemma, you've been making wild claims about Sophie. Conspiracy theories. She's genuinely concerned about your wellbeing, Em."

The betrayal stings fresh and sharp. Not just that Gemma chose Sophie's company over mine, but that she's been sharing our private conversations with Daniel, packaging my desperate attempts to be heard as symptoms of psychological breakdown.

"She doesn't understand the situation," I say

Daniel gestures around the hallway. "What situation, Emma? Sophie's really holding things together here." His voice carries an edge of irritation. "The house is clean, Josh is thriving, you actually have time to work on your designs without constant interruption. What exactly are you complaining about?"

Heat rises in my cheeks. Every point he makes is accurate, irrefutable evidence of Sophie's positive impact on our family. But it misses the fundamental violation.

"She's not just helping," I begin, then falter. How do I explain manipulation so subtle it looks like kindness? How do I describe being erased by someone who appears to be saving us?

Daniel leans against the kitchen doorframe, arms folded across his chest in the posture of someone whose patience is wearing thin. "You still haven't called him, have you?"

The accusation hangs in the air between us. Him. The counsellor whose details Daniel pressed into my hands, the professional intervention he's convinced will restore my perspective to something approaching rationality.

"I've been busy." I avoid his gaze by focusing on the neat pile of Christmas cards Sophie has arranged on the hall table.

Daniel's jaw tightens. "I gave you that number for a reason, Em. You can't keep ignoring this."

His tone isn't angry—it's worse than angry. It's weary, resigned, carrying the defeated quality of someone who's given up expecting his wife to take responsibility for her own mental health.

The accumulated weight of it all crashes over me like cold water. Sophie's revelation about being my half-sister. The playground mothers treating me like damaged goods. Gemma's betrayal disguised as concern. Josh's innocent drawing that erased me from our family portrait.

"She's not holding things together," I snap, my voice rising in the echoing hallway. "She's taking over! Can't you see what she's doing? She's claiming my life piece by piece while everyone stands around applauding her for it!"

The words bounce off the Victorian plaster with harsh clarity, my desperation amplified by the house's acoustic properties. Upstairs, the sudden silence suggests Josh has heard something that's broken through his post-bedtime contentment.

Small feet hit the floor above us, followed by the creaking descent of someone who should be asleep but has been drawn by the sound of raised voices.

Josh appears at the top of the stairs clutching his stuffed dinosaur. "Mummy?" His voice wavers, uncertain. "Why are you shouting?"

The sight of him—small, vulnerable, frightened by the conflict crackling between his parents—makes my chest clench with guilt. He'd been safe upstairs in his bed, insulated from the adult tensions that have been building like storm pressure throughout our house.

Now I've shattered that security with my inability to contain the panic that's been building since Sophie arrived.

Josh's face crumples, and he begins to cry—not the dramatic wails of a tantrum but the broken sobs of a child whose world has suddenly become unpredictable. His small shoulders shake as tears stream down his cheeks, the dinosaur clutched against his chest like a talisman against forces he can't understand.

"It's okay, sweetheart," I say, moving towards the stairs with my arms extended, ready to comfort the distress I've caused.

But Sophie appears from nowhere, materialising at the top of the stairs like she's been waiting in the shadows for exactly this moment. She scoops Josh into her arms before I can reach him, her movements fluid and maternal while mine feel clumsy, desperate.

"Shh, darling," she murmurs, her voice carrying the kind of calm authority that makes frightened children feel safe. "It's okay. Mummy's just tired."

Josh buries his face in Sophie's shoulder, his sobs already quieting under her gentle ministrations. She holds him with practised ease, one hand rubbing circles on his back while the other supports his weight with maternal competence.

The sight stops me cold on the third step.

Daniel's expression when I glance back carries quiet condemnation. His silence speaks volumes—disappointment, resignation.

Sophie continues her gentle reassurances while Josh's breathing evens out against her shoulder. She doesn't look at me triumphantly or offer pointed commentary about proper parenting techniques. She simply does what needs doing while I stand paralysed on the stairs, watching my family reorganise itself around my absence.

"I'll get him settled," Sophie says quietly. "He'll be fine once he's back in bed."

She disappears into the upstairs darkness, taking Josh's trust with her while I remain frozen on the stairs. The hallway below feels cavernous, echoing with the aftermath of raised voices.

Daniel doesn't look at me as he turns towards the kitchen, his shoulders carrying the weight of someone whose domestic problems have multiplied rather than decreased.

33.

Williamson Park spreads before me in shades of grey and brown, cold rain turning its Victorian pathways slick beneath my feet. Bare trees rattle in the wind that cuts across Lancaster from Morecambe Bay, their skeletal branches scratching at the pewter sky.

The Ashton Memorial looms ahead, its baroque dome a landmark I've been navigating towards since childhood, but today it feels like a gravestone marking everything I thought I knew about my family.

I clutch the slip of paper tighter, Aunt Margaret's address scrawled in my own desperate handwriting. The house number feels foreign despite being lifted from my mother's old address book, a connection I'd severed years ago when grief made maintaining family ties feel impossible.

The terraced houses on Balmoral Road huddle together against the weather, their Victorian facades weathered by decades of Lancashire rain. Net curtains twitch as I pass.

Number forty-seven sits halfway down the terrace, its front garden neat but sparse, a single rose bush struggling against the December cold. The paint on the front door has faded to a colour that might once have been green but now looks like old brass. When I press the bell, it rings with the tinny persistence of something that needs replacing but works well enough to ignore.

Footsteps approach from inside, slow and deliberate. The door opens to reveal a woman I barely recognise despite sharing blood with her. Aunt Margaret looks older than her sixty-eight years, her grey hair pulled back severely, a cardigan wrapped tightly around shoulders that seem smaller than I remember. The smell of woodsmoke clings to her, along with something that might be lavender or old tea leaves.

"Emma." Her voice carries surprise wrapped in wariness, as if she'd given up expecting to see me again. "I didn't think..."

"Hello, Margaret." The formality feels necessary, a barrier against the history that stretches between us like barbed wire. "I wondered if we could talk."

Her eyes narrow slightly, taking in my appearance with the clinical assessment that runs in our family. "About what?"

"About Dad. About things Mum never told me."

Something flickers across her expression—recognition, perhaps, or resignation.

"You'd better come in then."

The front room feels smaller than memory suggests, cramped with furniture that's seen better decades. Lace curtains filter the afternoon light into something pale and apologetic while a wood burner hisses in the corner, throwing orange shadows across the floral wallpaper. Everything smells of old tea and loneliness, the particular atmosphere of someone who has learned to fill silence with routine rather than conversation.

Margaret settles into what's clearly her chair, the cushions shaped by years of solitary evenings. She doesn't invite me to sit, but I perch on the edge of the sofa anyway, my coat still buttoned against the chill that seems to permeate the house despite the fire's efforts.

"Tea?" she asks, though she's already reaching for the pot that sits on a side table, clearly prepared for visitors who rarely come.

"Please."

The ritual of pouring gives us both something to do with our hands while we navigate the careful choreography of reconnection. Margaret's movements are precise, economical, the gestures of someone who's learned to find comfort in small ceremonies.

"How's Joshua?" she asks, though she's never met him, never been invited to meet him. Another casualty of the silence that's stretched between us since Mum's funeral.

"He's well. Four now. Starting to read."

"And Daniel?"

"Fine. Working hard."

The pleasantries feel brittle, performative, both of us aware we're delaying whatever conversation brought me to her door on a grey December afternoon. The tea tastes of familiarity and distance, brewed the same way Mum used to make it but somehow lacking the warmth that made it comforting.

"You look tired," Margaret says, studying my face with the frank assessment our family has always mistaken for affection.

"Everyone keeps saying that."

"Maybe because it's true."

I set down my cup with more force than necessary, the china rattling against the saucer. "Did my dad have another child?"

The words hang in the air between us.

Margaret's expression doesn't change, but something in her posture shifts—a stiffening, a preparation for impact.

She pours herself more tea with deliberate care. "Why are you asking?"

"Because someone's turned up claiming to be my half-sister. Because she knows things about our family that she shouldn't know. Because she's..." I struggle to find words that don't sound mad. "Because she's taking my life apart piece by piece and I need to understand why."

Margaret sets down the teapot and meets my eyes properly for the first time since I arrived. "What's her name?"

"Sophie."

Something flickers across her expression—not recognition exactly, but acknowledgement.

"Your father had affairs," she says, her voice carrying the weight of secrets kept too long. "Several of them, over the years. Your mother knew, towards the end. One woman in particular..."

She trails off, her gaze drifting to the fire as if the dancing flames might provide easier answers than the ones she's trying to voice.

"Go on."

"Her name was Carol. Worked in a shop on Penny Street, sold handbags and scarves. Pretty girl, but fragile. Unstable, your mother said." Margaret's voice grows steadier as she settles into the rhythm of confession. "She fell pregnant in 1991, claimed your father was responsible."

The dates align. Sophie would be thirty-four now, the same age the timing suggests. My stomach clenches as another piece of her impossible knowledge clicks into place.

"What happened to her?"

"She had the baby. A girl. But the strain of it—raising a child alone, your father refusing to acknowledge paternity, the whispers that follow unmarried mothers in places like Lancaster—it broke something in her."

Margaret's words paint a picture I don't want to see: a young woman destroyed by secrets my family helped keep.

"She was institutionalised when the child was about three. Couldn't cope anymore. The girl went into care, then to foster families." Margaret's voice carries the clinical distance of someone recounting facts rather than tragedies. "I told your mother about it at the time. Thought she deserved to know."

The betrayal hits from multiple directions. My father, carrying on affairs while pretending to be a devoted family man. My mother, learning about a half-sister I'd never known existed. Margaret, possessing this knowledge while I grew up in ignorance.

"That's why you stopped talking to us," I say. "Mum cut you off for telling her the truth."

"She said I was stirring up trouble where none existed. That some truths were better left buried." Margaret's smile carries decades of bitter vindication. "She chose to protect your father's reputation over acknowledging what he'd done."

The family mythology I'd built my understanding on—devoted parents, stable marriage, love that weathered ordinary difficulties—crumbles like damp plaster. In its place stands something uglier: lies, betrayals, a half-sister abandoned to protect secrets that were never worth keeping.

"Is she still alive? Carol?"

"Died about ten years ago. Still in care, from what I heard. Never really recovered from the breakdown." Margaret's matter-of-fact delivery makes the tragedy sound inevitable rather than preventable. "The girl would be grown now. Early thirties, I suppose."

Sophie's age. Sophie's desperate need to claim what was denied her. Sophie's careful infiltration of the family that cast her out before she was old enough to understand why.

My chest tightens with something that might be empathy or dread. The woman I've been fighting isn't just a manipulative stranger—she's my father's abandoned daughter, seeking recognition that was withheld until it was too late to matter.

"Why didn't you tell me?" The question comes out sharper than intended.

Margaret's expression hardens slightly. "When? At your mother's funeral, when you could barely look at me? In the years since, when you've made it clear our family connection was an obligation you'd rather avoid?"

The words sting because they're accurate. I'd blamed Margaret for the family fractures without understanding their true cause, made her the villain in a story where the real damage had been done by people I'd chosen to remember as heroes.

"I thought you might reach out eventually," she says, her voice softening slightly. "When you needed answers your mother couldn't give you anymore. But I wasn't going to force unwelcome truths on someone who'd made it clear they preferred comfortable lies."

The conversation dies there, smothered by the weight of revelations neither of us knows how to process. The fire hisses in the corner while outside, the December afternoon deepens into early evening. Families will be heading home from work and school, settling into the comfortable routines of ordinary happiness.

"I should go," I say, though leaving feels like abandoning something that might be important.

Margaret nods, rising to show me out with the careful courtesy our family has always used to paper over emotional chasms. At the door, she touches my arm gently.

"I'm sorry, Emma. For your father's choices, for your mother's silence, for my own part in not finding a way to tell you sooner. I only ever wanted you to know the truth."

34.

Frigid air hits my lungs as I stumble away from Margaret's terraced house, my legs barely steady enough to carry me across Balmoral Road. The park gates loom ahead through the drizzle, their Victorian ironwork black against the darkening sky. My body shakes with something deeper than cold—the cellular shock of learning that everything I've believed about my family has been built on carefully constructed lies.

I find an empty bench on the hillside overlooking the playground, the Ashton Memorial rising in the distance like a monument to certainties I no longer possess. The wooden slats feel damp through my coat, but I sink onto them anyway, clutching my handbag against my chest.

Sophie is my half-sister. The words circle in my head with the persistence of a stuck record, each repetition making them more real and more impossible simultaneously. My father's abandoned daughter, raised in care while I grew up in the family home that should have been partly hers.

Dad's mysterious absences during my childhood suddenly make sense, as do the arguments I overheard through bedroom walls—Mum confronting him about responsibilities he refused to acknowledge.

The tension that thrummed through our Chatsworth Road house wasn't just marital strain but the weight of secrets that ate at the foundations of our family.

Around me, Williamson Park continues its ordinary evening rhythm. Families stroll past despite the weather, children tugging at parents' coats while couples sip takeaway coffees from the visitor centre café. Christmas lights flicker to life near the playground, testing circuits that will soon transform the park into a seasonal wonderland.

Their normalcy feels like mockery.

I want to scream at them

But they can't hear the panic building in my chest, can't see the way reality has tilted off its axis while they go about their ordinary business. To them, I'm just another woman on a park bench, probably waiting for someone who's running late.

My heart begins to race without warning, pulse hammering against my ribs with increasing urgency. The sensation spreads outward like ripples in disturbed water—pins and needles in my fingertips, heat rising in my cheeks, vision blurring at the edges as if someone's adjusting the focus on a camera.

I know this feeling. Recognise it from other moments when reality has shifted too quickly for my mind to process.

The drowning sensation.

My breathing grows shallow, quick, insufficient. The park tilts around me while my hands shake with tremors I can't control. Families continue their evening walks, their voices growing distant as if I'm hearing them through thick glass.

This is how it felt before. Standing on that canal towpath while Josh struggled in water too deep for his small body, paralysed by the choice between jumping in to save him and staying safe on the bank. The terrible moment when maternal instinct warred with self-preservation and left me frozen while seconds ticked by like hours.

Someone else had pulled him out in the end—a jogger who'd appeared just in time, who'd acted while I stood useless with panic. Josh had been fine, coughing up river water but unharmed, while I'd pretended my delay had been reasonable caution rather than cowardice.

But I remember the feeling. The drowning sensation that came from being faced with choices too enormous for ordinary decision-making. The way time stretched and compressed while I failed to be the person my child needed me to be.

I curl forward on the bench, pressing my face against my knees, trying to make myself small enough to escape notice. Around me, the park continues its evening routine while I fall apart with as much dignity as I can manage.

My phone weighs heavy in my coat pocket. Daniel's number sits at the top of my contacts, the lifeline I should use when everything becomes too much to handle alone. He'll be home by now, probably wondering where I've gone, possibly worried enough to listen without immediately dismissing my concerns as symptoms of mental fragility.

The phone feels foreign in my shaking hands. It rings twice before his familiar voice cuts through the December evening.

"Em? Where are you? Sophie said you went out hours ago."

The sound of him—normal, concerned, unchanged by revelations that have shattered my understanding of everything—nearly breaks me completely. He exists in a world where Sophie is still just our helpful nanny rather than the half-sister I never knew existed, where my family history remains intact rather than revealed as elaborate fiction.

"Daniel." His name comes out as barely more than a whisper.

"What's wrong? You sound terrible."

I open my mouth to tell him everything. About Margaret's confession, about Sophie's impossible claim being rooted in truth, about our family being built on lies that left a daughter abandoned while I received everything that should have been partly hers.

But only sobs escape.

The words exist in my head with perfect clarity—explanations that would make sense of Sophie's infiltration, that would transform my paranoid fears into justified concern about a half-sister seeking recognition that was systematically denied. But they won't travel from my mind to my mouth, trapped by the magnitude of what acknowledging them would mean.

"Emma, talk to me. What's happened?"

"I can't—" The words break apart before they form properly. "I need—"

"Where are you? I'll come get you."

Through my tears, I manage to tell him about Williamson Park, about the bench near the memorial. His voice carries practical concern as he promises to drive over, to collect me and bring me home to safety and explanations that can wait until I'm capable of providing them.

The call ends, leaving me alone with the sound of families enjoying December evening walks while I fall apart on a park bench. I wipe my eyes with the back of my hand, trying to pull myself together enough to walk to the car park where Daniel will be waiting.

That's when I see her.

A lone figure stands beneath the park's main gate, silhouetted against the glow of street lights beyond. The posture is unmistakable—straight-backed, confident, the particular way Sophie holds herself that suggests ownership rather than observation.

Families pass between us, children racing ahead of parents who call gentle warnings about puddles and careful walking. But the figure doesn't move, doesn't acknowledge the life flowing around her. She simply stands, watching.

Watching me.

My pulse spikes again, panic returning with fresh intensity. How long has she been there? How much has she seen of my breakdown, my desperate phone call to Daniel, my complete collapse under the weight of truths I can't process?

I blink hard, trying to clear my vision, and when I look again the figure is gone.

Nothing beneath the gate but empty space and the ordinary flow of evening foot traffic. Couples heading home from work, teenagers cutting through the park to avoid main roads, dog walkers making final rounds before settling into television and takeaway dinners.

Had she been there at all? Or had panic conjured her from shadows and wishful thinking, my stressed mind creating threats where none existed?

The uncertainty gnaws at me with fresh horror. Either answer is terrifying—Sophie following me to witness my breakdown, or my grip on reality becoming so tenuous that I see her everywhere, even when she's safely at home preparing dinner and helping Josh with his bedtime routine.

I force my legs to carry me down the hill, past families who don't notice the woman falling apart amongst them.

Headlights slice through the gloom as Daniel pulls into the visitor car park.

His face shows genuine worry as I approach the car, his expression carrying the particular concern reserved for medical emergencies rather than domestic disagreements. He doesn't ask questions as I slide into the passenger seat, just turns up the heating and begins the careful drive home through Lancaster's evening traffic.

"Better?" he asks gently as we wait at traffic lights near the cathedral.

I nod, though better feels like the wrong word for the hollow space where certainty used to live. The revelation about Sophie hasn't made anything clearer—it's only added layers of complexity to a situation I already couldn't navigate.

She's not just the manipulative stranger I've been fighting. She's my father's abandoned daughter, seeking recognition from the family that cast her out before she was old enough to understand why. Her claim to Josh's affections, to Daniel's respect, to the domestic harmony I've failed to provide—it all carries the weight of historical injustice that makes simple opposition impossible.

Whether she'd been there or not, I knew one thing: Sophie was everywhere now—in my past, in my home, in my head.

35.

The front door clicks shut behind us, sealing me inside with the smell of rosemary and garlic. Sophie's voice drifts from the kitchen—something cheerful about timing, about dinner being almost ready, about Josh having been such a good boy while we were out.

Daniel shrugs off his coat, hanging it on the hook. His movements carry relief rather than tension, as if collecting his distraught wife from a park bench is just another item ticked off his evening to-do list.

"Smells incredible," he calls towards the kitchen.

"Just something simple," Sophie says, and I can hear her smile through the words.

I stand in the hallway still wearing my damp coat. The house feels smaller than when I left it, compressed by secrets that have nowhere to expand. My father's abandoned daughter moves through our kitchen while I hover by the front door like a stranger.

"Em?" Daniel touches my elbow. "You should get out of those wet things."

I climb the stairs without responding, my legs heavy. Each step creaks under my weight.

Our bedroom door closes behind me with a soft click. I sink onto the bed we've shared for eight years, still wearing my damp coat, still clutching my bag. The framed photographs on the dresser stare back at me—our wedding day, Josh as a baby, the childhood home that Sophie now inhabits like a rightful heir reclaiming stolen property.

The pillow smells of fabric softener and the particular scent Daniel leaves behind. I bury my face in it and let the sobs come.

They tear through me like physical wounds, each one carrying the weight of everything I've lost without realising I was losing it. My son's unconditional love, my husband's respect, my place at the centre of our family's story. All of it handed over to someone with a better claim—not through manipulation but through historical injustice I can't compete with.

They function better without my presence.

I push myself up from the bed, wiping my eyes with the back of my hand.

Josh's bedroom door stands slightly ajar. I push it open to find him sitting cross-legged on his bed, sorting through his collection of toy cars with the focused attention he brings to important tasks. He's arranging them by colour, his dark hair falling across his forehead.

"Josh?"

He looks up, his face brightening with the uncomplicated joy that makes my chest ache. "Mummy! Did you have a nice walk?"

I sit on the edge of his bed, reaching out to smooth his fringe. "I love you so much, sweetheart. More than anything in the whole world. You know that, don't you?"

Something in my voice makes his expression shift. The brightness fades, replaced by the particular wariness children develop when adult emotions become too large for them to navigate.

"Course I know," he says, but he's already pulling back slightly.

"I need you to remember that, always. Whatever happens, whatever anyone tells you, I love you more than my own life." My voice cracks on the words, desperation leaking through despite my efforts to sound normal. "You're the most important thing that's ever happened to me."

His small shoulders stiffen as my intensity washes over him like a tide he can't swim against. The cars scatter across his duvet as he scrambles backwards.

"Your eyes are funny, Mummy. You're scaring me."

"I'm sorry, love. I didn't mean—"

But he's already sliding off the bed, his bare feet hitting the carpet with soft thuds. He runs from the room without looking back, his small figure disappearing down the hallway towards the stairs.

Towards Sophie.

I follow, my legs unsteady on the Victorian boards. At the top of the stairs, I can hear Josh's voice, higher than usual with distress.

"Sophie! Mummy's being scary again!"

"Oh darling, she's just tired. Come here."

I descend slowly, gripping the banister. At the bottom, I find Josh wrapped in Sophie's arms while she rubs gentle circles on his back. Her movements are practised, maternal, exactly what he needs to feel safe again.

Daniel stands in the kitchen doorway, his phone pressed to his ear. "She's been under enormous pressure," he's saying. "The breakdown this afternoon was quite severe. I'm genuinely concerned about her mental state."

My stomach drops. He's talking to someone about me.

"Yes, I understand," Daniel says. "Tonight would be helpful. She's...not herself."

I step closer, close enough to catch fragments of the voice on the other end. Professional, calm, used to these kinds of conversations.

Daniel notices me listening and lowers his voice, but not quickly enough. "The crisis line, yes. I think she needs to speak to someone qualified."

Crisis line. Mental health emergency. Professional intervention for the woman whose grip on reality has become unreliable, whose paranoid fears about the helpful nanny have escalated into public breakdown and frightening her own child.

"Daniel." My voice sounds foreign, smaller than intended.

He ends the call quickly, turning to face me with the careful expression reserved for unpredictable situations. "They'd like to speak with you, Em. Just to check you're okay."

"I'm fine."

"You collapsed in the park. You terrified Josh." His voice carries exhausted patience. "You're not fine."

Behind him, Sophie continues comforting my son, her presence a calm counterpoint to the chaos I've created. Josh's breathing has already steadied against her shoulder, his trust in her ability to make things right absolute.

"They just want to help," Daniel says, extending his phone towards me. "Five minutes. That's all."

The phone waits in his outstretched hand like evidence of my failure. On the other end, a professional trained in managing psychiatric emergencies waits to assess whether I'm a danger to myself or others. Whether the mother who scared her own child needs immediate intervention.

I grab my handbag from where I dropped it by the stairs. "I'm going for a walk."

"Emma, no." Daniel steps forward, his voice sharp with alarm. "You can't just—"

"I need space." I push past him towards the front door, my movements clumsy with desperation. "I can't think here."

"You're not thinking clearly anywhere." His hand finds my arm, not roughly but with the firm grip of someone preventing a mistake. "Please. Just talk to them."

I shake him off, my fingers already on the door handle. "I'll be fine. I just need air."

"It's dark. You're upset. This isn't safe."

Behind him, Sophie watches our exchange with quiet attention, Josh still pressed against her shoulder. Her expression carries concern wrapped in calculation, as if she's cataloguing every moment of my breakdown for future reference.

"Let me go, Daniel."

Something in my voice makes him step back. His hand drops to his side, defeat written across his features. "How long?"

"I don't know."

The air hits my face like a slap as I step outside, sharp with frost and the promise of snow. I hear Daniel call my name once, but I don't turn back.

36.

Dalton Square glows with Christmas magic beneath the December drizzle, fairy lights strung between the wooden chalets casting everything in warm gold. The scent of mulled wine mingles with roasted chestnuts while families drift between stalls selling handmade crafts and seasonal treats. The town hall looms behind the market, its Victorian grandeur floodlit against the grey evening sky.

I drift through the crowd, clutching my handbag against my chest while trying to let the market's cheerful bustle calm the panic that's been building since Margaret's revelations. Around me, Lancaster settles into its evening rhythm—couples sharing steaming cups of mulled wine, children tugging parents towards the carousel, teenagers clustering around the sweet stalls.

The normalcy should comfort me. These are my neighbours, my community, people who share the particular satisfaction of living in a city that balances heritage with progress. But tonight, the warmth feels distant, as if I'm watching their contentment through thick glass.

Near the craft stalls, I spot Helen Marsden examining hand-knitted scarves. She's chatted with me countless times at school pick-up, comparing notes about Reception homework and sharing mild complaints about Lancaster's unpredictable weather.

I raise my hand in greeting as I approach.

Helen glances my way, her expression shifting from concentration to something cooler, more distant. Her smile feels perfunctory, delivered without warmth, before she turns back to the scarves with renewed interest.

The dismissal stings more than it should. Not because Helen and I are close friends, but because her sudden coolness suggests a shift in how I'm perceived by people who used to include me in their casual social geography.

I move on through the market, trying to shake off the interaction as seasonal stress rather than a deliberate snub. But at the mulled wine stall, another group of familiar faces cluster around steaming cups, their laughter bright against the evening air.

Sarah Whitworth stands at the centre of their small constellation, animated as she recounts some story that has the others leaning in with amused attention. I recognise two other mothers from Dallas Road Primary, women I've exchanged countless small conversations with about homework policies and playground politics.

Their laughter dies abruptly as I draw near, conversation stuttering to an uncomfortable halt. One of them glances at me with the particular expression reserved for people who might be unstable—careful, assessing, ready to deploy therapeutic kindness if necessary.

Sarah offers a smile that doesn't reach her eyes. "Emma. How are you?"

The question carries weight that should belong to medical inquiries rather than casual greeting. How are you feels loaded with subtext, as if my mental state has become a legitimate topic of community concern.

"Fine, thanks," I say, though the word sounds hollow even to me. "Lovely market this year."

They nod with the kind of careful enthusiasm people use around those who require gentle handling.

"Well," Sarah says eventually, her tone carrying the brightness of someone ending an interaction that's served its purpose. "Lovely to see you."

I step away from their group, my cheeks burning. Behind me, their conversation resumes with the particular energy of people who've successfully navigated a potentially awkward situation.

The market continues around me—families browsing handmade jewellery, couples sharing bags of roasted chestnuts, children racing between stalls with the particular freedom that comes from being outdoors after dark. But I feel ghostlike amongst them, haunting scenes of community contentment I can no longer access.

Snippets of conversation drift past as I wander between the chalets.

"...poor thing, really struggling..."

"...Sophie says she's quite fragile..."

"...lucky to have such good help..."

I pause beside a stall selling handmade candles, pretending to examine their wares while my ears strain to catch more of the conversation happening just beyond the display.

"She seemed fine at the summer fair," someone is saying. "But you never know with these things, do you? Sometimes it hits later."

"Sophie's been such a godsend," another voice replies. "Don't know what the family would do without her."

The careful pity in their voices suggests they've already written me off as someone whose grip on reality can't be trusted.

I fumble for my purse, intending to buy something—anything—to justify lingering near their conversation. But my hands shake as I try to count coins, my fingers suddenly clumsy.

The vendor looks past me to the next customer with barely concealed impatience, as if my presence is slowing down his evening's trade. Heat rises in my cheeks as I struggle with money that should be straightforward, wondering if I look as unstable as Sophie's narrative suggests.

Maybe the story is becoming true through sheer repetition. Maybe enough people believing I'm fragile, unreliable, prone to paranoid fantasies has begun to reshape reality itself. When everyone around you sees mental instability, how do you maintain confidence in your own perceptions?

The mulled wine I finally manage to purchase tastes like disappointment. I clutch the paper cup like a prop in a performance I no longer understand, wandering between stalls that offer everything except the community belonging I used to take for granted.

Near the carousel, children shriek with delight while their parents wave from the sidelines, phone cameras capturing moments that will become next year's Christmas card memories. The scene should warm me—evidence of the simple joys that make December magical despite Lancaster's grey weather.

Then I see her.

Gemma stands near the mulled wine stall, her blonde hair catching the fairy lights as she laughs with two other parents from Josh's school. The sound carries across the market noise.

I push through the crowd, dodging families with pushchairs and teenagers clutching paper cups of hot chocolate.

"Gemma!" I call, raising my hand to catch her attention above the market chatter.

She looks up from her conversation, her eyes finding mine across the square. For a moment, her expression flickers.

Then she looks straight through me.

The dismissal is so complete, so deliberately cruel, that for a moment I think I've imagined it. But Gemma's gaze has already returned to her companions, her laughter resuming as if I don't exist. As if twenty years of friendship can be erased by simply refusing to acknowledge someone's presence.

The noise of the market dulls around me, everything becoming muffled as if I'm hearing it underwater.

Memories surface with brutal clarity. Gemma holding my hand during Mum's funeral, her presence the only thing that made the service bearable. Coffee dates that stretched into afternoon wine, sharing fears about motherhood and marriage with the particular honesty that comes from being understood completely. Her shoulder to cry on when freelance work dried up, when Daniel grew distant, when the weight of failing at everything became too much to carry alone.

All of it erased by whatever narrative Sophie has spun about my deteriorating mental state.

Gemma doesn't glance back, doesn't offer even the courtesy of a polite nod. She's made her choice, and it doesn't include maintaining loyalty to someone who's become socially inconvenient. The woman who once promised we'd be friends forever has cut me loose.

If Gemma can be turned against me, then no one is safe from Sophie's influence.

Across the square, I spot Sophie chatting animatedly with two other mothers near a craft stall. Her red scarf provides a bright splash of colour against the December gloom while her companions lean in with the focused attention reserved for people worth listening to.

Her laughter carries across the crowd, confident and musical. She gestures as she speaks, her movements graceful and assured, everything about her suggesting someone who belongs exactly where she is. The other women nod with obvious agreement, their faces showing the particular warmth reserved for trusted friends.

To everyone else, she's the competent woman who stepped in when needed, while I'm the ungrateful recipient of help I should appreciate rather than question.

I force myself to remain where I am, willing Gemma to glance back, to break whatever spell has convinced her that abandoning our friendship is the reasonable choice. But she moves further into the crowd.

The physical sensation of being cut adrift hits with surprising intensity. Not just lonely but untethered, floating free of social moorings. Without Gemma's friendship, without the neighbours' casual acceptance, without even Daniel's reliable support, I'm truly alone in ways I hadn't imagined possible.

Nausea rises in my throat. Sophie hasn't just taken my home, my son's primary affections, my husband's respect. She's systematically severed every connection that might provide an alternative perspective on what's happening to our family.

I can't stay here anymore. Can't stand amongst families enjoying seasonal traditions while being treated like a cautionary tale they whisper about when they think I can't hear.

The fairy lights feel harsh, exposing, turning the square into a spotlight where my social exile is performed for anyone interested in witnessing it.

I push through the crowd, moving faster than the families with children can easily navigate.

Tears sting my eyes, blurring the fairy lights into streaks of gold and red.

By the time I reach the edge of the square, one truth is clear: I have no one left.

Sophie has taken them all.

37.

The house feels smaller when I push through the front door, as if the walls have shifted inward. The hallway stretches ahead with its familiar runner and coat hooks, but something fundamental has changed in the house's atmosphere. Not just the scent of Sophie's cooking—cinnamon and something else, mulled wine sachets she must have picked up at the market—but the quality of silence that suggests conversations have been happening without me.

Daniel sits at the kitchen table, papers spread in neat piles around his laptop. Bills, probably, or tax documents that need filing before the year ends.

He doesn't look up when I enter, his attention focused on columns of figures that apparently require more concentration than acknowledging his wife's presence. The deliberate snub hits harder than it should, coming so soon after Gemma's public dismissal.

"Did you call them?" he asks without preamble, his voice carrying the weary tone of someone who already knows the answer.

"I don't need help," I say.

Daniel's pen stops moving across whatever form he's completing. The silence stretches between us.

"You're spiralling, Em. Everyone's worried about you."

"I'm not paranoid."

Daniel finally looks up. "Then explain tonight. Gemma rang. She's genuinely concerned about your behaviour."

"She wouldn't even look at me," I say, hating how the words sound—petulant, desperate, exactly like someone whose grip on social reality has become unreliable.

"Because you were making a scene, Em. Standing in the middle of Dalton Square, waving and shouting like..." He trails off, but the unfinished comparison hangs between us.

Like someone having a breakdown.

Sophie appears in the doorway. She carries a tray with three mugs of tea. "I thought you might both need this."

She sets the mugs down with care, the ceramic clicking softly against the wooden table. As she moves past Daniel, her hand finds his arm—a brief touch, barely more than a brush of fingers, but intimate enough to make my stomach clench.

Daniel doesn't pull away. Doesn't acknowledge the contact, but doesn't reject it either. The small gesture carries more significance than any conversation could have conveyed.

"She's just under pressure," Sophie says. "It's been hard on her, with everything that's happened. Sometimes people need time to process difficult emotions."

Heat rises in my cheeks as Sophie's narrative reshapes the conversation around my supposed instability.

"Do you not see what she's doing?" The words explode from me with more force than intended, my bag hitting the kitchen counter with a sharp crack that makes both of them look up.

Daniel's expression hardens. "What I see is someone trying to help us, and you tearing our family apart because you can't accept that help gracefully."

A small sound from the doorway makes us all turn. Josh stands there in his pyjamas "Mummy?" His voice wavers with confusion and fear. "Why are you shouting?"

The sight of him—small, vulnerable, frightened—makes my chest clench.

"It's alright, sweetheart," Sophie says, gathering him against her shoulder. "Mummy and Daddy are just talking about grown-up things. Nothing for you to worry about."

Josh melts into her embrace with the unconscious trust of childhood, his small body relaxing as Sophie's gentle presence restores his equilibrium. She guides him towards the stairs while she whispers reassurances that make his tears stop flowing.

"I can't do this if you won't even try to get help," Daniel says once Josh's footsteps fade up the stairs.

His shoulders sag with something that might be defeat. Not anger anymore, but resignation.

"I don't need help," I say, but the protest sounds weak, unconvincing even to me.

"You do, Em. You really do." Daniel turns back to his paperwork, the gesture carrying more dismissal than any argument could have conveyed. "And until you're willing to admit that, I don't know how we move forward."

The conversation dies there, smothered by his refusal to engage further. Sophie's footsteps creak overhead as she settles Josh back into bed.

I flee upstairs to our bedroom, slamming the door with enough force to make the windows rattle in their frames. The room feels smaller than usual, compressed by the weight of conversations happening without me, decisions being made around my absence.

Through the floorboards, voices rise from the kitchen below. Daniel and Sophie, their tones too low to distinguish individual words but intimate in their careful consideration for each other's perspective. The sound carries through the old house's thin floors—not quite whispering but private enough to exclude anyone who might be listening.

I press my ear to the carpet, desperate to catch fragments of whatever they're discussing. My marriage, probably. My mental state. The professional help I'm apparently too proud or unstable to accept.

But the harder I strain to hear their words, the more they blur into indistinct murmur—as if the house itself had chosen a side, and it wasn't mine.

38.

I give up after three hours in the library café, my laptop screen still empty, my coffee stone cold.

The surface has a thin film now, wrinkled like skin, but I can't bring myself to drink it.

Every attempt at working on the new logo collapses beneath the hiss of the steamer, the clatter of cups, the steady drizzle tapping at the windows.

Frustration knots in my chest until I snap the laptop shut and shove it into my bag.

Outside, December rain needles through my coat, damp seeping into the fabric until it hangs heavy on my shoulders.

I keep my head down as I walk home, past rows of terraced houses with their glowing windows and ordinary warmth that feels a world away from mine.

By the time I reach my front door, my fringe is plastered to my forehead, my hands trembling as I fumble the key into the lock.

The house exhales silence around me as I push inside.

The hallway stretches ahead with its familiar runner and coat hooks, but something fundamental feels wrong in the house's atmosphere.

No voices. No *Octonauts* theme tune from the television. No patter of small feet across floorboards that creak with every step.

Josh's toys lie scattered across the living room floor—Lego bricks arranged in the elaborate fortress he'd been building yesterday, picture books splayed open to pages showing pirates and dinosaurs. Evidence of recent play, but no child.

"Josh?" I call. "Sophie?"

Nothing.

I race through the ground floor, checking every room with growing desperation.

The kitchen stands empty.

No warmth from recent cooking, no signs of the afternoon snack ritual that usually marks Josh's return from school.

The back door is locked from inside. No sign of hasty departure or struggle, just the ordinary emptiness of a house waiting for its occupants to return.

I bolt upstairs, taking the steps two at a time. Josh's bedroom lies undisturbed, his dinosaur duvet smoothed over pillows that still hold the impression of last night's sleep.

Sophie's room maintains its unsettling perfection—bed made with military precision, not a single possession out of place.

The silence presses against my eardrums.

I race back downstairs, grabbing my keys from the hall table with hands that won't stop shaking. The coat hooks by the front door confirm what I'd feared—Josh's bright blue jacket is missing, along with his wellies.

They've gone out. Without telling me. Without leaving a note or sending a text.

I pace the length of our hall, mobile clutched in my hand, debating whether to call the police or Daniel or simply scour Lancaster's streets until I find them. The rational part of my mind insists they'll return soon, but panic doesn't listen to rational arguments.

Minutes stretch as I imagine Josh frightened, calling for me while Sophie soothes him with promises I'll never hear. The woman who's already claimed so much of his affection, now having him completely to herself without my interference.

A key scrapes in the lock.

"...and the big duck, the one with the green head, he ate three pieces at once!"

Relief floods through me so completely my legs nearly buckle. But it's quickly replaced by fury that burns hotter than the panic that preceded it.

The front door opens, and they appear like figures from a storybook—Sophie with her cheeks pink from cold air, Josh bouncing beside her with the satisfaction of someone who's had an excellent afternoon.

"Where the hell have you been?" The words explode from me before they're fully through the door.

Sophie blinks with apparent surprise at my tone.

"We were feeding the ducks by the river. Josh loved it, didn't you, sweetheart?"

Josh nods. "The bread went spinning in the water like it was racing! And Gerald—the big duck—he caught most of it before the river took it away."

The River Lune. Racing water. Something spinning away too fast to catch.

My vision blurs as memory crashes over me with brutal clarity. Josh at three years old, slipping from the towpath while I stood paralysed by indecision. The terrible seconds when he struggled in water too deep for his small body while I failed to act, failed to jump in, failed to be the mother he needed when it mattered most.

Now Sophie has taken him back to that same stretch of water, to the place where my maternal failures are written in the landscape itself.

"We stood right by the edge," Josh says. "Sophie held my hand so I wouldn't fall in. The current was really fast—whoosh!—taking everything downstream."

The sound of rushing water fills my ears, drowning out Sophie's calm explanations about fresh air and healthy exercise. All I can hear is the Lune's relentless current, carrying away everything that slips from careless hands.

"You should have told me where you were going," I manage, my voice cracking with the effort.

Sophie shrugs with the casual dismissal of someone whose judgement rarely gets questioned. "It was harmless. He needs fresh air, Emma. Children can't live wrapped in cotton wool."

The criticism cuts deep because it carries truth.

The front door opens again as Daniel arrives home from work, his face lighting up when he sees Josh's animated state.

"Someone's had a good afternoon," he says. "Nice to see him outside instead of glued to the television."

Throughout dinner, Josh regales Daniel with stories about their adventure. The ducks' feeding hierarchy, the way bread crusts float differently than whole slices, the joggers and dog walkers who shared the towpath with them. His enthusiasm is infectious, making the outing sound like the kind of wholesome childhood experience any parent would encourage.

"Sophie says we might see kingfishers next time," Josh announces between mouthfuls of the shepherd's pie that appeared while I was upstairs changing clothes. "They're blue and orange and really fast. Mummy Sophie says we'll live together forever."

My fork clatters against the plate, the sound sharp in the sudden quiet. Daniel's chewing slows.

Sophie continues eating with serene composure, her face showing nothing but gentle affection as she reaches over to stroke Josh's hair.

"That's just children's talk," she says. "He knows I care about him."

But her hand lingers on his head with maternal possessiveness, and her eyes meet mine across the table with calm satisfaction. She's not embarrassed by Josh's revelation—she's pleased he's shared it, pleased I've heard the future she's been whispering into his willing ears.

Forever. Not until he's older, or until I'm back on my feet, or until our family crisis resolves itself. *Forever*, as if their bond transcends the temporary employment arrangement that brought her into our lives.

Daniel clears his throat, clearly uncomfortable with the direction of the conversation but unwilling to challenge Sophie directly. "Well," he says, "we're lucky to have Sophie helping us for now."

For now. Not forever, but the distinction feels meaningless when Josh beams.

After dinner, I help Josh into his pyjamas while Sophie clears the table. But my hands shake as I guide his arms through fabric sleeves, the simple mechanics of bedtime routine requiring concentration they shouldn't need.

The river's sound still roars in my ears, mixing memory with present panic until I can barely distinguish between past trauma and current threat.

39.

Rain streaks the sash windows while I pad downstairs in bare feet, the floorboards creaking against the morning's first footsteps. The house holds that particular quiet of early winter days—central heating humming against the cold while outside, Lancaster settles into another grey morning.

The post lies scattered across the doormat. Gas bill with its ominous red print, takeaway flyers promising meals I'll never order, Christmas cards from relatives whose faces I struggle to recall.

But nestled amongst the familiar clutter sits a plain white envelope with no stamp, no postmark, no handwriting to identify its sender. Just my name printed in block letters across cream paper.

I tear open the envelope, extracting a single sheet of paper that's been folded once.

Truth drowns eventually.

The ink looks rushed, as if written by someone whose hands weren't entirely under control. But the letters are deliberate, carefully formed, designed for maximum impact rather than hurried communication.

My stomach drops as the word 'drowns' seems to pulse on the page, underlined by my mind's desperate attempt to make sense of what I'm seeing. Not threatens or disappears or gets buried—drowns. The specific verb that connects directly to memories I've been trying to suppress.

I read the message again, hoping repetition might reveal innocent explanations for what feels like targeted cruelty. But the words refuse to transform into anything benign.

Someone knows about the river, about the choice I made when courage was required and I found only paralysis.

My hands shake as I shove the note back into its envelope, terrified Daniel might appear from the kitchen and see evidence of whatever campaign is being waged against our family.

Images flood through me with brutal clarity, as if the note has unlocked memories I've kept carefully sealed.

The terrible moment when I should have acted, should have jumped in without hesitation, should have been the person someone needed me to be. Instead, I stood frozen while seconds stretched like hours, while my paralysis made me complicit in whatever followed.

The rush of the Lune's current fills my ears again, mixing past trauma with present panic until I can barely distinguish between memory and immediate threat. The silence that followed still echoes in my chest—not peaceful quiet but the hollow absence that comes after irreversible choices.

Now someone else knows. Someone who's chosen this particular weapon to torment me, who understands that some guilts never fade but only sink deeper until the right pressure brings them floating back to the surface.

But who would send such a message? A neighbour who's tired of keeping secrets? Sophie, escalating her psychological campaign? Aunt Margaret, finally tired of protecting family members who don't deserve protection? Daniel?

The uncertainty gnaws at me. Not knowing who sent the message makes every face suspect, every casual encounter potentially loaded with knowledge I can't acknowledge without admitting truths that would destroy what's left of my carefully constructed life.

Could Sophie have delivered the note herself, slipping it amongst legitimate post before Daniel or I could witness the deception?

The timing would be perfect—arriving just as yesterday's trauma at the River Lune towpath has reopened wounds I thought had healed. Sophie taking Josh to the exact place where my maternal failures are written in the landscape, then following up with targeted psychological pressure designed to keep me off balance.

How would she have known?

I move towards the sitting room door and watch her with Josh.

Her expression shows only gentle focus as she helps him select the right crayon for his dinosaur drawing. Nothing in her demeanour suggests someone who's just delivered anonymous threats, no tell-tale signs of guilt or anticipation.

Footsteps on the stairs announce Daniel's descent. He appears in the hallway still adjusting his tie.

"Morning," he says absently, scanning the scattered post. "Anything important?"

For a moment, I consider telling him everything. The note, the growing certainty that someone knows about the river, the weight of carrying secrets that eat at you from the inside until even ordinary mornings feel like battlefields.

But Daniel's distracted mood, his constant refrains about counselling and professional help, silence me before the words can form. How do I explain that anonymous messages are arriving to torment me about events he doesn't know happened? How do I confess to failures of character that would change how he sees me as wife, mother, human being worthy of basic respect?

"Just bills," I say. "Nothing urgent."

Daniel nods, already reaching for his coat. "I'll be late tonight."

After Daniel leaves, I stand in the hallway clutching the envelope while Sophie's voice drifts from the living room—gentle encouragement about staying inside the lines, praise for Josh's artistic choices, the easy warmth that makes children feel valued and understood.

I shove the note deep into my work files, burying it amongst client invoices and design sketches like I'm hiding evidence of crimes I can't admit to committing.

Truth drowns eventually. Not disappears or gets forgotten, but drowns.

40.

The night air bites at my cheeks as I walk through Lancaster's empty streets, Christmas lights strung between lamp posts casting everything in shades of gold and red.

Sleep had become impossible after another evening of watching Sophie orchestrate our domestic harmony while I played the role of grateful recipient.

Another bedtime where Josh reached for her instead of me, another conversation between her and Daniel that stopped when I entered the room.

The walls of our home felt like they were closing in, suffocating me with the scent of her cooking and the sound of her laughter.

I'd slipped out after midnight, leaving them all sleeping peacefully while I sought air that didn't taste of my own redundancy.

The city centre lies quiet at this hour, pubs closed and restaurants shuttered while Lancaster settles into the particular stillness that comes after midnight. My footsteps echo off cobblestones as I navigate streets that lead inevitably towards the water, drawn by something I can't name but can't resist.

The Millennium Bridge spans the River Lune in its elegant arc of steel and glass, Christmas lights reflecting off the black water below in fractured patterns of colour. During the day, families stroll across its walkways while joggers and dog walkers use it as a shortcut between the city's divided halves. At night, it feels exposed, windswept, the kind of place where thoughts echo louder than they should.

I grip the rail with hands that have gone numb from cold, staring down at water. The Lune's current carries Lancashire towards the sea, taking with it whatever gets swept into its flow—branches, litter, secrets that were meant to stay buried.

The sound rises from below like a promise and a threat. Not the gentle babble of streams but the deeper roar of water with purpose, water that's carved this landscape for millennia and will continue long after human concerns have been forgotten.

My breath clouds in the frosty air while memories I've tried to suppress surface with increasing clarity. Another riverbank, another winter evening, the terrible moment when courage was required and I found only paralysis.

Footsteps echo on the bridge behind me, measured and deliberate. At this hour, in this cold, most sensible people are safely indoors with central heating and hot drinks.

I turn to see Sophie approaching through the bridge's pools of light, her coat dark against the reflections from the water below.

"Couldn't sleep either?" she asks, settling beside me at the rail as if we're old friends.

"Why are you following me?"

"Following you? I was just walking." She gazes down at the river's surface. "You always end up here, don't you? The river draws you back."

How does she know about my nocturnal wanderings? How long has she been watching, cataloguing my movements, mapping the geography of my guilt?

"I don't know what you mean," I say, but my voice lacks conviction.

Sophie steps closer, her proximity making the bridge feel smaller, more confined. "I know what you did by the river. Or, more precisely, what you didn't do."

My grip tightens on the rail until the metal bites into my palms, but the pain feels distant compared to the panic rising in my chest.

"That's not— I never—" The denials fragment before they can form properly, dissolved by the weight of what Sophie apparently knows.

"One word from me, and your perfect life is over. Daniel, Josh, everyone you care about—they'll know exactly what you are."

The river surges below us, its sound amplifying until it drowns out everything except Sophie's voice and the hammering of my own pulse. Water that's witnessed secrets, carried away evidence, provided the perfect burial ground for guilt I thought would stay submerged forever.

But nothing stays buried permanently. The river gives up its secrets eventually, depositing them downstream where they can be found by people who know how to look.

Images overwhelm me with brutal clarity. Not just memory but the full weight of choices that seemed rational in the moment but look monstrous in retrospect.

"How did you—" I begin, then stop. The how matters less than the what. She knows. Somehow, impossibly, she's discovered the one secret that could destroy my marriage.

The bridge sways slightly in the December wind, or perhaps it's just my legs losing their ability to support my weight. Below, the Lune continues its relentless journey towards the bay.

Sophie's smile plays at the corners of her mouth like someone enjoying a private joke. "You don't own this life anymore," she says. "I do. The house, Josh's affections, Daniel's respect—all of it. The more you fight me, the more everyone will see what you really are."

In the distance, the cathedral bells begin to toll midnight, their bronze voices carrying across Lancaster with the authority of centuries. Each chime feels like a sentence being pronounced, marking the end of whatever illusions I'd maintained about fighting back.

Sophie doesn't need to make explicit threats or demands. The knowledge she possesses is weapon enough, hanging over every interaction like a sword suspended by the thinnest thread. One wrong move, one moment of defiance, and everything I've built collapses into ruin.

She straightens, adjusting her coat. "I should get back. Early morning tomorrow—Josh wants to visit the Christmas market again."

I watch her walk back towards the city centre, her footsteps echoing off the bridge's steel until they fade into the night.

The river roars below, and with Sophie's words still in my ear I know the truth wasn't buried anymore.

She owns it—and she owns me.

41.

Grey skies press against Lancaster, while the River Lune runs dark and swollen with winter rain. I pull my scarf tighter against the damp wind that cuts through the bare branches lining the towpath, each gust carrying the particular bite that comes when weather systems roll in from Morecambe Bay.

My footsteps echo dully on the wet stone, each step carrying me further from the warmth of homes where people are addressing Christmas cards and planning Boxing Day dinners. Normal concerns. Manageable anxieties.

Sophie's words from last night pulse in my head with metronomic persistence: *You don't own this life anymore. I do.*

The churning water below drags memory to the surface.

Josh, drowning.

Me, unable to move.

Sophie has dragged the memory back into focus, ensuring my guilt stays fresh enough to weaponise.

I watch debris swept along by the current—branches torn from riverside trees, plastic bottles that catch the weak light, a piece of red Christmas ribbon that spirals past like spilled blood.

Truth drowns eventually. But watching the river's relentless flow, I understand she meant something different. Not that truth disappears, but that it gets swept along by forces stronger than human control, surfacing wherever the current decides to deposit it.

Everything I've tried to bury keeps rising back to the surface, carried by currents I can't predict or contain.

If Daniel ever hears even a whisper of what happened. That my burnout wasn't exhaustion from work, but guilt from almost letting our son drown, my marriage collapses.

If Josh learns his mother failed to leap to his rescue, my relationship with him becomes another casualty.

If clients discover I'm the kind of person who can't save my drowning child, my work disappears along with our financial security.

Sophie owns my secret now, and through it, she owns me.

For the first time, I wonder if she'll force me to confess publicly. Not just holding the knowledge as leverage but demanding I admit my cowardice to Daniel, to Josh, to the community that's already convinced I'm mentally fragile.

Being made to destroy myself rather than simply being destroyed.

The towpath curves past St George's Quay, where a small group works to string Christmas lights along the rails of a narrowboat moored against the stone. Their laughter carries across the water, bright and uncomplicated.

I wish I could step into their reality, trade my knowledge for their ignorance, swap the weight of buried secrets for the simple pleasure of decorating boats with fairy lights. But the gap between their contentment and my paranoia feels unbridgeable.

The ordinary cheer jars against my internal landscape of panic and guilt. While they prepare for joy, I spiral towards ruin orchestrated by someone who's made destroying lives into an art form.

I turn away from their seasonal preparations and head back along the towpath towards Scotforth. Behind me, their voices fade into the general murmur of wind and water while ahead, the terraced houses of home glow with their own Christmas preparations.

That's when I hear them. Footsteps on the path behind me, steady and deliberate.

The steps match my pace exactly—not hurrying to overtake, not falling behind, but maintaining precise distance. When I slow to examine a bare tree whose branches create interesting shadows on the water, the footsteps slow as well.

Coincidence, perhaps. Another walker admiring the same view, taking time to notice details that usually pass unobserved in our rush towards destinations. But the synchronisation feels deliberate rather than accidental.

I stop completely, pretending to adjust my scarf while listening for confirmation. The footsteps stop too.

My pulse spikes with recognition I don't want to acknowledge. This isn't coincidence—it's surveillance.

The wind carries no sound except the river's constant murmur and the distant hum of traffic on the main road. But the silence feels charged, loaded with presence rather than absence. Someone watching from whatever cover the winter landscape provides.

I spin around, breath caught in my throat, expecting to see Sophie's familiar figure on the path behind me. But the towpath stretches empty in both directions, nothing visible except drizzle and shadows cast by bare trees.

No footsteps now. No movement except the river's endless flow towards the sea.

But the certainty remains, lodged in my chest like a splinter that can't be extracted. Whether real or imagined, those footsteps have joined the chorus of paranoid thoughts that follow me everywhere now.

42.

Home feels smaller when I push through the front door, my hair damp from December drizzle and shoes muddy from the towpath.

Warm light spills from the dining room where Daniel sits at the table with his laptop open, papers spread in careful piles.

From the living room comes the sound of Josh's delighted laughter mixed with Sophie's gentle encouragement.

I linger in the hallway. This should be my home, my family, my evening routine. Instead, I feel like I've walked into someone else's domestic harmony, a carefully orchestrated scene where I'm the intruder rather than the inhabitant.

Daniel looks up when I enter, closing the laptop. "Em. We need to talk."

I slip off my damp coat, buying time while my pulse spikes. "About what?"

Daniel gestures to the chair across from him. "You're not well. Everyone can see it, Em. Everyone's worried." He shakes his head. "And you still haven't called that counsellor I found for you."

"I don't trust her."

"Don't trust who? Sophie?"

"There are things about her you don't know."

"What things? That she keeps this house functioning while you wander the streets in the rain talking to yourself."

I can't bring myself to respond.

Daniel pulls a printed sheet from his papers. "I've arranged a weekend away. Windermere. Just Josh and me. It'll give you space to think, time to rest properly."

A weekend away. Without me. While Sophie presumably remains to manage whatever domestic emergencies might arise in our absence—or rather, in my husband and son's absence, since I'm apparently staying behind.

"Space to think about what?" I ask, though I already know the answer.

"About getting the help you need. About calling that counsellor. About whether you're ready to admit this situation has become bigger than you can handle alone."

His tone is soft, therapeutic, designed to ease the blow of what feels like exile from my own family.

Heat rises in my cheeks as the full implications crash over me. Not a family holiday but a trial separation. Daniel removing Josh from whatever toxic influence I supposedly represent, giving our son access to quality time with his father while protecting him from his mother's deteriorating mental state.

"You can't just take him away from me," I say, my voice rising despite my efforts to remain calm.

"It's just two nights, Em. He'll be safe—" Daniel stops himself.

Safe. Safe from what? From me. From the paranoid woman who sees threats where none exist, who creates domestic crisis from innocent help, whose grip on reality has become so unreliable that her own husband can't trust her alone with their child.

"I'm his mother," I say, the words scraping my throat raw.

"I know you are. But right now, you're not well enough to be the mother he needs."

I push back from the table, my chair scraping. But this isn't a negotiation—it's Daniel informing me of decisions that have already been made.

As I storm towards the hallway, seeking escape from his clinical assessment of my inadequacy, something catches my eye beside the front door. Sophie's overnight bag, navy blue with wheels, the same case she'd arrived with months ago when this nightmare began.

From the living room, Josh's excited chatter carries clearly: "Sophie says there's boats and mountains and we can feed the ducks without them trying to steal our sandwiches!"

She's going with them. The weekend away isn't father-son bonding—it's family time that includes everyone except me.

Daniel has arranged a trial run of life without Emma, complete with the woman who's systematically replaced me in every aspect of our household. Josh will experience what it feels like to have a mother who's competent, calm, enthusiastic about adventure rather than paralysed by anxiety about water and risk.

They'll explore Windermere's shores while I remain in Scotforth, alone with my paranoid fantasies and my refusal to seek professional help.

The perfect contrast between functional family and damaged individual, between healthy relationships and whatever psychological wreckage I've become.

The Lake District trip wasn't about giving me space. It was about replacing me completely.

43.

I wake to silence.

Not the comfortable quiet that settles over houses when everyone sleeps peacefully, but the hollow absence that follows evacuation.

They've gone.

The knowledge sits in my chest like swallowed glass, sharp and indigestible. My family—or what's left of it—is driving through the Lake District while I lie in a bed that feels too large, in a house that echoes with abandonment.

I drag myself downstairs, each step creaking against the morning silence. The kitchen stands pristine, surfaces wiped to Sophie's exacting standards. Even her absence feels organised, deliberate, superior to the chaos I'd leave behind.

Her coffee mug sits in the drying rack—the blue one with tiny flowers that Josh picked out for her during one of their shopping expeditions. A cream scarf drapes over the back of the chair.

Josh's toys lie arranged in neat piles rather than the scattered explosion I'm used to navigating. Sophie's influence extends even to his play—everything contained, purposeful, reflecting the kind of childhood where imagination comes with boundaries and guidance.

I pour tea with hands that shake, the mundane ritual feeling foreign in the absence of my usual audience. No one to butter toast for, no one to chase about finding lost socks, no one to need me for anything at all.

The house presses against me with its emptiness until I can't breathe properly.

Outside, December drizzle turns Lancaster's streets silver, but I push through the front door anyway. Movement feels necessary, even if I've nowhere particular to go.

The city centre hums with festive energy despite the weather. Christmas shoppers hurry between Penny Street's boutiques while the sound of brass instruments drifts from Dalton Square. I follow the music, drawn by noise that might drown out the silence in my head.

Near the carousel, a father lifts his daughter onto his shoulders so she can see the Christmas tree. She squeals with delight, her mittened hands tangling in his hair while her mother captures the moment on her phone. The scene should warm me—evidence of the simple love that makes parenting worthwhile.

Instead, it cuts like a blade.

This time last year, Josh rode that same carousel while Daniel and I stood watching. We'd felt like a proper family then, united in the simple goal of creating happiness for someone we both adored.

Now Sophie holds Josh's hand through similar moments in Windermere, claiming experiences that should be mine. She's not just invaded my home—she's usurped my role in the memories still being made.

I push through the market crowd, dodging pushchairs and shopping bags, trying to escape the cheerful assault on my isolation. But everywhere I look, families demonstrate the bonds I'm losing.

Near the craft stalls, I spot Sarah Whitworth examining hand-knitted scarves with two other mothers from Josh's school..

Sarah glances up as I approach, her smile faltering slightly. The warmth that used to mark our casual conversations cools to polite tolerance.

"Emma," she says, her voice carrying careful distance. "How are you?"

"Fine, thanks," I manage.

The other mothers nod with uncomfortable sympathy, their expressions suggesting they've discussed my situation in detail.

"Lovely market this year," I say, desperate to find normal ground.

"Yes, isn't it?" Sarah's enthusiasm feels performed, delivered for my benefit rather than genuine appreciation. "Well, we should—"

"Of course. Don't let me keep you."

I retreat before they can finish the dismissal. Behind me, their conversation resumes.

The market swirls around me. Every laugh feels like mockery, every family tableau a reminder of what I've lost. I duck down Church Street, seeking escape.

The narrow lane offers shelter from the crowds but not from the thoughts that chase me.

Maybe they're right. Maybe I am broken, unstable, the kind of person who sees threats where none exist. Maybe Daniel's exile isn't punishment but protection—keeping Josh safe from whatever poison I've become.

My mother's voice echoes from memory, sharp with the particular disappointment she reserved for my failures: *Stop making such a fuss, Emma. There's nothing worse than someone who can't cope properly.*

But I couldn't cope, could I? Not with motherhood, not with marriage, not with the simple task of accepting help when it was offered.

I'd turned Sophie's assistance into a conspiracy, her competence into a threat, her presence into evidence of my own inadequacy.

The street tilts around me as the full weight of self-recrimination crashes down. My legs carry me without conscious direction, away from the market's cheerful noise, towards the river that's always drawn me when thoughts become too heavy to carry alone.

St George's Quay opens ahead, its facades dark against the grey sky. The River Lune runs high and swift beneath the bridge, swollen with winter rain.

I sink onto the cold stone bench where courting couples usually sit during warmer weather. Now it's empty, abandoned to winter's bite and the particular loneliness that comes with watching water flow towards destinations you'll never see.

The thought arrives unbidden: *they're better off without me.*

Daniel, freed from the burden of a wife whose paranoia creates domestic crisis from innocent help. Josh, guided by someone whose patience never falters, whose competence never wavers, whose love comes without the weight of maternal failure. Sophie, finally claiming the family position she's earned through daily service while I provided nothing but resistance.

The water surges past, dark and purposeful, carrying debris towards Morecambe Bay.

For a moment, the pull feels almost irresistible. The simplicity of letting go, of stepping into current that would carry away guilt and inadequacy and the crushing weight of being unwanted in your own life. The river that's witnessed my failures offering final absolution through obliteration.

Children's voices cut through the December air—teenagers racing along the opposite bank, their laughter bright against the grey afternoon. One stumbles and the others help him up, their care for each other casual and absolute.

The sound snaps something back into place. Josh still calls me Mum, even if he prefers Sophie's stories. He still reaches for my hand sometimes, still brings me drawings that I stick to the fridge with religious devotion. Whatever Sophie has claimed, she hasn't erased me completely.

Not yet.

I stand, wiping my eyes with the back of my hand. The tears are cold against my skin, but the despair that produced them has crystallised into something harder, more useful.

Sophie has spent months positioning herself as the solution while painting me as the problem.

She's turned my husband against me, charmed my son away from me, convinced my community that I'm mentally unstable.

She's claimed my past, colonised my present, and planned a future where I don't exist.

But she's made one crucial mistake.

She's left me with nothing to lose.

I walk back through Lancaster's streets with steady steps.

If Sophie wants a war, I'm ready to fight.

44.

The house breathes around me as I push through the front door, my coat dripping rain onto the Victorian tiles. The silence hits differently now—not just empty but expectant, as if the walls themselves are waiting to see what I'll do.

Sophie's perfume still clings to the hallway air, that subtle floral scent she wears that makes everything smell like competence. Daniel's work shoes are gone from their usual spot by the stairs. Josh's bright wellies no longer sit beside the radiator.

They've taken pieces of the house with them, leaving behind spaces that feel deliberately vacant rather than accidentally empty.

I make tea with hands that have finally stopped shaking, the ritual grounding me in something approaching normality.

The dining table sits beneath the window, scattered with the debris of our interrupted life. Bills that need paying, Josh's abandoned colouring sheets, the Christmas cards I've been meaning to write for weeks. Evidence of the chaos Sophie's been quietly managing while I spiralled into paranoid accusations.

But today the mess looks different. Not shameful evidence of my inadequacy but raw material for something more purposeful.

I clear space with deliberate ceremony, stacking bills and smoothing Josh's artwork until the surface emerges.

The notebook comes from the kitchen drawer—one of those black composition books Josh uses for school projects. I open it to a fresh page, uncap a pen, and stare at the blank lines that wait to give structure to months of accumulated suspicion.

"If I can write it all down, it'll make sense," I whisper to the empty room. "It has to."

The first entry comes easily: *Sophie knew Mum's lullaby.* Impossible, but there it sits in black ink, undeniable.

Found in our bedroom with childhood photo. Not just tidying but studying, memorising details from a life she had no business accessing.

Living in my childhood home. The key sliding smoothly into that Chatsworth Road lock, her casual familiarity with streets I'd navigated as a teenager. Coincidence stretched past breaking point.

The bruise on Josh's arm. Finger-shaped, precisely placed, accompanied by stories that shifted under examination. A four-year-old who couldn't remember falling hard enough to leave marks.

Diary entries rewritten. My private thoughts contaminated by her neat handwriting, my safe space violated. *Remember you're lucky*, as if gratitude could be prescribed like medication.

Anonymous notes. Messages that arrived when I was most vulnerable, designed to break whatever confidence remained intact. Someone knew about the river, about choices I'd never confessed to anyone.

I pause, studying the growing list. Each item alone might be explained away—stress, coincidence, the paranoid imaginings of someone under pressure. But together, they form a pattern too deliberate to dismiss.

At the top of the page, I write "Coincidences" in careful capitals. Then I cross it out with three sharp strokes, replacing it with a word that tastes like vindication: "Evidence."

The act of writing calms something frayed in my chest. For weeks, these concerns have rattled around my skull like loose change, creating noise without purpose. Now they sit organised on paper, transformed from symptoms of breakdown into components of a case.

I create columns across the page: *Fact, Sophie's Version, My Version.* The framework forces precision where confusion had reigned.

Fact: Josh had bruising on his upper arm. Sophie's Version: Playground accident during walk. My Version: Deliberate injury, story fabricated.

Some entries wobble under scrutiny. The humming could be chance, the bedroom intrusion might have been innocent tidying. But others—the documents I'd glimpsed in her room, the impossible knowledge of my family history—resist rational explanation.

I whisper to the empty dining room: "It's not paranoia if it's true."

The words feel like absolution, like permission to trust instincts I'd been taught to doubt. Everyone said I was imagining threats where none existed, but here's the evidence laid out in neat columns, undeniable as arithmetic.

Reading through the completed list, one absence glares back at me like an accusation: Sarah.

Sarah Whitworth, who'd recommended Sophie with such confident enthusiasm. Sarah, who'd positioned Sophie as the perfect solution to problems I'd been too proud to admit. Sarah, who'd never explained how she knew Sophie's qualifications, never mentioned where their paths had crossed.

I'd been too grateful at the time to question the gift of competent help. Too desperate for domestic rescue to examine the source of my salvation. But now the gap in my knowledge feels deliberate, strategic, designed to prevent the kind of investigation I should have conducted from the beginning.

Why did Sarah have Sophie's details readily available? Why this particular nanny for this particular family? Why did she speak about Sophie's qualifications with such specific certainty?

I underline "SARAH" three times, the pen pressing deep enough to score the paper beneath. The name pulses on the page like a heartbeat, like an accusation waiting to be voiced.

If Sarah knew something—if she'd placed Sophie deliberately rather than coincidentally—then she's part of whatever conspiracy has been dismantling my family piece by careful piece.

The notebook sits open before me, pages filled with evidence that transforms months of gaslighting into something approaching a case file. Sophie hasn't been helping us—she's been studying us, collecting intelligence, executing a plan that required insider knowledge to succeed.

And Sarah provided that knowledge.

I close the book with hands that shake from fury rather than fear, the composition binding slapping shut with the sound of a decision being made.

Tomorrow, I'll make Sarah talk.

45.

My phone feels heavy in my hands as I scroll through contacts, thumb hovering over her number. The rational part of my mind whispers warnings: *What if you're wrong? What if she thinks you've lost your grip completely? What if this makes everything worse?*

But the evidence sits there in black ink, undeniable. Sarah recommended Sophie without explanation, vouched for qualifications she shouldn't have known, positioned herself as the helpful neighbour while orchestrating my family's destruction.

I press call before doubt can paralyse me again.

The phone rings twice before Sarah's voice cuts through, brisk and distracted. Behind her, I can hear the familiar chaos of family teatime—children arguing over something, the clatter of dishes being cleared, the comfortable noise of a household that functions properly.

"Emma? Is everything alright?"

The question carries weight it shouldn't. Not casual concern but genuine alarm, as if my calling represents some kind of emergency that needs immediate management.

"I'm fine," I say, trying for casual. "Just wondered if we could have a chat sometime. About Sophie, actually. I'd love to know more about how you found her."

Silence stretches across the line. The background noise from Sarah's kitchen continues—her children's voices, the sound of running water—but Sarah herself has gone completely quiet.

"I'm sorry?" she says eventually, her tone shifting from distracted friendliness to something cooler, more guarded.

"Sophie. You recommended her, didn't you? I just wondered where you'd heard about her work, what made you think she'd be perfect for our family."

"Emma, I'm rather busy just now." Sarah's voice carries the particular crispness that marks the end of unwelcome conversations. "Just heading out, actually. Perhaps we could chat another time?"

But I can hear her kitchen sounds continuing in the background. No rustling of coats being retrieved, no footsteps moving towards doors. She's lying, and we both know it.

"It would only take a minute. I'm just curious about her background, her previous families. You spoke so highly of her experience."

"Because she's been wonderful for you, hasn't she?" Sarah's tone grows sharper, defensive. "Josh is thriving, Daniel seems more relaxed. I don't understand what you're driving at."

There's something beneath her irritation though—a tremor that suggests nerves rather than mere annoyance. The confident Sarah who commands playground hierarchies with effortless authority has been replaced by someone who sounds genuinely rattled.

"I just want to understand how you knew her," I say, hearing my own voice rise slightly. "Where she worked before, who recommended her to you. Basic references, really."

"Emma." Sarah's voice drops to something approaching concern. "Are you quite well? You sound...stressed."

"I'm perfectly well. I just think it's reasonable to want to know more about someone living in our house, caring for our son."

"She came highly recommended," Sarah says, but there's something evasive in her tone now. "Very experienced with children Josh's age. I thought she'd be perfect for your situation."

"Recommended by who?"

Another pause, longer this time. "Look, I really can't talk now. The children need—"

"Sarah, please. Just tell me where you heard about Sophie. It's a simple question."

"It's not that simple, actually." The words come out sharp. "Some things are better left alone, Emma."

My pulse spikes at the admission hidden in her deflection. She knows something. Something she's actively choosing not to share, something that makes my questions dangerous rather than merely inconvenient.

"What do you mean by that?"

"I mean—" Sarah stops herself mid-sentence, and I can hear her breathing change, as if she's caught herself on the edge of saying too much. "I mean you should focus on the positive. Sophie's helped your family enormously. Why complicate that with unnecessary questions?"

"Because they're not unnecessary," I snap, my carefully maintained composure finally cracking. "Because I have a right to know who's living in my house, who's influencing my son, who's—"

"Emma, just...drop it. Please."

The line goes dead with a click that feels like a door slamming shut.

I stare at my phone. That final "please" echoes in my head—not the irritated dismissal of someone whose time is being wasted, but something that sounded almost like pleading.

Or fear.

I flip open my notebook, pen already moving across the page: *Sarah knows more than she's saying. Deflected questions about Sophie's background. Seemed nervous, almost frightened. Told me to "drop it" - why?*

The evidence accumulates, transforming vague suspicions into something approaching certainty. Sarah isn't just the helpful neighbour who happened to know the perfect nanny. She's complicit in whatever

Sophie's been orchestrating, part of a conspiracy that requires my silence to succeed.

But why would Sarah participate in destroying my family? What could she possibly gain from my suffering, from Sophie's systematic replacement of me in every aspect of my domestic life?

The questions multiply faster than answers, creating new layers of paranoia that threaten to overwhelm the clarity I'd gained from writing everything down. But one truth remains solid beneath the speculation: Sarah knows something she's determined not to share.

I grip the phone tight, fury simmering in my chest like something that could boil over at any moment. If Sarah won't talk on the phone, hiding behind false busy-ness and therapeutic concern about my mental state, then she'll have to explain herself face-to-face.

I slide my coat from the peg by the front door, my movements sharp with purpose rather than desperation. The December afternoon has already begun its slide towards darkness, but there's still time to corner Sarah before she can prepare more deflections.

46.

The drizzle turns Lancaster's streets silver under the yellow streetlamps, each step carrying me deeper into the residential maze of Moor Lane. Christmas lights twinkle through front windows while families settle into their evening routines, their warm domestic scenes playing out behind glass like advertisements for lives I can no longer access.

My notebook weighs heavy in my bag, evidence of Sophie's systematic infiltration burning against my ribs. The phone call with Sarah had confirmed what I'd suspected—she knows more than she's saying, something that makes my questions dangerous rather than merely inconvenient.

Sarah's terrace sits halfway down the street, its Victorian facade glowing with the kind of restrained Christmas cheer that marks proper middle-class celebration. Tasteful white lights outline the front window, a wreath hangs on the freshly painted door, everything suggesting the domestic competence I've been failing to achieve for months.

I hesitate on the doorstep, doubt creeping back despite my determination. What if I'm wrong? What if Sarah's evasiveness comes from embarrassment rather than complicity, awkward social manoeuvring rather than conspiracy?

But the alternative—accepting that I'm paranoid, delusional, the problem that requires professional intervention—feels impossible now. I've seen too much, documented too many violations, felt the systematic erosion of my place in my own family.

I knock hard before courage can desert me.

Sarah opens the door with surprise written across her face, her expression shifting quickly from confusion to something approaching alarm. She's still in the clothes she wore for school pick-up.

"Emma. What are you doing here?"

"I thought we could finish our conversation properly," I say, my voice steadier than I feel. "Face to face."

Sarah glances past me into the street, checking whether neighbours might witness this unexpected visit. The gesture feels telling—not concern for my wellbeing but anxiety about her own social positioning.

"I suppose you'd better come in," she says reluctantly, stepping aside to let me pass.

The hallway smells of dinner and furniture polish, the comfortable scents of family life functioning properly.

"Tea?" Sarah asks, though she's already moving towards the kitchen where the kettle sits ready on its base.

"Please."

Sarah's movements are precise but nervous, her hands slightly unsteady as she retrieves mugs from cupboards.

"Lovely home," I say, settling onto the edge of a sofa that actually matches its cushions.

"Thank you." Sarah perches across from me, not quite relaxed, her posture suggesting someone prepared for flight rather than conversation. "How have you been? You sounded rather stressed on the phone earlier."

The deflection stings—immediately positioning me as the unstable party rather than someone seeking reasonable answers.

"I just want to understand how you knew Sophie. Where she came from, who recommended her to you."

Sarah's grip tightens on her mug, knuckles showing white against the ceramic. "I don't understand why this is coming up now."

"Because she's living in our house, caring for our son. I think I have the right to know her background."

"Her background is excellent. Very experienced with children, particularly boys Josh's age."

"Yeah. You said that."

"I thought she'd be perfect for your...situation."

"My situation?" Heat rises in my cheeks at the careful phrasing. "What exactly is my situation, Sarah?"

Sarah shifts uncomfortably, avoiding my gaze. "Well, you've been under enormous pressure, haven't you? Work stress, Josh's needs, managing everything while Daniel's so busy. The burnout. Anyone would struggle."

"Who recommended her to you? It's a simple question, Sarah."

"I don't remember exactly. Word of mouth, you know how these things work."

"No, I don't know. Tell me."

Sarah sets down her mug with enough force to make the coffee table rattle. "Emma, what's this really about? You're making me uncomfortable with all these questions."

"Because you won't answer them. Because every time I ask about Sophie's background, you deflect or change the subject or tell me I should just be grateful."

"Maybe because you should be grateful," Sarah snaps, her carefully maintained composure finally cracking. "Your house is clean, Josh is thriving, Daniel seems happier than I've seen him in months. What exactly are you complaining about?"

"How would you know how Daniel seems?" I ask, leaning forward. "When have you seen enough of him to judge his happiness levels?"

Sarah's face flushes, caught in revealing more than she'd intended. "I just mean—from what I've heard—"

"From who? From Sophie?"

The name hangs between us like an accusation. Sarah's expression shifts, becoming guarded in a way that confirms my suspicions.

"We're friends. Good friends."

"For how long?"

"A few years. Sophie's fond of you all."

"She talks to you about us? About our private family life?"

"Not in detail. Just...she cares about Josh, wants to make sure he's happy."

"And you discuss this with her regularly?"

"Emma, you're being ridiculous. You're making something sinister out of perfectly normal—"

"Then why won't you tell me where she came from? Why won't you explain how you knew her qualifications, her experience, her references?"

"Because it doesn't matter!"

"It matters to me!"

"Well maybe that's the problem!" Sarah stands abruptly, pacing to the window. "Maybe that's what's destroying your family, not Sophie."

"She told you not to get involved, didn't she?" I say, the words emerging from instinct rather than conscious deduction.

Sarah freezes by the window, her reflection caught in the glass. "What?"

"Sophie. She warned you not to talk to me about her background. That's why you're so evasive."

"That's not— I never—"

"She told you not to get involved, and you agreed. You know something about Sophie that you're actively choosing not to share."

Sarah turns from the window, her face pale in the lamplight. "Emma, you need to stop this. You need help."

"What kind of help, Sarah? The same kind Sophie's been providing? The kind that makes everyone think I'm losing my mind while she takes over my life piece by piece?"

"Enough!" Sarah moves towards her phone. "You come barging into my house, making wild accusations, interrogating me like some kind of criminal. If you don't leave right now, I'm calling the police."

"You do know something," I say, backing towards the hallway. "And she's made sure you won't tell me. What's she got on you? Blackmail?"

"Get out, Emma. Before I make that call."

I fumble for the front door.

Sarah follows, her proximity feeling threatening rather than concerned.

"This isn't over," I say, stepping back outside.

"Yes, it is," Sarah says, already closing the door. "It's over because you're going to get the help you need and stop harassing people who've done nothing but try to support you."

The door slams with finality that echoes down the empty street.

I stand on her doorstep, rain soaking through my coat while my pulse hammers against my ribs. The confrontation had confirmed what I'd suspected—Sarah knows more than she's willing to share, and Sophie has made sure that information stays buried.

But it had also revealed something more disturbing. The careful way Sarah had avoided my eyes, her intimate knowledge of Daniel's happiness levels, her defensive protection of Sophie's reputation—it all suggested collaboration rather than simple complicity.

47.

My feet carry me without conscious direction, following familiar pathways that bypass the city centre's Christmas cheer. Past the cathedral's floodlit stones, over the Millennium Bridge where the Lune runs black beneath the streetlights, into the maze of terraced streets that climb Skerton's hill.

These pavements know my footsteps from childhood. The same uneven stones I'd navigated on my way to school, the corner shops where Mum sent me for emergency milk, the bus stops where I'd waited each morning with my grammar school blazer pristine and my stomach churning with teenage anxiety.

Everything looks smaller than memory suggests, shrunken by the particular alchemy that turns childhood landscapes into miniature versions of themselves. But the streets pulse with recognition despite their diminished scale, every junction triggering fragments of the girl I used to be.

I turn the corner onto Chatsworth Road without meaning to, my legs carrying me towards the house that shaped my understanding of family, love, disappointment. The house that contained my first sixteen years sits halfway down the terrace.

I freeze on the pavement opposite.

The house looks exactly as it should—cream render, brown window frames, the small front garden. But the windows stare back like dead eyes, no warm glow spilling through curtains, no movement behind glass that once framed my childhood world.

It sits empty. Dark. Waiting.

Through the dark windows, I can see nothing—just the faint outline of furniture. The front room where I'd opened Christmas presents, the kitchen where Mum taught me to make pastry, the hallway where Dad's coats used to hang before work became an excuse for absence.

All of it claimed by someone whose presence contaminates every memory I've stored in those walls, even when she's not physically there to defend her territory.

The house that witnessed my mother's lullabies now echoes with Sophie's version of the same melody, as if she's rewriting history from the inside out.

Memory floods through me with brutal clarity. Christmas mornings in that front room, fairy lights reflecting off the bay window while Mum supervised present-opening with the particular mixture of joy and exhaustion that marks parental love. Dad's laughter echoing from the kitchen before disappointment taught him to withdraw behind newspapers and silence.

The tree that used to stand in the corner where Sophie's probably placed her own, decorations accumulated over years of family tradition rather than purchased in a single shopping expedition. The armchair by the fireplace where Mum used to sit with her endless cups of tea, watching me colour in books spread across the carpet.

Now those spaces sit empty but somehow occupied, breathed in by someone who sleeps in bedrooms where my dreams took shape.

The dark windows reflect nothing back but my own pale face, ghostly against the December night. But I can imagine Sophie's possessions arranged inside—ornaments chosen to replicate the domestic atmosphere that made this house a home rather than just accommodation.

Sophie will return from the Lake District with stories about my family, my son, the memories she's building in my absence. She'll settle back into my childhood bedroom, claiming dreams that should have remained mine, living a life that spans both past and present while I'm locked out of both.

Worse—she probably knows things about those final years that I never discovered. Secrets Dad kept, truths Mum buried, the full extent of the family dysfunction I'd escaped to university without understanding. Sophie has access to evidence I've never seen, documents I never knew existed, the complete picture of why our family fractured along lines I could never quite map.

The house keeper of my childhood secrets, currently occupied by the woman who's systematically dismantling my adult life.

But houses left empty become vulnerable. Security systems can be bypassed, locks can be picked, windows can be opened by people who know their weaknesses from childhood exploration.

If Sophie has secrets—and she must have secrets—then she's probably keeping them here.

In my house. My childhood bedroom, my father's study, my mother's kitchen where family truths used to surface during late-night conversations I was too young to understand.

I pull my hood up against the drizzle, stepping back into shadows. My pulse hammers with something that might be terror or excitement—the particular cocktail that comes with decisions that can't be undone.

For the first time since Sophie arrived, I'm not running from her presence or reacting to her manipulation. I'm preparing to go on the offensive.

48.

Midnight settles over Lancaster. Frost glints on car windscreens while streetlamps cast everything in amber pools separated by darkness. The city sleeps around me.

My hands shake as I pull on gloves, the fabric catching on fingernails I've bitten to the quick. The screwdriver weighs heavy in my coat pocket—borrowed from Daniel's toolbox.

Chatsworth Road lies quiet, terraced houses dark except for the occasional porch light or Christmas decoration blinking on timer switches. My childhood home sits halfway down the row, windows black.

The side gate still sticks where it always did, the metal latch corroded by decades of rain. I slip into the back garden, my feet finding familiar pathways between flower beds Mum planted before disappointment made her stop caring about beauty.

The apple tree I used to climb stretches skeletal branches against the December sky. The cracked paving stones where I'd chalked hopscotch squares still show the same uneven gaps. Everything smaller than memory suggests but achingly recognisable, like photographs that capture truth without context.

The kitchen window latch gives after tense minutes of pressure that makes my gloves slip against the metal.

I push the sash open, the familiar groan of wood against wood that used to signal my teenage adventures in sneaking out after curfew.

I climb through, my legs remembering the precise distance from sill to floor.

A line has been crossed. I'm no better than a common burglar. I just hope I haven't been spotted.

The house breathes around me. Sophie's absence fills every room like a presence waiting to return.

The kitchen smells wrong. Furniture polish and bleach.

I stand in the kitchen where Mum used to make endless cups of tea while waiting for Dad to come home with increasingly elaborate excuses for his absence. The layout remains identical—sink beneath the window, cooker against the far wall, the table where I'd done homework while family tensions simmered around me.

But Sophie's possessions contaminate every surface even in her absence. Her mug sits clean in the dish rack, her tea towels hang folded above the radiator, her presence transforming my childhood geography into something alien.

I creep through the hallway, each floorboard creak amplified by the house's emptiness until every footstep sounds like gunfire. The stairs rise ahead, the same seventeen steps I'd counted during sleepless nights when parental arguments leaked through thin walls.

Upstairs, the landing feels narrower than memory allows. My old bedroom door stands ajar, darkness beyond suggesting Sophie has claimed it as her own. The thought makes my stomach clench with violation—her sleeping in my childhood bed when she returns, dreaming in the room where I'd first understood that families could fracture along fault lines too deep to repair.

But it's the back bedroom that draws me, the room that used to be Dad's study where he'd disappear with whisky and paperwork when family life became too much to endure.

The door opens to reveal a space transformed into something resembling a showroom. Bed made with hospital corners despite no one sleeping in it tonight, surfaces polished to reflection, every object positioned with the precision of someone who allows no chaos to contaminate their environment.

Too perfect. Too sterile. Like a stage set awaiting actors rather than a room where actual life gets lived.

My hands move through drawers filled with clothes folded into perfect squares, wardrobe hangers spaced evenly. Nothing personal, nothing that suggests the accumulated debris of ordinary existence.

Then my fingers find something in the back of the wardrobe. A shoebox wrapped in brown tape.

I pull it free, setting it on the bed. The tape peels away reluctantly, as if whatever's inside has been sealed against discovery for years rather than months.

The box opens to reveal my life laid out like evidence at a crime scene.

Notebooks with my name written inside the covers. Newspaper clippings—Dad's obituary, Mum's funeral notice, even my university graduation announcement from *The Lancaster Guardian*.

I find notes on my family tree, names and dates connected by red lines that map relationships with obsessive detail. My father's name appears repeatedly, underlined and annotated with question marks that suggest gaps in her knowledge. My mother's maiden name, our old addresses, even details about relatives I'd forgotten existed.

Photographs lie beneath the papers. Me as a teenager outside Boots. Me in my wedding dress.

Dozens of images spanning decades, taken from distances that suggest telephoto lenses and careful stalking.

Sophie hadn't just recently developed an interest in my family—she'd been watching me for most of my adult life.

But it's the photographs at the bottom that make my knees buckle.

Josh. At nursery, his face bright. On the swings at Williamson Park. Walking home with me from school.

Evidence that Sophie's obsession extends to my son, that she's been cataloguing his existence with the same methodical attention she'd devoted to mapping mine.

Then I find a manila envelope tucked beneath everything else, my name written across it in Sophie's careful script. My hands shake as I lift the flap.

The photographs spill across the bedspread in accusation and proof. The River Lune on that terrible afternoon when Josh slipped from the towpath while I stood frozen by indecision. Image after image showing his small body struggling in water too deep, too fast, too indifferent to his need for rescue.

But it's the final photograph that makes the room tilt around me.

Josh in the water, arms reaching desperately for help that seems impossibly distant. The stranger who'd appeared like divine intervention, hauling him back to safety while I failed to act. And there, in the background, blurred but unmistakable—my own figure rooted to the bank, paralysed by terror that turned maternal instinct into useless observation.

The moment I've hidden from Daniel, from Josh, from everyone who matters in my life. The failure that defines me as a mother, captured in digital permanence by someone who's been using it as leverage.

Sophie has the evidence that could destroy my marriage, my relationship with Josh, my right to be trusted with the safety of the person I love most in the world.

My legs give out completely. I sink onto the bed, clutching the photograph while my vision blurs with tears. This isn't paranoia or mental breakdown or the stress-induced fantasies everyone's been suggesting. This is calculated psychological warfare waged by someone who's devoted years to collecting ammunition.

The house remains silent around me, holding its secrets while I shove everything back into the box with hands that shake so violently I nearly drop the photographs. The evidence needs to be preserved, documented, shown to Daniel as proof that I'm not delusional but the victim of systematic stalking.

Standing to leave with the envelope clutched against my chest, I pause at the bedroom door and listen to the empty house breathing around me.

I glance towards the stairs, half-ready to flee, but something draws my eyes upward to the top of the wardrobe.

The corner of a card folder.

For a moment I freeze, my throat dry, pulse hammering.

I take it down and stare at the label: *Josh - Custody Plan*.

Inside, typed notes outline strategies for positioning Sophie as Josh's primary carer. Arguments about my mental instability, evidence of my inadequate parenting, documentation of every moment when I've failed to meet the standards of competent motherhood.

A legal blueprint for removing Josh from my care, complete with character references from neighbours who've been charmed into seeing Sophie as the solution to problems they didn't know existed.

Daniel's likely support is noted. His frustration with my behaviour, his gratitude for Sophie's intervention, his growing belief that professional help might be necessary. All of it positioned to support a custody claim that would leave me with supervised visits rather than shared parenting.

My phone buzzes against my leg, the vibration startling in the quiet.

A text from Daniel, sent from whatever Lake District hotel they've chosen for their family weekend.

Josh is fine. Sophie's a star.

49.

I stand at our bay window watching for headlights. My home feels hollow around me, three days of solitude having amplified every creak and whisper until I've memorised the house's repertoire of settling sounds.

My hands shake as I grip the folder of evidence I've assembled—photographs, documents, proof of Sophie's systematic infiltration of our lives. Everything I need to expose her manipulation, to show Daniel what she really is, to reclaim my place in my own family.

If he'll listen. If he'll look at what I've found instead of dismissing it as more evidence of my deteriorating mental state.

Headlights sweep across the street, illuminating raindrops that cling to glass like suspended tears. Daniel's Mondeo pulls up outside our gate, the engine's familiar rumble cutting through the evening quiet.

The passenger door opens first. Sophie emerges with fluid grace, immediately opening an umbrella to shield herself and Josh from Lancaster's persistent drizzle. She moves with the kind of thoughtful efficiency that marks competent people—umbrella positioned perfectly, Josh's hood adjusted.

They look like a unit. Mother and child navigating the world together while Daniel unloads bags from the boot, his movements suggesting the satisfied tiredness of someone who's had a successful weekend away.

I'm already excluded from their tableau, watching through glass like an audience member observing a play about family happiness she'll never be invited to join.

Josh clutches what appears to be a stuffed sheep—Lake District souvenir, probably bought during one of those spontaneous moments that make childhood magical. His face glows with the particular contentment of someone who's been thoroughly entertained, properly looked after, made to feel special without effort.

Sophie's hand rests lightly on his shoulder as they approach the front door, the gesture so natural it looks rehearsed. Daniel follows with their weekend bags, his expression carrying none of the tension that usually marks his homecomings. The successful family man returning from successful family time, problems temporarily solved by competent delegation.

I step back from the window before they can see me watching, my pulse hammering with something that might be panic or fury. This is my chance—perhaps my last chance—to show Daniel what Sophie really is. To prove that my accusations aren't paranoid fantasies but documented truth.

The front door opens with its familiar scrape, followed by Josh's excited chatter about sheep and mountains and something involving a boat that made Sophie laugh. Their voices fill the hallway with the comfortable chaos of people who've shared adventures, created memories, bonded over experiences I wasn't part of.

"Mummy!" Josh barrels into the hallway, his wellies still damp from Lake District puddles. "Look what Sophie bought me!"

He brandishes the stuffed sheep with the pride of someone displaying treasure. The toy looks expensive—proper wool rather than synthetic stuffing, the kind of thoughtful gift that demonstrates someone paying attention to a child's interests. "It's a Herdwick!"

"It's lovely, sweetheart," I manage, crouching to his level while my chest aches. "Did you have a wonderful time?"

"The best time ever! Sophie knows all about sheep, and she let me help feed them proper grass, and we saw a real waterfall that made rainbows!"

Each detail cuts deeper than the last. Sophie sharing knowledge I don't possess, creating magical moments I couldn't have provided, building memories that will outlast whatever pathetic attempts I make to reclaim my maternal role.

Daniel appears behind Josh. He looks older than when he left, lines around his eyes suggesting the weekend wasn't entirely restful despite Josh's obvious happiness.

"Hello, Em," he says, his tone carefully neutral. "Good weekend?"

"Fine, thanks." The lie tastes like dust. "Daniel, I need to speak with you. Alone."

His expression shifts, wariness replacing the tentative warmth he'd carried from the car. "If it's about Sophie, you should say it in front of her. She's part of this family now."

Part of this family. The words hit like physical blows, confirming what I'd feared—that in three days, Sophie has consolidated her position while I've been relegated to outsider status in my own home.

Sophie appears in the doorway behind Daniel, her travel coat still damp from the drizzle, her expression carrying the particular serenity of someone whose conscience is clear. She doesn't speak, doesn't insert herself into our conversation, but her presence fills the hallway.

"This is important," I say, my voice higher than intended. "Private. Between husband and wife."

"There's nothing you can't say in front of Sophie," Daniel says, his tone hardening. "She's been nothing but helpful, Em. If you've got issues with her, address them directly."

Heat rises in my cheeks as Sophie's gaze settles on me with something that might be pity or satisfaction. She's positioned herself perfectly—the reasonable party while I'm cast as the one making unreasonable demands for privacy in my own home.

"She's replacing me," I blurt, the words escaping before I can package them in rational argument. "Can't you see what she's doing? Taking over my role piece by piece while you stand there thanking her for it?"

Daniel's jaw tightens, his patience visibly fraying. "She's helping us, Emma. Helping you. Because you haven't been coping."

"I've been coping fine."

"Have you? Because from where I'm standing, it looks like you've spent the weekend spiralling into whatever paranoid fantasy you've constructed."

The accusation stings because it carries enough truth to wound. I have been alone, have been spiralling, have been constructing narratives that sound increasingly desperate even to my own ears.

But I have evidence now. Proof.

My hands shake as I retrieve the folder from where I'd left it on the hall table, pages of evidence that will vindicate every suspicion, every moment of unease I've felt since Sophie arrived. Daniel will have to believe me when he sees what she's really been doing.

"Did you sleep with her?" The question escapes before I can stop it, raw jealousy making me reckless. "At the hotel? Is that what this is about?"

Daniel's face flushes with something that might be guilt or outrage. "Jesus Christ, Emma. How can you even—"

He pulls his wallet from his jacket pocket with sharp movements, extracting a folded piece of paper. The hotel receipt unfolds to show two separate room charges, proof of the propriety he wants to establish.

"Two rooms," he says, his voice shaking with fury. "Separate beds, separate bathrooms, separate everything. I thought this weekend might help you get some perspective, but instead you've made yourself worse."

The receipt should reassure me, but instead it highlights how far my marriage has deteriorated—that Daniel feels the need to provide documentary evidence of his fidelity, that I've become the kind of wife who makes such accusations necessary.

"I found something," I say, opening the folder with hands that won't stay steady. "Evidence of what she's really been doing."

The photographs spill across our dining table. Sophie's fake references, printed on letterhead designed to fool rather than inform. Surveillance photographs spanning decades—my childhood, my wedding, Josh's early years—all captured by someone who'd been watching from shadows I never suspected.

The photograph of my greatest failure, captured with digital clarity by someone who understood exactly how to use shame as a weapon.

"Look at this," I say, my voice cracking with desperation. "Look at what she's been doing. The surveillance, the fake documents, the—"

Daniel recoils, but not at the evidence. His horror focuses on me, on what I've become in his eyes—the wife who creates elaborate conspiracy theories from innocent help, who plants evidence to support her delusions.

"This is insane, Emma," he says, stepping back from the table as if the documents might contaminate him. "You've made this up. Planted these photos, forged these papers. This is exactly the kind of behaviour that proves you need professional help."

"I didn't make anything up!" The protest comes out as a shriek, my composure finally shattering under the weight of being disbelieved. "She's been stalking us for years, Daniel. Building a case, collecting evidence, positioning herself to take my place!"

"Listen to yourself. You're talking about elaborate conspiracies, long-term surveillance, professional-level document forgery. Does any of that sound remotely plausible?"

It doesn't, when he phrases it like that. The evidence that felt so compelling in isolation sounds absurd when subjected to rational analysis. What are the chances that our helpful nanny is actually a master manipulator with decades-long obsession and unlimited resources for surveillance equipment?

But the photographs don't lie. The documents exist. The violation is real, even if I can't make Daniel see it.

"She's dangerous," I whisper, hating how desperate I sound. "She's got plans, Daniel. Legal documents about taking Josh away from me. A custody strategy that—"

"Enough!" Sophie's voice cuts through my rambling with quiet authority. She stands in the doorway, having shed her damp coat, looking every inch the competent woman who steps in when others fall apart.

"Josh, sweetheart," she says, her tone gentle but firm. "Why don't you run upstairs and have a wash before bed? Your daddy and I need to help Mummy with something grown-up."

Josh obeys without question, clutching his stuffed sheep while casting worried glances at the scattered papers that have turned our dining room into a crime scene. His footsteps fade up the stairs, leaving the three of us in silence that feels charged with possibility and threat.

Sophie moves into the room with careful steps, surveying the evidence I've spread across our table. Her expression shows none of the shock or guilt I'd expected—just the mild concern of someone observing a friend's mental breakdown.

"She's been under such enormous strain," Sophie says softly, her voice carrying to Daniel rather than addressing me directly. "I hate seeing her like this, but I suppose it was inevitable. The pressure, the isolation, the guilt about not coping—it has to surface somehow."

Her words reframe everything. Not evidence of her manipulation but symptoms of my instability. Not proof of conspiracy but manifestation of breakdown. She doesn't deny the documents or dismiss the photographs—she simply repositions them as products of my deteriorating mental state rather than discoveries of her criminal behaviour.

"I know you're trying to help," she says, settling her gaze on me with something that looks like compassion. "But fabricating evidence, creating elaborate scenarios to explain away your struggles—that's not helping anyone, especially Josh."

Daniel's expression hardens as Sophie's interpretation takes hold. I can see him processing her words, applying her framework to everything he's witnessed over recent months. My accusations, my paranoia, my increasing isolation—all of it recontextualised as symptoms rather than responses to legitimate threats.

"I can't do this anymore, Em," he says, his voice shaking. "Either you get help—real help, professional intervention—or I take Josh somewhere safe while you sort yourself out."

The ultimatum hangs between us. Not a negotiation but a final warning, delivered by someone who's reached the end of his capacity for managing a wife whose grip on reality has become unreliable.

Sophie doesn't speak, doesn't need to. Her presence behind Daniel provides silent validation for his assessment, wordless agreement that drastic measures might be necessary to protect Josh from whatever I've become.

"You can't take him away from me," I whisper, but the protest sounds hollow. "He's my son."

"He's our son," Daniel corrects. "And right now, you're scaring him. These accusations, this obsession with Sophie, the way you look at us like we're enemies in our own home—that's not the mother he needs."

Josh's footsteps echo from upstairs, his small voice calling down to ask if everything's alright.

Sophie immediately moves towards the stairs. "Everything's fine, darling," she says. "Mummy and Daddy are just talking about boring grown-up things. You get ready for bed, and I'll be up in a minute to read your story."

She returns to our standoff with the quiet satisfaction of someone who's just demonstrated superior parenting while the actual mother remains frozen in crisis. Daniel's expression softens as he watches her handle Josh's concerns with competence I should have shown but didn't.

"I'll take him to my sister's tomorrow," Daniel says, his decision apparently made. "Give you space to think about whether you're ready to accept help or whether this situation needs to become more permanent."

The threat crystallises everything I've been fighting against. Not just losing Josh's daily affections but losing him completely, relegated to supervised visits while Sophie claims the maternal role I've been failing to fill adequately.

I gather the scattered evidence with shaking hands, photographs and documents that were supposed to prove my sanity but have instead confirmed my husband's belief that I need professional intervention. The folder closes on everything I'd hoped would save me.

Sophie watches my retreat with an expression that never shifts from gentle concern. She's won without saying a word, without making a single accusation, simply by embodying stability while I perform instability in front of the person whose opinion matters most.

50.

Christmas lights blink weakly on our tree, casting fractured patterns across the living room walls. Each flash illuminates surfaces that should feel familiar but somehow don't—as if Sophie's presence has altered the very light in our home.

We've just returned from dinner at the Wagon and Horses, an awkward family meal where Josh chattered happily about his Lake District adventure while Daniel and I maintained careful politeness across the table. Sophie played the perfect intermediary, smoothing conversational gaps and ensuring Josh felt included while his parents struggled to find common ground.

The evening hangs heavy with unspoken tensions that even Josh seems to sense.

Daniel busies himself in the kitchen, stacking plates while the dishwasher hums its familiar cycle. His movements carry the controlled energy of someone using mundane tasks to avoid difficult conversations, each gesture a small act of domestic procrastination.

Sophie shepherds Josh upstairs, her voice carrying from the landing as she negotiates bedtime routines with the kind of patience I wish I could summon more consistently. The sound of running water, Josh's delighted squeal as she makes bathtime entertaining, the comfortable murmur of someone who knows exactly how to make a four-year-old feel safe and cherished.

I linger in the living room, unable to settle into any chair that feels properly mine anymore. The fairy lights pulse with their programmed rhythm.

Everything looks like someone else's home now. Not unfamiliar exactly, but performed rather than natural. As if Sophie's influence has transformed our domestic space into a showroom displaying the kind of family life we used to have rather than the one we're actually living.

The silence stretches until I can't bear it anymore. Daniel emerges from the kitchen, tea towel in hand.

"Daniel." I take a deep breath. "We need to talk."

He sighs, draping the towel over the back of a chair. "If this is about Sophie again—"

"She isn't who she says she is." The words tumble out before I can package them in rational argument. "She's my half-sister. She's been stalking me for years, building up to this moment when she could take everything I have."

Daniel freezes, his hand still resting on the chair back. The Christmas lights continue their relentless blinking while my accusation hangs between us.

"Emma. Not this again."

"Listen to me," I say, desperation making my voice higher than intended. "She's been watching me since childhood, collecting information, preparing for this invasion."

Daniel rubs his forehead with both hands. "Do you hear yourself?"

"I have the evidence—"

Sophie appears in the doorway. "Josh is all settled. He wanted to show you his drawings from the trip tomorrow, Daniel. He's very proud of his sheep pictures."

"Thank you," Daniel says. "You're brilliant with him."

Her gaze settles on me. "Does Daniel know about Josh?" Sophie asks, her voice soft with apparent concern. "About the river?"

"What about the river?" he asks.

"Sophie, don't—" I begin, but she's already speaking.

"The day Josh nearly drowned...and you just stood there."

Daniel's face goes completely still, his expression cycling through confusion, recognition, and something that might be dawning horror. "Emma?"

The room tilts around me as the secret I've been guarding crashes into the open air.

"I can explain," I whisper, though no explanation could possibly be adequate.

"Explain what?" Daniel's voice rises. "Emma, what is she talking about?"

Through tears that blur the fairy lights, I stammer out the truth I've been hiding since Josh was barely walking.

"He slipped from the towpath," I say, my voice barely audible above the blood pounding in my ears. "One second he was beside me feeding ducks, the next he was in the water, and it was moving so fast—"

"And you pulled him out."

"I froze." The confession escapes like something expelled from diseased tissue. "I stood there on the bank watching him struggle, and I couldn't move. Couldn't think. Couldn't do anything except watch the current carry him downstream while I remained rooted like some useless statue."

Daniel's face cycles through expressions I can't read—shock, disappointment, something that might be disgust. "Someone else pulled him out?"

"A jogger. Some stranger who acted while I stood there." My voice cracks completely. "Josh was drowning, and I failed him. Failed in the most basic way possible. I let someone else save my own child while I did nothing."

"But he was fine," Daniel says, though his tone suggests he's trying to convince himself rather than me. "He's fine—"

"He was fine because someone else made him fine. Because a stranger proved to be a better parent in thirty seconds than I managed to be in three years." The admission tastes like poison, but also like relief. "I broke down afterwards, Daniel. Completely. That's why I couldn't work for months, why I kept crying, why everything felt impossible. Not because I was overworked or stressed, but because I'd discovered what kind of mother I really am when it matters."

Daniel stares at me with an expression I've never seen before—not anger exactly, but something colder. More final. "You never told me."

"I was ashamed. I didn't know how to explain that your wife, the mother of your child, could watch that child drown while self-preservation kept her safely on dry land." I wipe my eyes with the back of my hand. "I told you it was burnout, work stress, normal parental anxiety. Everything except the truth."

"The truth," Daniel repeats, his voice flat. "That you lied to me about the most important thing that's ever happened to our son."

Sophie stands silently throughout this exchange, her presence somehow both invisible and overwhelming. She doesn't speak, doesn't offer commentary or judgement, doesn't need to. My confession damns me more thoroughly than any accusation she could make.

Daniel begins pacing, his movements sharp with contained energy. "Jesus Christ, Emma. You let me think you were struggling with ordinary parenting stress while you were actually covering up—what? Criminal negligence? Child endangerment?"

"It wasn't criminal."

"Wasn't it? You were responsible for keeping him safe, and you failed so completely that a stranger had to save him while you stood there doing nothing. And then you lied about it. Let me blame myself for not supporting you properly when the real problem was that you're fundamentally unfit to be trusted with our son's safety."

I was responsible. I did fail. I have been lying by omission, allowing Daniel to believe my breakdown stemmed from ordinary pressures rather than extraordinary failure of character.

"I've been a good mother since then. I learned from it, became more careful, more protective—"

"More paranoid," Daniel corrects. "More convinced that everyone else is a threat when the real danger was you all along."

The Christmas lights continue their programmed sequence, oblivious to the family disintegrating beneath their cheerful glow. Gold, green, red, white—colours that should represent joy and celebration but now feel like evidence lighting up everything I've tried to keep hidden.

"I should have told you," I whisper. "I know I should have. But I was terrified you'd leave, that you'd take Josh somewhere safe and I'd never see him again."

"Maybe I should have," Daniel says, his voice carrying conviction that makes my stomach drop into free fall. "Maybe that would have been the responsible thing to do instead of trusting someone whose judgement clearly can't be relied on."

"I'm so sorry you've been carrying this alone," Sophie says. "The guilt must have been unbearable."

Her sympathy feels more devastating than Daniel's anger. She understands the burden I've been carrying while positioning herself as the competent alternative, the person who would never hesitate when action is required.

From the doorway comes a small sound—footsteps padding down the stairs. Josh appears in his dinosaur pyjamas, clutching his stuffed sheep against his chest, his face crumpled with the particular confusion that comes from being woken by raised voices.

"Mummy?" His voice wavers, uncertain. "Daddy? Are you fighting about something?"

The sight of him—small, vulnerable, trusting—makes my chest clench with love and shame in equal measure. This is what's at stake: not just my marriage or my pride, but his security, his understanding of himself as someone worthy of protection.

"We're just talking, sweetheart," I manage, though my voice cracks.

Josh pads closer, his bare feet silent on our wooden floors. "Are you talking about when the man pulled me from the river? When I fell in and got all wet?"

51.

I remain hunched on the sofa, drained by confession but oddly relieved to have the truth finally exposed. The weight I've been carrying for more than a year feels lighter now that it's shared, even if sharing it has destroyed whatever remained of Daniel's trust in my competence as a mother.

Josh hovers near the doorway, clutching his stuffed sheep. His dark eyes move between his parents with the instinctive wariness that comes from sensing adult emotions too large for his understanding.

Sophie stands perfectly still beside the Christmas tree, her expression unreadable in the fairy lights' shifting glow. She doesn't speak, doesn't offer comfort or judgement, doesn't need to. My confession has done her work more effectively than any accusation she could have made.

"The photo," I whisper, scrambling for the folder. "Daniel, there's something you need to see."

The photograph hits our dining table with the soft sound of paper against wood, but its impact feels seismic. Josh flailing in water too deep, the stranger reaching towards him, and there on the bank—my own figure rooted in paralysis while crisis unfolded around me.

"This is real," I say, my voice cracking with desperation. "She took this photo, Daniel. She was there, watching, documenting my failure while I stood frozen. She knew about the river because she's been stalking us for years."

Daniel stops pacing. His eyes find the photograph, and something in his expression shifts. The colour drains from his face. "Where did this come from?"

"Sophie's collection. Hidden boxes full of surveillance photos, fake references, custody plans." The words tumble out in a desperate rush. "She's been building a case against me, documenting every failure, every moment of weakness. This photograph is proof that her interest in our family predates her employment."

Daniel picks up the image with trembling fingers, studying it with the focused attention he'd refused to give before.

"This shouldn't exist," he says slowly, his voice carrying the bewildered tone of someone whose worldview is reshaping itself around new information. "How?"

"She's been watching us, Daniel. Collecting evidence, building profiles, preparing for the moment when she could step in and claim what she thinks should have been hers all along."

Sophie steps forward, and something in her posture has changed—the careful composure she's maintained for months cracking like ice under pressure. "You ruined everything!"

"Sophie—" Daniel begins, but she cuts him off.

"You stole him from me. Just like you stole our father. Just like you stole everything that should have been mine." Her voice rises to a scream that makes Josh whimper and press himself against the doorframe. "You had the house, the family, the Christmas mornings, the bedtime stories—everything I watched from across the street while I grew up in care homes and foster families that never wanted me."

The mask has finally slipped.

"I spent years planning this! Years watching, learning, preparing to take back what you stole from me. And you're going to ruin it with your pathetic confession about being too cowardly to save your own child?"

Daniel stares at her, his mouth gaping. The woman he's been defending, the solution he thought would save our family, stands revealed as something else entirely—obsessed, unhinged, dangerous.

Sophie lunges towards the kitchen counter where our knife block sits beside the microwave. Her hand closes around the largest handle, the chef's knife we use for Sunday roasts and Christmas dinners, its blade catching the fairy lights' glow.

"Sophie, don't—" Daniel starts, but she's already turning back towards us, the weapon raised.

Instinct kicks in before conscious thought can interfere. I move between Sophie and Josh, my body forming a barrier while my son presses against my back with trembling hands. The paralysis that kept me frozen on the riverbank evaporates, replaced by something fierce and protective that makes my muscles coil with readiness.

"Stay behind me," I whisper to Josh, my voice steady despite the terror flooding my veins. "Whatever happens, stay behind Mummy."

Sophie steps closer, the knife trembling in her grip.

"You don't deserve him," she whispers, taking another step forward while Daniel remains frozen in place. "You couldn't even save him when he was drowning. What kind of mother are you?"

"The kind who won't let you hurt him," I say, surprised by the steadiness in my own voice. My hands find Josh's shoulders, keeping him safely positioned behind me while I face down the woman who's been systematically dismantling our lives.

Daniel finally breaks from his paralysis. "Sophie, stop! Put the knife down!"

But she doesn't stop.

52.

Sophie lunges forward, teeth bared, eyes wild with something that's moved far beyond rational anger.

The knife arcs through the air towards my chest, close enough that I can see my reflection distorted in the blade's surface.

I jerk sideways, dragging Josh with me, his small body colliding with mine as we stumble against the dining table.

The knife misses by inches, the displaced air brushing my cheek with the promise of what could have been.

"Take him!" I shout at Daniel, shoving Josh towards his father while Sophie recovers her balance for another strike.

Daniel scoops Josh up, but our son fights against his grip, small fists beating at his father's chest. "Mummy! Mummy!" His voice cracks with terror, reaching a pitch that makes my chest ache even as adrenaline floods my system.

Sophie swings again, her movements unpractised but desperate enough to be deadly.

The blade scrapes across our dining table's surface.

I grab the nearest chair, swinging it awkwardly between us like a shield.

The crash of wood against steel echoes through our kitchen while Christmas lights continue their relentless blinking.

"Sophie, stop this!" Daniel yells from the doorway.

Sophie doesn't even acknowledge him. Her attention stays locked on me with laser intensity, as if Daniel and Josh have ceased to exist and only we remain.

She lunges again, forcing me backwards until my spine hits the kitchen counter.

Plates crash to the floor as we collide, ceramic shattering across the floor.

"You stole everything," Sophie says, forcing me back against the cupboards while I struggle to keep the knife away from my throat. "Everything that should have been mine."

Her wrist twists in my grip, muscles corded with strength I hadn't expected.

The blade flashes close to my face, close enough that I can smell the metallic tang of sharpened steel.

"Mummy!" Josh's voice cuts through the struggle, high and thin above the sound of our breathing, our grunting, our feet scrabbling for purchase on the floor tiles.

The sound of my son's terror gives me strength I didn't know I possessed.

I twist Sophie's wrist harder, feeling something give under the pressure.

The knife wavers, nearly slips free, but she snatches it back with her other hand before it can fall.

We crash to the floor in a tangle of limbs, rolling across our kitchen while Daniel remains frozen in the doorway.

Sophie's hair tangles with mine, her knees finding my ribs while I try to keep the blade away from anything vital.

The knife tip scrapes against the tiles.

For a moment I feel Sophie's strength overpowering mine, her fury giving her advantages my exhaustion can't match.

She's been planning this for years while I've been struggling just to survive each day.

But desperation makes people capable of things they never imagined.

I rear back and drive my forehead into Sophie's nose with all the force I can muster, feeling cartilage give way beneath the impact.

Sophie's scream pierces the kitchen's chaos.

The knife clatters loose from her grip, spinning across the tiles.

We both scramble after it, knees scraping against the floor while our breath comes in ragged gasps.

My fingers brush the handle just as Sophie's hand tangles in my hair, yanking me backwards with enough force to make stars explode behind my eyes.

The knife skitters further across the kitchen, sliding beneath our Welsh dresser where it disappears into shadow.

Out of reach for both of us.

We freeze, staring at each other across the wreckage of my kitchen.

My cheek stings where her nails found purchase, warm blood trickling down my face.

Sophie's knuckles are scraped raw, her nose streaming crimson that spatters her cream jumper with evidence of what we've done to each other.

Between us, plates lie shattered in patterns that speak of violence.

Josh's sobs echo from the doorway where Daniel still holds him, both of them witnessing the complete breakdown of everything they thought they knew about the women in their lives.

53.

We circle each other in the wreckage of our domestic battlefield, both breathing hard, both waiting for the other to make the fatal mistake that will end this.

Josh's sobs echo from the doorway where Daniel holds him, my son's terror cutting through the adrenaline that's kept me fighting. His cries bounce off the walls and up the stairwell, filling our home with the sound of childhood trauma being carved into memory.

"It's over, Sophie," I gasp, though I'm not sure which of us I'm trying to convince. "Just stop. Please."

"I won't let you have him," she says, wiping blood from her nose with the back of her hand. "He should be mine. He was always meant to be mine."

She lunges again, not towards the knife but directly at me, her hands clawing at my face while incoherent sounds tear from her throat.

Pure fury rather than strategy.

I brace myself against the doorframe, feeling the old wood creak under the impact as Sophie's weight crashes into me.

Her fingernails rake my neck, seeking soft tissue while I try to protect my throat.

Panic floods my system—not the paralysis that kept me frozen on the riverbank, but something that galvanises every muscle.

I think of Josh watching this unfold, of Daniel's horrified face, of everything that will be destroyed if I don't end this now.

With a surge of strength I didn't know I possessed, I shove Sophie backwards with both hands against her chest.

Not calculated, not strategic—pure maternal instinct translated into physical force.

Sophie stumbles towards the cellar stairs.

I shove her again and her arms flail as she reaches desperately for the banister, her fingers grasping at carved wood.

Her body twists as gravity claims her, shoulder colliding with the wall hard enough to crack the plaster.

Then momentum carries her backwards, down the cellar steps. Her head strikes the wooden edge with a dull crack that makes my stomach lurch, the sound of bone meeting timber with force that suggests permanent damage.

The silence that follows feels enormous, pressing against my eardrums with the weight of what's just happened.

Sophie lies crumpled at the bottom of the cellar stairs, her body twisted in ways that speak of breakage, her cream jumper now stained with more than just blood from her nose.

Josh's screams pierce the silence, his voice rising to a pitch that makes the house's windows rattle in their frames. Daniel curses under his breath, his footsteps heavy on the floorboards as he rushes forward while still maintaining his protective grip on our son.

I grip the banister with hands that won't stop shaking, my knuckles showing white against skin that feels clammy.

Bile rises in my throat as I stare down at Sophie's motionless form. Her dark hair spreads across the cellar floor, one arm bent beneath her body at an angle that suggests her shoulder has separated from its socket.

The guilt hits with the force of revelation. Not self-defence but murder, delivered by someone whose maternal instincts had finally overwhelmed her paralysis. I've become capable of violence I never imagined, protecting my child with methods that will destroy us all.

Daniel reaches the bottom of the stairs, his face pale as he takes in the extent of Sophie's injuries. "Christ, Emma. What have you done?"

My ears ring with the aftermath of adrenaline, my own breathing loud in the hollow space that used to feel like home

At last, the faintest sound breaks through the terrible quiet.

A wet, rasping breath from Sophie's chest, barely audible but unmistakably present.

The sound of lungs that are damaged but still functioning, of someone hovering between life and death.

She wasn't dead. Not yet.

54.

Sophie stirs, her eyelids fluttering as consciousness returns to limbs that should probably stay still.

Relief and dread collide in my chest with equal force.

Alive means I haven't become a murderer, haven't crossed that final line that separates desperate mothers from actual killers.

But alive also means dangerous—means Sophie can still speak, still manipulate, still reshape whatever narrative emerges from tonight's violence.

Blood streaks her forehead from where her skull met our steps, but her eyes focus with disturbing clarity when they find mine. Even injured, even broken, she possesses the kind of alertness that suggests her mind remains perfectly functional despite her body's damage.

"Sophie?" Daniel's voice cracks as he kneels beside her, Josh still clutched in his arms while our son's sobs echo up the stairwell. "Can you hear me? Don't try to move."

She manages what might be a nod, though the movement makes her wince with pain that looks genuine rather than performed.

Whatever else Sophie might be—stalker, manipulator, threat to my family—she's undeniably hurt in ways that will require professional medical attention.

That's when the pounding starts.

Heavy fists against our front door, the kind of urgent knocking that means someone's heard things they shouldn't have heard.

"Are you alright in there?" Mrs Hopkins' voice cuts through the wood. "We heard banging, shouting—is everyone safe?"

More voices join hers—Mr Ellis from next door, the young couple from across the street, people whose names I barely know but whose judgement will matter more than I'd like.

The facade of domestic normality has cracked beyond repair, spilling our family crisis into the street where it becomes public property rather than private shame.

"Everything's fine," Daniel calls back, though his voice shakes. "Just a small accident. Nothing to worry about."

But the neighbours don't disperse. Their murmured conversations seep through our front door, and I catch fragments that make my chest tight with dread. Someone mentions calling for help, someone else suggests the police might be needed.

"Daniel," I whisper, my voice barely audible above Josh's continued crying. "We need to call an ambulance. She's badly hurt."

He nods, already reaching for his mobile while Sophie makes another attempt at speech.

"She tried to kill me."

Daniel freezes with his phone halfway to his ear, his face cycling through expressions I can't read.

"Sophie, that's not— you attacked me first, with the knife—" I begin, but she's not finished.

"She pushed me," Sophie whispers, her voice gaining strength as she finds her rhythm. "Down the stairs. Tried to murder me because I knew her secrets."

"That's not what happened!" The protest tears from my throat with desperate force. "Daniel, you saw the knife, you saw her attack me first!"

But Daniel's expression suggests he's no longer certain what he saw. The kitchen chaos, the struggle over the blade, my shove that sent Sophie tumbling—it could be interpreted multiple ways depending on who's telling the story.

Blue light suddenly spills through our stained glass panels.

Someone's already called the police, made the decision Daniel was still debating.

The front door bursts open without ceremony. Two uniformed officers step through. Radio chatter crackles from their belts while their eyes assess the scene.

"Everyone stay exactly where you are," the taller officer says.

Daniel doesn't move, shock apparently pinning him in place. Josh continues crying in his arms, clutching his stuffed sheep while chaos unfolds around him.

The officers move with practised efficiency—one approaching Sophie while the other positions himself where he can observe everyone present.

"Can you tell me your name, love?" the first officer asks Sophie, kneeling beside her with the kind of gentle professionalism reserved for obvious victims.

"Sophie," she manages, then adds with deliberate precision, "Sophie Hartwell. She's Emma Cartwright. She pushed me down the stairs."

The surname hits like a physical blow. Not the random identity she's been performing for months, but my maiden name—claiming kinship while simultaneously accusing me of attempted murder.

"Right, Sophie, we're going to get you sorted," the officer says, pressing gauze against her bleeding forehead. "Paramedics are on their way. Can you tell me what happened here tonight?"

Sophie's version emerges in carefully measured fragments. How she'd been trying to help with family problems, how I'd become increasingly unstable and violent, how tonight's confrontation had escalated when I'd accused her of impossible conspiracies.

"She said I was stalking her family," Sophie whispers, her voice carrying just the right note of bewildered hurt. "When I tried to calm her down, she attacked me. Pushed me backwards down the stairs."

"That's not true!" I step forward, desperation making my voice shrill. "She attacked me with a knife! There's evidence upstairs, photographs, documents that prove she's been—"

"Ma'am, step back please," the second officer says, his hand moving to his belt with casual readiness. "Let's all keep calm while we sort this out."

But I can't keep calm. Not when Sophie's rewriting history with every word, not when the officers' expressions suggest they're already forming opinions about who's credible and who's hysterical.

"She's been stalking me," I say, my words tumbling over each other in desperate haste. "Living in my childhood home, collecting photographs, planning to take my son away from me. The knife's still in the kitchen—you can see where she attacked me first!"

The officers exchange glances. To them, I probably sound exactly like someone whose grip on reality has become unreliable—making elaborate accusations while Sophie lies bleeding at the bottom of our stairs.

"Emma Cartwright?" the taller officer says, consulting his notebook. "I'm arresting you on suspicion of grievous bodily harm. You don't have to say anything, but it may harm your defence if you do not mention when questioned something which you later rely on in court."

Cold steel snaps around my wrist with a sound that seems to echo through the entire house, the handcuff's bite sharp against skin that's already scraped from our struggle.

"Mummy!" Josh's voice cuts through everything else, high and thin with terror that will probably require therapy to process. "Don't go! Don't leave me!"

His reaching arms break something fundamental in my chest.

I've fought to protect him, killed part of myself to keep him safe, and now I'm being taken away while he watches the last of his security crumble.

Daniel remains frozen by the stairs, his face ashen as he watches his wife being arrested. In his eyes I see something that might be doubt—not about Sophie's guilt, but about mine.

The woman he married, the mother of his child, being led away in handcuffs while her supposed victim bleeds on their cellar floor.

Paramedics arrive as the officers guide me towards the door, their equipment clattering against our narrow walls while they begin the process of stabilising Sophie for transport.

Professional voices discuss potential spinal injuries, the need for CT scans, the kind of serious medical intervention that transforms domestic disputes into criminal cases.

Sophie catches my eye as they lift her onto a stretcher, and despite her injuries, despite the blood and the obvious pain, her expression carries something that might be triumph.

Not the wild fury that drove her to attack with a knife, but the satisfied calculation of someone whose long-term planning has finally paid off.

55.

The police station entrance swallows me with the kind of institutional authority that makes even innocent people feel guilty. Christmas Eve drizzle clings to my coat while the officers march me through sliding doors that seal shut behind us.

Through the reception windows, Lancaster Castle looms against the grey sky.

The corridor stretches ahead in shades of beige and institutional green, past bustling desks where officers type reports and answer phones with the weary efficiency of people working through the holidays. The air smells of stale coffee and the particular desperation that accumulates wherever people's lives fall apart in public.

My handcuffs are removed at the custody desk, but the relief is temporary. Freedom to move my wrists doesn't extend to freedom to leave, to return home, to hold my son while he processes whatever trauma tonight has carved into his four-year-old understanding of family safety.

The interview room door closes behind me with a sound like a tomb sealing.

Harsh strip lights hum overhead while blank walls reflect nothing back.

I sit with my hands folded in my lap, trying to look calm despite the trembling that won't stop. My hair sticks to my face with dried sweat from our struggle, my cheek throbs where Sophie's nails found purchase, my throat feels raw from screaming explanations no one seemed to hear.

The door opens to admit a woman in her forties with the kind of steady competence that suggests she's heard every possible variation of domestic crisis. Her partner follows, younger and quieter, already reaching for the recording equipment that will turn my words into evidence.

"I'm Detective Inspector Hughes," the woman says. "And this is Constable Sharma."

I nod.

"Right then, Emma," Hughes says, settling into her chair with the easy authority of someone whose judgement matters. "You're here on suspicion of attempted murder. Tell us what happened tonight."

The formal accusation hits like ice water. Attempted murder. Not domestic dispute or assault, but the kind of charge that transforms confused wives into criminals whose children get taken into care while courts decide their fate.

"She attacked me first," I stammer, my voice cracking despite my efforts to sound rational. "With a knife from our kitchen. I was defending myself, defending my son."

"And this woman—Sophie Hartwell—she lives in your house? Works as your nanny?"

"She says she's my half-sister. She's been stalking my family for years, collecting photographs, forging documents, building some kind of case to take my son away from me."

Hughes makes notes. "That's quite an accusation. Any evidence to support these claims?"

"Surveillance photographs going back decades, fake references, custody plans—"

I stop mid-sentence as Hughes exchanges a glance with her colleague.

"And you believe these items prove she was stalking you?" Hughes asks.

"I know they do. She had custody plans, legal strategies for taking Josh away from me. Documents that show this has been orchestrated for years."

Constable Sharma looks up from his notepad. "How did you come to see these items?"

The question hangs in the air like a trap. Admitting to breaking into Sophie's house—even if it's my childhood home—adds another criminal charge to whatever they're already building against me.

"I...I went there. To understand what she was doing."

"And where would 'there' be?"

"Her house..."

"You entered her residence without permission?"

"It's my family's house. I grew up there." But the words sound pathetic even to me, the kind of justification that reveals guilt rather than innocence.

Hughes makes another note. "So you unlawfully entered her home, rifled through her possessions, and then returned to your house where you assaulted her and pushed her down a flight of stairs."

"She attacked me with a knife first! The knife should still be under our Welsh dresser where it fell during the struggle."

"We'll certainly examine the scene thoroughly," Hughes says, though her tone suggests she's already formed opinions about my credibility. "Is there anything else you'd like to tell us about tonight's events?"

My mind races through everything I need them to understand—Sophie's confession about being my half-sister, her years of surveillance, her systematic replacement of me in my own family. But the words feel inadequate, desperate, exactly like someone whose grip on reality has become unreliable.

"She told me she was my half-sister," I say, trying one more time. "My father apparently had an affair in the nineties. Sophie's been seeking revenge ever since."

Hughes closes her notepad with the soft sound of finality. "Right then. We'll need to verify these claims, examine the evidence you've mentioned, speak with the other parties involved." She stands. "Interview terminated at twenty forty-seven."

The recording equipment clicks off, sealing my words into digital storage where they'll be analysed, dissected, used to build whatever case the Crown Prosecution Service decides to pursue.

Constable Sharma escorts me back through corridors that feel longer now. Officers work at their desks, processing the debris of other people's Christmas disasters with resigned professionalism.

The custody sergeant books me with efficient indifference—personal effects sealed in plastic bags, photographs taken from angles that make everyone look guilty, fingerprints pressed onto cards that will remain in some database forever.

"Phone call?" he asks, already reaching for the handset.

"My husband," I whisper. Though Daniel's probably at the hospital with Josh, following the ambulance that carried Sophie away from our wreckage. Would he even answer? Would he want to hear from the wife who's just been arrested for attempted murder?

The phone rings once, twice, three times before going to voicemail. His recorded voice sounds cheerful, normal, from a time when our biggest concern was remembering to pick up milk on the way home from work.

"Daniel, it's me," I say to the machine. "I'm at Lancaster police station. They've arrested me for—for what happened to Sophie. I need you to know that everything I told you was true. Please—please look after Josh. Tell him Mummy loves him."

The custody sergeant leads me down another corridor, past cells where other people's lives have reached their lowest ebb on Christmas

Eve. Drunks singing carols with slurred enthusiasm, domestics sobbing into tissue paper, the usual seasonal casualties of too much alcohol and too little patience.

My cell door clangs shut.

The space measures perhaps eight feet by six, containing a narrow bed with a mattress thin as cardboard, a steel toilet without a seat, walls painted that particular shade of institutional green that's designed to prevent excitement of any kind. A small window set high in the wall shows nothing but December darkness.

Christmas Eve.

Josh should be asleep while dreams of Father Christmas fill his head with anticipation. Instead, he's probably crying in some hospital waiting room, confused by violence he shouldn't have witnessed, traumatised by seeing his mother led away in handcuffs.

I sink onto the bed, the mattress barely yielding under my weight. Through the walls, I can hear sounds of the station continuing its night shift—phones ringing, doors slamming, the occasional burst of laughter from officers who've found something amusing in the debris of human failure.

56.

The cell's fluorescent light never dims, creating a perpetual artificial day that makes sleep impossible.

I lie on the thin mattress staring at the walls while my mind churns through the events that brought me here.

Midnight comes and goes without ceremony. Christmas Day arrives in a police station that smells of disinfectant and desperation, marked only by the distant sound of church bells tolling across Lancaster.

Josh should be safe in his dinosaur pyjamas, but where? Daniel's sister's house, probably, surrounded by cousins and the comfortable noise of a family that functions properly. Or maybe still at the hospital, curled up on waiting room chairs while doctors assess the extent of Sophie's injuries.

The uncertainty gnaws at me with physical intensity.

Footsteps echo in the corridor outside—officers doing their rounds, checking on the seasonal collection of drunks and domestics who've found themselves spending Christmas Eve in custody. Their voices carry through the walls, professional and weary, discussing shift changes and overtime pay with the resignation of people working while everyone else celebrates.

I'm drifting towards something that might be sleep when my cell door opens.

"Emma Cartwright?" The custody sergeant stands silhouetted in the doorway, his bulk blocking most of the corridor's harsh light. "You're wanted in Interview Room Two."

My pulse spikes as I sit up, the mattress springs creaking beneath me. "What time is it?"

"Just gone midnight. Come on then."

The corridor feels different at this hour—quieter, more charged with possibility. Most of the earlier bustle has faded, leaving only skeleton staff and emergency calls.

The interview room door opens to reveal DI Hughes waiting with her notes spread across the metal table.

Constable Sharma isn't present this time.

"Take a seat, Emma," Hughes says, her tone carrying none of the formal authority from our earlier session. "We need to talk."

I take a seat and swallow hard, my mouth dry.

Hughes reaches beneath the table and slides a file across its metal surface. "These were found during our search of your property."

I stare at Sophie's forged references. Surveillance photographs spanning my entire adult life—graduation, wedding day, walks with Josh through Lancaster's familiar streets. Me at the river.

But seeing it presented as official evidence rather than personal shame transforms its meaning somehow—not proof of my inadequacy but documentation of Sophie's violation.

"She's been watching you for approximately fifteen years," Hughes says, consulting her notes. "Long before she approached your family about employment. The level of surveillance suggests obsession rather than casual interest."

Fifteen years of my life catalogued by someone whose motives I still don't fully understand.

"There are detailed notes about your daily routines," Hughes says, turning pages. "Your work schedule, Josh's nursery arrangements, even records of conversations you had with neighbours. She formed friendships with people you know. She knew intimate details about your family life that no casual acquaintance could have accessed."

The evidence continues—custody plans, character assessments that position me as unstable while elevating Sophie to parental sainthood, strategies for removing Josh from my care that suggest months of careful preparation.

"Jesus Christ," I whisper, pressing my hands against the table's cold surface. "She really was planning to take him."

Hughes nods grimly. "The documentation suggests a systematic campaign to undermine your parental rights while positioning herself as the superior alternative. Very sophisticated, very calculated."

The door opens to admit Daniel, escorted by another officer who guides him to the chair beside me. He looks older than he did this morning, his face grey with exhaustion and something that might be dawning comprehension.

"Daniel." My voice cracks on his name, desperate for connection with the person who should know me well enough to believe in my sanity.

He doesn't meet my eyes immediately, his attention caught by the files spread across the table. Hughes slides the evidence towards him with the same professional detachment she'd shown me.

"Mr Cartwright, you might want to look at what we found in your home."

Daniel reads slowly, his colour draining with each page. Forged documents that had fooled him completely, surveillance photographs that prove Sophie's interest in our family predates her employment, custody plans that name him as likely supporter of her claim to Josh.

"She said Emma was making it all up," he mutters, his voice barely audible above the strip lights' persistent hum. "Said she was having some kind of breakdown."

"Classic manipulation technique," Hughes says. "Discredit the victim's testimony by questioning their mental stability. Very effective when combined with positioning yourself as the helpful solution to problems you've actually created."

Daniel continues reading, his jaw working silently as he processes evidence that reshapes everything he thought he knew about the woman who'd been living in our house.

"The level of preparation suggests this wasn't impulsive," Hughes says. "Your nanny—or rather, this woman posing as your nanny—spent considerable time and resources building this operation. Fake credentials, manufactured references, detailed psychological profiles of your entire family."

"But why?" Daniel's voice carries bewilderment that matches my own. "What could she possibly want badly enough to justify years of surveillance?"

Hughes closes the file. "That's what we intend to find out. But first—Emma, do you still maintain you acted in self-defence?"

"Yes." The word comes out steadier than I'd expected. "She attacked me with a knife from our kitchen block. I pushed her away to protect myself and Josh. I never intended for her to fall down the stairs, but I won't apologise for defending my family."

Daniel sits back in his chair, shoulders slumping as the full weight of Sophie's deception settles over him. For the first time since her arrival in our lives, he looks at me without the careful concern reserved for people whose mental stability requires monitoring.

"Do you believe me now?" I whisper, my voice barely audible above the strip lights' electrical hum.

57.

Christmas morning arrives without fanfare, seeping through our curtains like something reluctant to be witnessed. The living room sits in half-darkness despite the tree lights blinking their relentless sequence, casting fractured patterns across walls that still bear invisible scars from last night's violence.

Presents huddle beneath the tree in neat piles, their wrapping paper gleaming with promises no one feels ready to unwrap. The sight should trigger excitement, the particular magic that makes Christmas morning worth anticipating all year. Instead, the unopened gifts feel accusatory, evidence of celebrations that require energy none of us possess.

The house feels gutted despite our efforts to restore order. Daniel and I swept up the broken crockery, mopped blood from the tiles, returned overturned furniture to positions that approximate normality.

But something fundamental has been damaged beyond our ability to repair—the sense of safety that makes a house feel like home rather than just accommodation.

The air hangs heavy with unspoken trauma, weighted with memories that will require more than housework to eliminate. Every creak of the floorboards echoes with violence, every shadow holds the possibility of threat, every silence stretches long enough for doubt to take root.

Daniel sits in his usual chair but nothing about his posture suggests comfort. The newspaper lies open across his lap, but his eyes don't move across the pages with the focused attention that marks actual reading.

He's performing the role of someone having a normal Christmas morning.

Josh appears in the doorway wearing his dinosaur pyjamas.

"Morning, sweetheart," I say, my voice carrying forced brightness that fools no one. "Happy Christmas."

He pads across the room but doesn't race towards the presents with his usual Christmas morning enthusiasm. Instead, he climbs onto the sofa beside me, pressing his small body against my side while his thumb finds his mouth—a comfort habit I thought he'd outgrown months ago.

"Are we having Christmas?" he asks, his voice muffled against my jumper.

The question breaks something in my chest.

"Yes, love," I manage, stroking his hair with fingers that still shake slightly. "We're together, and that's what matters most."

Josh shifts against me, his breathing steady but his body tense in ways that suggest he's absorbing adult anxieties he shouldn't have to process. The trauma of watching his mother arrested, of seeing violence in spaces that should represent security, won't disappear simply because Sophie's deception has been exposed.

"When's Mummy Sophie coming back?"

My heart clenches. "She's not coming back, sweetheart," I say, forcing my voice to remain steady. "It's just us now. Just our family."

But even as I speak the words, their fragility becomes obvious. Daniel's distance, Josh's confusion, the cracks that run through our domestic foundation—we're together but not whole, present but not healed, surviving but not thriving.

Josh nods against my chest but doesn't look convinced. At four years old, he lacks the context to understand why the woman who read him bedtime stories and made bath time magical has suddenly vanished from his life. All he knows is that someone he trusted is gone, leaving behind absence that feels like abandonment.

Daniel sets aside his unread newspaper and reaches for one of Josh's presents, a package wrapped in paper covered with reindeer that I'd chosen during a more optimistic moment weeks ago. "Shall we see what Father Christmas brought you?"

Josh shakes his head, burrowing deeper against my side. Even presents can't compete with the confusion and loss that's reshaping his understanding of family stability.

We sit in silence while the tree lights continue their programmed sequence, three people bound by blood and history but separated by trauma that will require time and patience to heal.

The unspoken truth settles over us: Sophie may be gone, but she's left damage that will take years to repair.

I look around our living room, cataloguing details I usually take for granted. The half-moon scar on the wooden table where Sophie's knife gouged the surface. The spot near the doorway where Josh stood crying while his parents fought over truth and sanity. The stairwell beyond, where someone I'd trusted fell with sounds that will echo in my memory forever.

This is my home again. Sophie's possessions have been removed by police as evidence, her presence erased from surfaces that had begun to reflect her taste rather than mine. But winning feels hollow when the victory comes at such cost.

The terror of almost losing Josh still sits fresh in my mind, mixing with the exhaustion of fighting battles everyone insisted existed only in my imagination.

Even vindication carries weight—proving I was right about Sophie's manipulation doesn't undo the damage her presence caused to my marriage, my confidence, my son's sense of security.

Daniel picks up another present. "Emma? This is for you."

I accept the package but don't unwrap it immediately. The gesture feels premature somehow, as if celebrating Christmas requires emotional energy I haven't recovered yet. My hands trace the ribbon he'd tied with care.

"Thank you," I whisper, setting it aside for later when gift-opening won't feel like performance.

Daniel's face shows hurt at my rejection of his offering, but also understanding. Christmas morning should represent joy, gratitude, the particular contentment that comes from being exactly where you belong.

Instead, we're three damaged people trying to navigate traditions that require wholeness none of us currently possess.

The silence stretches until even the tree lights' blinking feels accusatory.

Outside, Lancaster settles into its Christmas rhythm—families gathering for celebrations that probably include laughter, genuine affection, the comfortable chaos of people who trust each other completely.

Josh's breathing evens against my chest, his small body finally relaxing into sleep despite the morning hour. I hold him carefully, grateful for his weight, his warmth, his continued presence in my arms. This is what I fought for—the right to keep holding my son, to be his sanctuary when the world becomes too much to handle.

"We'll be alright," I whisper, more to myself than to Daniel or sleeping Josh. "We have to be."

58.

The kitchen holds its breath around me on this grey January morning, Lancaster drizzle streaking the bay window while the boiler hums its familiar tune against the cold. The sound should comfort me—evidence of ordinary domestic life resuming its rhythm—but nothing feels entirely safe anymore.

I sit at our dining table sorting through the morning's post, a mundane ritual that represents something approaching normality. Bills that need paying, charity appeals I'll probably ignore, takeaway menus for restaurants I'll never order from. The kind of everyday debris that accumulates when life continues despite the chaos that tried to destroy it.

Josh's laughter drifts from upstairs where he's building something elaborate with his Lego, his voice bright with the particular concentration that marks serious four-year-old construction projects. The sound should fill me with maternal satisfaction, but instead it highlights how fragile this peace feels.

We're rebuilding, piece by careful piece.

Daniel helps with the evening routine now, reading bedtime stories with genuine attention rather than distracted obligation. We cook meals together while Josh stands on his step stool, stirring sauces with intense focus. Small gestures that suggest we might survive this, that families can heal from wounds that seemed fatal.

But the scars remain visible despite our efforts. Josh still asks about Sophie sometimes, his questions delivered with the casual curiosity that makes parental hearts ache. Daniel remains careful around me, his trust rebuilding slowly through daily evidence that I'm competent rather than delusional.

I tell myself we're standing again, finding our feet on ground that felt unsteady for so long. That the worst is behind us, that Sophie's influence has been neutralised by truth finally emerging through official channels.

The post sorting continues until one envelope stops my hands mid-motion. No stamp, no postmark, no return address. Just Josh's name written across cream paper in neat script that makes my stomach clench with recognition.

My fingers shake as I tear the envelope open, though part of me knows I should call the police instead.

A photograph slides out, edges slightly curled, surface bearing water damage that suggests it's been stored somewhere damp. The image resolves into focus with sickening clarity—Sophie and Josh standing together on the River Lune towpath, her hand holding his with casual possession while he looks up at her with trusting affection.

The picture must have been taken during one of their walks, those innocent afternoon expeditions I'd been grateful for at the time. Josh appears tiny beside her, his bright coat making him look like a beacon against the winter landscape. Sophie's face is half-turned towards the camera, her expression carrying the satisfied smile of someone whose plans are proceeding perfectly.

But it's not just a photograph. It's proof that even from hospital beds and police custody, Sophie can still reach into our lives. That the safety I've been trying to rebuild remains an illusion sustained only by my desperate need to believe we've escaped.

I flip the picture with hands that won't stay steady, already knowing I'll find words that will shatter whatever peace we've managed to create. Sophie's neat handwriting fills the blank space: *Sisters look out for each other.*

The message hits like ice water flooding my veins. Not past tense, not acknowledgment of defeat, but present commitment. Active intention to continue the relationship I've spent weeks trying to escape.

My pulse thunders while the kitchen fades around me, ordinary domestic sounds disappearing beneath the imagined roar of river water that carries everything downstream. The radiator's steady ticking becomes the sound of time running out, of safety dissolving like sugar in rain.

I stare at Sophie's careful script, my throat closing with the certainty that whatever legal consequences she's facing won't stop her. Prison sentences end, restraining orders expire, but obsessions that span decades don't simply vanish because courts declare them inconvenient.

She's still out there. Still planning, still watching, still committed to the narrative that casts us as family rather than victim and predator. The photograph proves she's kept mementos of her time with Josh, trophies that maintain emotional connection despite physical separation.

The clock on our kitchen wall clicks over to the next minute while I sit frozen with evidence of ongoing threat clutched in my shaking hands.

Outside, Lancaster continues its January routine—people heading to work, children walking to school, the ordinary bustle of lives that feel secure in their predictability.

But I know better now. Know how easily that security can be penetrated by someone with patience, resources, and the particular kind of determination that comes from believing your cause is just.

Sophie isn't finished with us.

The photograph trembles in my grip as understanding crystallises with terrible clarity. The trial, the restraining orders, the police protection—all of it represents temporary inconvenience rather than permanent solution. Sophie sees herself as my sister, Josh as her rightful nephew, our family as something she deserves rather than something she's stolen.

I grip the photo tighter, knowing normality is an illusion—Sophie is still out there, waiting for her moment.

THE END.

Thank you for reading *The Nanny's Secret*. If you've followed Emma's story this far, you've stepped into the quiet streets of Lancaster—where terraced houses watch each other, school-gate hierarchies matter more than they should, and the boundaries between safety and threat blur behind closed doors.

I live in Morecambe, so Lancaster is part of my daily rhythm. I walk its streets, cross the Millennium Bridge, and pass through its snickets and cobbled alleys. When I planned this novel, I knew Lancaster had to be the setting.

It's a city in name, but it moves with the intimacy of a small town. You can walk from one side to the other in under half an hour, and that closeness carries a sense of scrutiny—of lives intertwined, secrets leaking across walls and through whispers.

I've spent time in the Gregson pub, in Dalton Square under Queen Victoria's stern gaze, and around Lancaster Castle's looming walls. I've wandered Williamson Park, where the Ashton Memorial rises above like a silent witness. These places all carry history and atmosphere, and they fed directly into the mood of *The Nanny's Secret*.

Lancaster has a dual nature. On bright days, it's lively with markets, students, and Georgian charm. But when the rain sweeps in from the Bay, the streets glisten with unease. The city becomes something different—familiar yet unsettling, respectable yet shadowed. That duality was perfect for Emma's story: a place where the everyday can tip so easily into menace.

If you've enjoyed *The Nanny's Secret,* it would mean the world if you left a review. Reviews not only help authors like me keep writing, but they also help other readers find the books that will grip them.

And if you'd like more, I'd love to give you a free novella. You can download *The Lodger*—a psychological thriller about trust, betrayal, and the stranger in your home—direct from my website: jcronshaw.com[1].

Thank you again for reading. I hope Emma's fight to hold onto her family stays with you long after you've turned the final page.

J. Cronshaw

October, 2025

P.S. Turn the page for a sneak-peek at *I Know What I Saw*.

---

1. https://jcronshaw.com/

I Know What I Saw – Chapter One

"Mum, I saw Dad kill Kevin Jacobs."

My fork freezes halfway to my mouth. The shepherd's pie falls back onto the plate with a wet slap.

Hannah sits across from me, her voice flat. No tremor. No tears. Just that terrible certainty teenagers wield like weapons.

The silence stretches between us. The old carriage clock on the mantel ticks loud enough to hammer nails. Outside, a car door slams. Mrs Dawson calling her cat in. Normal sounds from a normal Tuesday evening.

But nothing about this is normal.

Matt's knuckles have gone white around his wine glass. For a heartbeat, he looks like a stranger sitting at my kitchen table. Then he blinks and becomes my husband again.

"Honestly, Hannah." He forces a laugh. "Drama queen as always."

He lifts the glass to his lips.

Hannah leans forward, elbows on the scratched pine table. Her eyes lock on mine, not Matt's.

"I saw him, Mum. At the Serpentine Path."

Her tone carries no trace of teenage exaggeration. No breathless excitement at being the centre of attention. Just facts, delivered like a weather report.

Goosebumps prickle my arms. "You must've mistak—"

"I know what I saw."

The words slice through my stumbling denial. Hannah's gaze doesn't waver. She has Matt's stubborn chin, my green eyes. Right now, she looks older than fifteen.

From Agnew Street comes the distant hum of evening traffic, commuters heading home to their own families, their own problems. The sound feels wrong somehow, too ordinary for this moment.

Matt pushes back his chair. The legs scrape against the kitchen tiles. "She's making things up, Vicky." He stands, smoothing down his shirt. "Attention-seeking nonsense."

But sweat beads along his hairline despite the December chill seeping through our single-glazed windows.

Hannah stays seated. Her hands clench into fists on the table.

"Kevin Jacobs is dead, isn't he?" she asks.

I want to laugh it away, to tell her she's watched too many crime dramas, that Kevin is probably at home right now watching the news or polishing those awful model ships he collects.

But Kevin Jacobs. The man who organised the street's Christmas lights competition. Who always waved when he trimmed his hedge. Who knew exactly which wine to bring to dinner parties and never stayed past ten o'clock.

Dead?

My mind scrambles for logic. When did I last see him? Yesterday morning, maybe. Or was it Sunday? The days blur together lately—freelance deadlines, Hannah's school drama, Oliver's nativity, Matt's long hours at the office.

"This is ridiculous." Matt moves towards the doorway. "I won't sit here and listen to this rubbish."

Hannah doesn't flinch. She watches him go, then turns back to me.

"He came home late last night. After eleven. His shirt was dirty."

Matt's footsteps pound up the stairs. A door slams. The house shudders.

Hannah and I sit in the sudden quiet. The shepherd's pie congeals on our plates. The smell of mince and onions that felt comforting twenty minutes ago now turns my stomach.

"Hannah—"

"He threw his shirt in the washing machine straight away." Her voice stays level, matter-of-fact. "He never does the washing."

She's right. Matt considers the washing machine a mysterious feminine appliance, like my hair straighteners or the air fryer his sister bought us last Christmas.

"There could be any number of reasons—"

"Ask him where he was."

The challenge sits between us. Hannah's eyes burn into mine, waiting.

From upstairs comes the sound of Matt pacing. Back and forth across our bedroom floor.

I think of his recent mood swings. The whispered phone calls that stop when I enter the room. The way he checks his mobile constantly, jaw tight with tension.

The distance that's grown between us, subtle as frost forming on windows.

"There was no trace of a joke in her eyes. Only certainty."

Hannah pushes her plate away, food untouched.

"Ask him, Mum."

But I'm not sure I want to hear the answer.

The Serpentine Path runs behind our terrace, dark and narrow between the houses and the train station car park. I've walked it hundreds of times, cutting through to the Tesco Express.

Now it feels different. Dangerous.

Hannah stands, scraping her chair back.

"I'm going to my room."

She pauses at the kitchen door, hand on the frame. For a moment, she looks like the little girl who used to crawl into our bed during thunderstorms, seeking comfort in the space between Matt and me.

"I know what I saw, Mum."

Order *I Know What I Saw* by J. Cronshaw today[1].

---

1. https://geni.us/iknowwhatisaw

Find J. Cronshaw online

Amazon: amazon.com/author/jcronshaw[1]
    BookBub: bookbub.com/profile/j-cronshaw[2]
    Facebook: facebook.com/jcronshaw[3]
    TikTok: tiktok.com/@jcronshaw
    Newsletter: subscribepage.com/thelodger[4]
    Website: jcronshaw.com[5]

---

1. https://amazon.com/author/jcronshaw

2.   https://www.bookbub.com/profile/j-cronshaw?follow=true

3.   https://facebook.com/jcronshaw

4.   https://subscribepage.com/thelodger

5.   https://jcronshaw.com

About the Author

J. Cronshaw is a British author raised in Wolverhampton who moved to Leeds for university. He worked as a journalist across the region for titles including the Halifax Courier, Yorkshire Post, Yorkshire Evening Post, and Wakefield Express, specialising in court and political reporting.

His years covering trials and magistrates' hearings gave him insight into the quiet tragedies that unfold when family secrets surface and ordinary people make extraordinary choices. These experiences inform his fiction, which explores the psychological tensions beneath domestic life.

He now lives with his wife and son in Morecambe, writing fiction full-time.

Read more at https://jcronshaw.com.

Printed in Dunstable, United Kingdom